WILD wild WEST

Charlene Teglia

St. Martin's Griffin 🦁 New York 📖

This is a work of fiction. All of the characters, organizations, and events portrayed in this novel are either products of the author's imagination or are used fictitiously.

www.stmartins.com

Library of Congress Cataloging-in-Publication Data
Teglia, Charlene.
    Wild wild west / Charlene Teglia.—1st ed.
        p. cm.
    ISBN-13: 978-0-312-36835-7
    ISBN-10: 0-312-36835-6
    1. Montana—Fiction. I. Title.
PS3620.E4357W55   2007
813'.6—dc22

2007012996

First Edition: August 2007

10 9 8 7 6 5 4 3 2 1

For Kyle and the entire Montana contingent.
Thank you for your support and encouragement!

ACKNOWLEDGMENTS

No book is a solo project, so thanks are due to many people. My husband for baby-sitting while I wrote and cheering me on; my agent for dealing with the details; my wonderful editor, Rose, for pointing out the places where the story needed work; Eliani Torres for making sure the story's shirt was tucked in with all the commas where they belonged; the cover geniuses for delivering a fantastic design; Angie and Chrissy for supporting me in this venture; and the Playground for giving me a place to de-stress. Thank you!

A man's WORD IS HIS BONDAGE

1

In all of Montana, from the heights of the Rockies to the width of the plains sprawling under the Big Sky, surely there were worse places to be.

Staked out naked on one of the reservations, for instance.

Gabe Wilson tipped back his sweat-stained Stetson and considered that possibility. He added his comfortably broken-in Tony Lamas to the mental picture. And his Stetson. To a Western man, there was naked and then there was *naked*.

"Tell me again why we're here," he said.

Chet Andrews raised a sardonic brow. There wasn't an ounce of compassion in his face or in his eyes. Eyes that reflected the same deep blue as the wide Montana sky.

"We're here for the culture."

He delivered this statement in a way that Gabe found difficult to trust. No, make that impossible. As impossible as trying to think of a worse place they could be in than the Seattle-light coffeehouse called Lemon Espresso, according to the fancy sign outside, and more appropriately "the Lemon" by Missoula's old-guard Montana element.

The other element, the renegades of new Montana who kept drifting over the border from the general direction of degenerate Seattle, surrounded and outnumbered the cowboys. The locals blamed John Updike for mouthing off to the world about Missoula as a center for artists and intellectuals, dubbing it the new Paris. Word spread and the newcomers kept coming.

"You mean we're here to raise some hell," Gabe stated in a flat voice. Not that he had any objection, in principle. It was just that somebody might have seen them come in. Somebody besides the group of flakes assembled for the poetry reading. Somebody they knew.

Right this very minute, rumors of his advanced mental deterioration could be flying like sand on the wind.

He'd never be allowed to live it down. The next time he walked into the Alibi, he'd get a tiny little china cup of coffee instead of a long cold beer. Served with roaring laughter from Eric the Red, the big Scandinavian-looking bartender with a long memory and a short imagination.

In fact, Eric was so short on imagination that the gag could conceivably continue each and every time he walked through the door. For the rest of his life.

He'd have to start drinking at The Hole in the Wall Saloon.

Gabe leaned back in his seat, depressed at the very thought of The Hole in the Wall. There were worse places to be than the Lemon after all.

Reuben Black, the third member of the trio they'd formed back in childhood, didn't say anything. Coming to the Lemon this Saturday night had been his idea, but whatever his reason, the former Army Ranger was keeping it to himself.

The sweet smell of clove cigarettes mingled with the scent of rich coffee and incense. Honest-to-God incense. It was like a bad sixties flashback, not that he'd been around in the sixties.

Love beads hung in the doorway off the main room, roping off the hall to the bathrooms, which were marked with the symbols for masculine and feminine. Little circle, little arrow. On the plus side, the bathrooms did have real doors that closed and locked instead of more of the long beaded strings.

Gabe wondered idly how many times those doors had been closed to conceal a hurried and clandestine coupling. It seemed like the kind of thing that would happen at the Lemon. If so, it would certainly liven up the evening.

Here in the coffeehouse's center, cushions and chairs and tables were scattered in an eye-jolting geometry and clash of colors. Fabrics in orange and purple, in patterns that must have been conceived by a blind man on acid, were matched with chartreuse and screaming yellow.

The inhabitants of the cushions and chairs were similarly hard on the optics.

Young women with hair in colors nature never intended and low-riding jeans that exposed pierced navels. Skinny intellectual guys with hair that would have embarrassed any sane man and pallor that could mean the onset of some wasting disease. Not one of them looked like they'd last a day on a ranch.

Gabe winced at the sight and directed his attention to the stage out of self-preservation.

An emaciated reader who appeared to be in the full-blown frenzy of either poetic ecstasy or epilepsy was finishing up his godawful poem, punctuated by wild gestures as he clutched at his heart and tore at the black shirt and suit jacket that must have been incredibly hot, considering the weather. Montana summers weren't as hot as, say, hell. Or Texas. But hot enough.

"Love—love—love—for love, I die."

"For love of my ears, I'd get a gun and help him," Chet volunteered.

"For love of poetry, he deserves to die," Gabe agreed. Teaching English to junior high kids should have steeled him to any abuse of the mother tongue, but his students wrote better stuff than this.

Reuben scowled at both of them. He probably didn't consider guns or death laughing matters. Or maybe it was love he was touchy about. Hard to tell with Reuben.

The enthusiastic applause that greeted this public massacre of the English language was proof of the crowd's low taste.

The human crow bowed and retired to a faux fur beanbag chair.

And then it happened.

Gabe heard music. He saw the room slow and spin in a soft-focus fantasy with white lights that faded and blurred everything except the vision that filled his sight.

Beauty. She was beauty, Byron's poem, come to life. Gabe cheered up. If women who looked like that hung out here, maybe Reuben was on to something.

Long dark hair sweeping behind her, she walked to the stage dressed in a filmy white shirt and sinfully tight, low-riding hip-hugging blue jeans that showcased her heart-shaped ass.

When she turned to face the room, Gabe imagined he could see a hint of the darker rose of her nipples under the white fabric. Not wearing a bra? By the time she opened her mouth to read, he would have forgiven her assaulting his ears with any awful verse for the pleasure of resting his eyes on her.

Her introduction told him her name, Willow Daniels. That she was a poet in residence with an impressive string of publishing credits, including two small volumes of poetry. And then she read.

Her voice was as lovely as her face and her body, but it was the poem that commanded Gabe's attention. Her poem was an invitation for a lover to seduce her, first in words and then in deeds.

By the time she was done reading, he had to shift lower in his chair to hide the fact that his jeans were suddenly too tight for comfort. She had an impressive command of the language. She'd seduced him with a poem. Made him hot. Made him want to answer her invitation and then let their bodies do the talking.

Ease down, cowboy, he thought. It was just a poem. Words. No need to take them to heart as if she'd written them for him, a personal invitation.

Then again, she had made eye contact with him while she'd read. She'd looked at him a bit longer than was strictly polite. A sign of interest. Maybe it wouldn't hurt to introduce himself to her later on.

Although if she really wanted an eloquent man, Montana wasn't exactly the place to find one. It was a place of vast silences. In the West, a man's word was his bond. It wasn't given lightly. A man said only what needed to be said, and actions spoke louder than words. Although action was what she really wanted, if he understood her poem correctly.

"What's he doing?" Chet interrupted his thoughts, nudging him with an elbow to the ribs and indicating Reuben with the tilt of his head.

Gabe leaned back to see their friend making his slow, steady way toward the coffee counter. Two women were behind it, both in blue jeans and identical lemon yellow tank tops.

One of the women, a blonde, was operating the espresso machine with expert speed and no wasted motions, her body swaying to the beat of the music playing in the background.

The other, with brown hair too light to be called brunette, was reaching up to get a five-pound bag of coffee beans on a high shelf above her head, arms outstretched and extended to the limit, and it wasn't quite enough. The tips of her fingers brushed against the bag, unable to grasp it.

Reuben walked up behind her, close enough that his body brushed against hers, and took the bag down. As he lowered it in front of her, his arms enclosed her on either side.

"Being helpful," Gabe said.

"The hell he is. He's hitting on her. He never does that. He never notices women." Chet eyed the pair in some consternation. "No wonder he kept dragging me in here all the time and then insisted we come here tonight. He was getting ready to make his move. Should we warn her?"

"That he hasn't had a relationship in recent memory and she should check the expiration date on his condoms?"

Chet frowned at him. "No, that he's not a man to mess around with."

Gabe considered the woman and the way Reuben's body enfolded her. Protective. Whatever Reuben intended, it wasn't dangerous. Well, possibly to her heart, but that was the way of things. She was slender with delicate features, so she created the illusion of fragile. But her hands were work worn and the clearly defined muscles in her bare arms told the real story.

"He doesn't hurt women. And she's stronger than she looks." Gabe shifted to the more important point, in his mind. "If Reuben's been bringing you to this place for a while, why drag me along tonight, too?"

"Because if I have to listen to bad poetry, you have to suffer with me," Chet said. "This is the first time he's wanted to come to a reading."

Reuben's head dipped down, putting his mouth level with her ear. He said something to her. Probably a suggestion to get a stepladder from the hardware store in the morning, knowing Reuben. Then he placed the bag in her hands, let her go, and walked back to their table.

Gabe let his attention drift back to the poet. The more he considered it, the more Gabe thought he needed to pursue this

Willow Daniels. He wasn't much of a conversationalist, but she was inspiring.

His thoughts were interrupted once again, this time by a woman's voice.

"Problem, cowboy?" The blond woman who'd worked the espresso maker like a pro was now standing in front of their table, hands on her hips, giving Chet a challenging look.

He scowled at her.

That was so uncharacteristic of the man's normal easygoing charm that it got Gabe's attention, dragging it away from his mental debate over whether or not Willow had a bra on and if her nipples were a deep, dark berry or a light dusky rose and what he might have to say to her to find out.

"You were speeding on the highway again," he accused the barista. "I saw you."

She gave him a long look. "Montana had fewer fatalities when there was no highway speed limit."

"Doesn't mean you can drive like you're trying to put your foot through the floor. Cattle get loose and wander onto the highway. You hit one, your sweet little tattooed ass is in a sling."

Chet, ranting at a stranger for speeding? A man who risked broken bones on a daily basis? And how did he know she had a tattooed ass, anyway?

A downward glance showed him that her tank top had ridden up and her jeans rode low enough to expose the beginnings of a colorful design that wrapped around and disappeared under the denim. Not too much of a deduction to guess that the tattoo did in fact decorate her backside. Still, the two of them had obviously met before tonight.

Chet and Reuben were both acting out of character, now that Gabe thought about it. And he'd known them long enough to judge. They'd been raised on neighboring ranches, gone to school together, grown up together. The three of them now worked their own ranches, although Gabe was the only one with a regular job.

Chet broke horses for extra cash, not exactly a low-risk occupation. He wasn't known to get worked up over little things like risking life and limb. Why did he care if some city woman who'd moved to Montana drove too fast? And why was Reuben suddenly making moves? What the hell was in the Lemon's damn designer coffee?

"My ass isn't your business and neither is my driving," Chet was told.

"How about if I make it mine?"

The blonde leaned forward, putting her cleavage at Chet's eye level, lifted his Stetson off, and trailed a long-nailed, red-tipped finger through his hair. "You think you're up to my speed?"

"Think you're up to mine?" Chet came around the table and planted his hat on her head.

She tilted her head back. "I'm ready to cowboy up and ride."

"You off work now?"

"Yes."

"Good." Chet scooped her up into his arms and headed for the door. "Night, Gabe, Rube," he called over his shoulder.

Just like that, Gabe thought, bemused. He still hadn't gotten to hello with the luscious Willow, and Chet was carrying off a hot blonde with a tattoo. Some men had it easy.

Before he'd recovered himself, Willow walked over. "Are you going to read tonight?"

"Yes," he said before he could stop himself.

Which was how he came to be standing on the stage at the Lemon, looking straight into Willow Daniels's dark eyes, delivering the old and well-memorized lines, "She walks in beauty like the night . . ."

This better get him into Willow's good graces, because it was going to destroy his reputation completely.

2

Crazy from the heat, thought Willow.

Lemon Espresso wasn't air-conditioned, and the ceiling fans did only so much. She'd left her bra off and worn her loosest, coolest shirt for tonight's reading and she still felt sweat trickling between her breasts. But the summer heat didn't explain why she'd taken one look at a tall, quiet cowboy with hazel eyes and sandy hair and felt her body go hot and tight.

She wasn't the only one, either. Jolie had gone off with the blond, blue-eyed cowboy, wearing his hat. She hadn't wasted any time making good on her vow to go wild before summer ended and she had to sit for the bar exam, cover up her tattoo with suits, and bury her high spirits in legal briefs. By now his boots were probably under her bed.

Unless they hadn't made it farther than his pickup truck. Willow imagined the two of them entwined, half-naked, not even taking the time to finish undressing before satisfying that hot aching need, and she felt her sex clench with want.

Lucky Jolie.

Even Laura, Lemon Espresso's hardworking owner who never flirted with customers, had let that third cowboy with eyes and hair so dark, they were nearly the color of espresso take a bag of coffee beans down for her and practically rub his cock into her ass in the process. She'd relaxed back against him like she wanted him to.

All three of them were suffering from the heat and an unwanted stretch of celibacy, and it was turning their brains, because for some reason the only men around who even looked like the right gender were those three Montana natives who'd come into the espresso house tonight looking like raw, hard sex in well-worn leather boots and sweat-stained cowboy hats.

The two cowboys who seemed to have laid claim to Jolie and Laura had been in several times before, but the one Willow had locked eyes with was new.

She could have sworn her cowboy wouldn't get up and read when she'd asked, but she hadn't been able to stop herself from asking. And then he'd surprised her completely. He didn't look like the type of man who read poetry, let alone went around with whole verses memorized. But he obviously was.

He'd recited every line of a classic poem straight at her. Then he'd touched the brim of his hat, nodded, and left.

Leaving her irritable, overheated, and envious.

Jolie was off making up for the long grind of law school that left no time for fun, let alone relationships. Laura was starting to do the tasks that led up to closing her business for the night with a very good reason to close early watching her work. She was making a success of the venture, but she worked long hours. It looked like the man waiting for her to finish up planned to help her unwind.

Dammit. She didn't begrudge her friends their good fortune, but they were getting lucky while her cowboy had left without a word and she was going home alone to a cold shower or a long masturbation session. Or both.

What she wouldn't give to be going home to a man who would whisper in her ear all the naughty, forbidden things he was going to do to her. And then do them. One by one. All night long.

She bit her lip to keep from groaning out loud.

It was too hot inside. She couldn't wait to be outside the confines of the building, feeling the cooling night air on her skin. Time to take her bad mood and her unfulfilled desires and go home.

"Good night, Laura," she said as she stood up to gather her purse and keys.

"You're leaving?" Laura brushed back the curtain of straight brown hair that had fallen into her eyes.

"Yes, it's getting late. We had a good turnout, though."

As usual. From the time she first opened the doors, Laura had planned a series of events that included readings from famous authors in the area on vacation, local authors, a broad range of talents and genres and literary affiliations.

She also alternated with other types of events like tarot card readers, and displayed artwork by local painters and photographers, rotating to feature a new artist each month as an added attraction to the coffee shop. The result was a brisk business.

Willow had been scheduled for several readings over the course of the summer. She'd come to look forward to them. Whenever she had an appearance at Lemon Espresso, it was well organized, well attended, and Laura made her feel comfortable and at home.

She'd gotten to know the owner and her assistant, Jolie, as the weeks and the heat of summer wore on. Usually the three of them had a good round of girl talk at the end of the night.

But tonight, the last thing Laura needed was her loitering when there was a man she clearly wanted to be alone with.

And the last thing Willow needed was to be around other people right now. She wasn't fit company for anybody.

It wasn't just the heat, or the lack of male companionship, although she was ridiculously disappointed that the one man who'd captured her interest in longer than she cared to think about had left without another word.

Her residency was coming to an end. So was the leave of absence she'd taken from her job. A job she wanted less, in a place she had less desire to ever go back to, with each day she spent in Missoula. But quitting meant taking an enormous risk. Keeping her job was safer. Smarter. Willow was so tired of doing the safe, smart thing.

She was leaving Montana in two weeks and going back home, though. She'd already started packing. Tonight had been her last reading for the poet-in-residence program, and soon her Missoula experience would be over completely.

Outside the coffee shop, she took a deep breath of night air and felt instantly better. The wide open sky glittered with stars, more than she could see in a big city even on the darkest nights.

What she didn't expect to find outside, leaning against the building smoking a cigarette, was the man who'd recited Byron to her. She thought her heart actually skipped a beat at the sight of him. He wasn't gone, after all.

"Were you waiting for me?" Willow asked. Then wished she could take the words back. Dumb question—he was probably waiting for his friend.

"Yes." He put out his cigarette, field-stripped it, and tucked the butt into his pocket. No littering, no risk of fire. The movements were the clear result of long-standing habit from a man who spent a lot of time outdoors and took care to leave nature as he found it.

For some reason, that careful habit struck her as significant.

"I'm Willow," she said. He already knew that, but she didn't know what else to say.

"I heard. I'm Gabe Wilson." He walked toward her and stopped inches away, close enough for her to imagine that the heat from his body was warming her skin. "That was some poem you read tonight."

Oh. Yes. She swallowed, thinking of what she'd written and how it might sound. Somehow it seemed a lot more suggestive with him around than it had before. Graphic, even. An outright erotic invitation. Maybe he wanted to take her up on it.

She should be so lucky.

"I'm glad you liked it," she said, figuring a neutral answer was probably best.

"It made me want to ask you a question," he said.

Oh, Lord, Willow prayed, *don't let this man ask me if I believe free verse is real poetry, or how it can be a poem if it doesn't rhyme.*

"Go ahead," she said.

"Do you just want words, or do you want a man who can back them up?"

Her prayer was answered. Along with her every erotic dream, maybe. Willow felt her pulse kick up and felt a low throb between her legs at the possibility. She had to lick suddenly dry lips before she could answer him. "I want a man who can back them up."

In a burst of uncharacteristic daring, she lifted her hand and placed her palm against his chest, feeling the heat of his body through the thin fabric of his shirt and the work-hardened muscles underneath and went on, "Can you?"

He could. She was certain of that. The real question was, did he want to?

"Yes, ma'am."

The words shouldn't have sounded erotic. It should have sounded like he was talking to somebody's grandmother. It didn't. It sounded like a sexual promise made by a man who knew exactly how to deliver and was confident in his abilities.

It would be reckless to go off with a stranger for a night of hot sex. Getting to know him first or saying no would be the mature, responsible thing to do. Willow thought of the mature, responsible, safe choices that seemed to be strangling her life, and her increasing desire to rebel against them, do something else, welled up.

Start with a small rebellion here? Say yes to this man who commanded her attention with his mere presence. Say yes to her own wants and desires and too-long-unfulfilled needs.

Yes.

She didn't have time to get to know him, anyway.

"I'm leaving in two weeks," Willow said, wanting to make sure he didn't misunderstand what she wanted. They didn't have a future, but that didn't mean they couldn't have tonight.

"Then we'd better not waste time." Gabe lifted a hand to cover hers, keeping it against his chest, and continued, "I believe the next question is, your place or mine?"

Willow thought about it. Where did she want to go? Her place? His?

She was curious about where he lived, what it would tell her about who he was. She might not get another chance to find out. He wasn't promising her forever or even a string of dates. Even if he had been, there wasn't time.

He was promising to fulfill her sexual desires. And there was a certain appeal to the idea of being in unfamiliar masculine surroundings while he told her what he was going to do to every inch of her body and then did it.

"Your place," she said.

His hand was warm, strong. His heartbeat under her hand was steady and solid. She swayed a little closer to him.

"I'd better warn you," Gabe told her, "I intend to take my time and be thorough."

That throbbing sensation between her legs wasn't alleviated by this warning in the least. She could feel herself growing damp and slick in anticipation of his touch. His hands. His mouth. All of him.

"I'll consider myself warned," Willow answered.

A group of people coming down the sidewalk made her realize they weren't alone yet. Gabe put his free hand on her waist and guided her to the side, letting the group pass. His hand felt so good there, and at the same time she felt impatient for it to slide up her rib cage to cup one full, aching breast. Or to slide down her hip to cup her sex in the palm of his hand.

"You want me to drive?" Gabe asked.

He was making sure she considered her choices, Willow realized. Letting her choose where they'd go. How they'd get there. If she wanted to drive her car, he'd agree. He was being careful not to rush her or put her in a position that made her uncomfortable.

That made her feel confident in letting him do the driving. In more ways than one. He was letting her establish the boundaries, set the limits. That told her that she could put herself in his hands safely.

"Yes," Willow said. "I want you to drive."

Gabe turned her in the right direction, guiding her with light pressure on her waist. He released her hand and walked beside her, keeping his arm around her and his hand against her waist. He was as relaxed and natural as if he'd known her for years and it was the way they always walked.

She, on the other hand, was very aware that a stranger was touching her and leading her away. It didn't alarm her. It excited her. Every step made her thighs brush together, making her conscious of the throbbing ache between them. That light pressure combined with anticipation made the simple act of walking with him arousing.

He stopped her beside a recent model Ford pickup. It had

an extended cab, she noted. Four doors. Two seats. Big enough to accommodate anything that might come up. The long truck bed was empty, and she wondered what it would be like to fill it with blankets and lie under the starry night back there with him.

Gabe opened the passenger door for her and helped her in. His hands supported her waist as she climbed up to the unaccustomed height, slid down her hips to guide her in, and then withdrew as he closed the door.

Willow wanted to tell him to keep touching her, but she'd been warned. He was going to take his time.

She sat back on the seat, drew the seat belt over her shoulder, and buckled it out of habit. Although if they had an accident before she got to experience Gabe taking his time, the universe was a crueler place than she could imagine.

3

Gabe didn't say anything when he climbed in beside her and turned the engine over. He wasn't the type for small talk, Willow realized. He wouldn't feel the need to fill the air with empty chatter. When he had something to say, he'd say it.

That was the mystique of the Western man, something she'd observed during her months in Montana. In contrast to the urban men she'd always known, the West bred quiet, capable men who saw what needed to be done and did it. Strong and reliable. And sexy as hell.

She thought Gabe probably wouldn't complain if her hair was messy in the morning. He might complain if there wasn't any coffee. *No wonder women go crazy for cowboys,* Willow thought. That basic nature was a powerful attraction.

Although a woman who constantly wanted to be told that her butt didn't look big would probably be a bad match. She couldn't imagine Gabe lying. She could easily imagine him wondering what started the fight if he told a woman her jeans didn't flatter her assets.

They made the trip to his place in silence. They turned off the highway and then made another turn onto a dirt road. After they'd driven for several minutes without passing anything, she saw a mailbox marking a long graveled driveway. Gabe turned onto the drive and she watched for her first view of his place. Not that she expected to see much of it in the dark.

She saw twin carriage lamps illuminating the front porch that seemed to run all along the front of the sprawling ranch house. For some reason, that porch attracted her. Did he have a porch swing?

Willow imagined sitting on Gabe's lap, facing him, wearing a loose skirt raised up in front and floating over his legs behind her as he rocked his cock into her slick, welcoming flesh on a front porch swing in the quiet night air with nobody around for miles.

She filled out other details in the imaginary picture. She'd wear a shirt that buttoned down the front, and he'd undo the buttons and leave it on her, open, her breasts bared to him and to the night air. He'd draw one taut nipple into his mouth while he used a hand to toy with the other. All the while gliding in and out of her in an unhurried rhythm.

Willow swallowed. The image was so vivid, the idea so erotic. Maybe she'd be able to live that fantasy tonight.

Gabe parked the truck. She could see the shape of a barn off to one side. Did he have cattle? Horses? She should ask. But when he opened up the door and took her hand to help her out, she found herself unable to say anything.

He put his hands on her waist and looked down into her eyes. The shadowy night lay hushed around them. He tugged her closer, until her nipples brushed against his chest. Then a little closer yet, so her hips were tucked against his, her pelvis cradling the unmistakable shape of his erection.

"I'm going to kiss you, Willow," he told her.

Yes. She waited for it, feeling her heart race. What was it about this man? She could have been sixteen again, on her first date, racked with nerves over the kiss to come.

He bent his head toward her, unhurried, and let his mouth close over hers. She breathed him in, the earthy masculine scent of him, and tasted the rich flavors of coffee and tobacco and man all mingled together in one erotic cocktail.

His mouth was firm and warm and in control. He directed the kiss, nudging her lips open, sliding his tongue into her mouth to taste her more deeply.

Willow pressed closer to him, her hips lifting into him just a little, urging that hard male part of his closer. Gabe wrapped his arms around her and slid his hands down to cup her ass. He squeezed and she felt her sex growing slicker.

He kissed her thoroughly, letting his hands roam over her back, her hips. He lifted the fabric of her shirt and tugged it up and broke off the kiss to look down.

"I didn't think you were wearing a bra," he said. His voice sounded deep and husky. "I tried to guess what color your nipples would be."

His hands slid up under her shirt and caressed her naked breasts. His fingers closed on her nipples and pinched. Not hard enough to hurt. Just enough pressure to feel really, really good.

Willow let out a soft moan of delight.

"Too dark to tell," Gabe said. "Let's get closer to the light."

He released her nipples, ending the delicious pressure, and she sighed in disappointment. He gave her a light slap on the butt that made her muscles tighten. "I warned you. I'm going to take my time."

"You warned me," Willow agreed. She walked beside him to the lit porch, her hip bumping against his as he kept her close to his side with one hand on her arm.

They climbed the steps and when they were in the lighted

circle of the carriage lamps, Gabe stopped her. "Now satisfy my curiosity. Take off that shirt and show me your pretty nipples."

The filmy white shirt buttoned down the front. She'd forgotten. Or maybe she hadn't. Was it coincidence that she'd fantasized about wearing an open, unbuttoned shirt with him while she was bare and braless underneath?

Willow undid the buttons, one by one. Then she opened the sides of the fabric to display her naked breasts and her nipples to his full view, as requested.

"Pink little roses," Gabe said. "I'm going to taste them now." He took her hips in a firm hold and lowered his head to draw one nipple into his mouth. He took his time, tasting her, drawing more of her breast into his mouth, lapping at her nipple with his tongue, then letting it slide out of his mouth. The night air hit her heated skin, damp from his tongue, and her nipples tightened even more in response.

She closed her eyes and relaxed into his hold, surrendering her breasts to the stranger who was going to be her lover tonight. When he drew on her nipple, it made heat curl through her, increased the throbbing between her thighs, made her go liquid and soft.

He gave both breasts equal treatment, tasting both as if she were some exotic candy he wanted to sample and savor, while she grew lost in the sensations of his mouth and the air on her bare skin and the promise of what was to come.

When Gabe finally finished and raised his head, he took his Stetson off and said, "I want to taste more of you. I want to get you out of those jeans and put my mouth between your legs. I want to suck your clit the way I sucked your nipples. And then I want to fuck you with my tongue."

Willow's knees nearly collapsed.

"Where would you like that, Willow? Inside? Outside? Standing? Sitting?"

Outside, she thought. In the back of his truck bed. She was

pretty sure she'd see shooting stars even if there weren't any meteor showers.

"Could we make a bed in the back of your truck?" she asked. "I want to watch the stars."

"Whatever you like. I'll do it. You have a seat while I fix it up."

Gabe led her to a bench by the door and she sat down, glad her knees didn't have to keep her upright for a little while. Her cowboy made her go weak with his words and with the far more interesting things he did with his mouth.

He disappeared inside the house carrying his hat and came back without it, his arms full of quilts. He carried them around to the back of the truck and was hidden briefly from view. A few minutes later she watched him walk back toward her.

The way he walked fascinated her. A sort of rolling gait, easy strides. She could watch him all day. He didn't do anything in a rush, and the relaxed power in his body was such a contrast to the stressed-out, hurried posture and jerky movements of a man living in the fast-paced business world.

He seduced her just by walking, Willow realized. With the simplest movements. Watching his body in motion, long, lean frame, corded muscles. She wanted to see that body naked and run her hands over every inch of it.

She was suddenly glad they were moving at his unhurried pace because every little thing he did reminded her that life was too frantic and rushed. And it didn't need to be. Gabe's wasn't.

Did she want hers to be rushed anymore? She had a choice. She didn't have to stay stuck with the old choices she'd made in her early twenties and outgrown. It was just that making life changes at thirty-two seemed so much more radical than at twenty-two. It was harder now.

But if she didn't make the changes she needed now, would she ever? How much harder would it be at forty-two? Willow felt almost certain that if she didn't make different choices and take the risks she longed to take now, she never would.

Too late for second thoughts, she told herself. Her decision had already been made.

"Ready." Gabe extended a hand to her and Willow put hers in it, letting him pull her to her feet. They walked to the bed he'd made and he lifted her up onto the open tailgate. She crawled forward on hands and knees and then rolled onto her side. He'd padded the truck's bed well enough that nothing dug into her hip. If she ended up on her back with him riding her, she wouldn't get bruised.

Gabe lay next to her. "Take your pants off for me, Willow."

She undid her jeans, lifted her hips to tug them down, kicked her shoes free, and drew the denim all the way down her legs and off. She pulled her panties off next and set her clothes off to the side. Her open shirt slipped off easily, and she set that next to the rest of her clothes.

"Lay back and spread your legs. I want a taste of you."

Shivering with anticipation, Willow lay back and opened her legs. She was slick with her own moisture already. Gabe moved between her thighs. His hands slid under her and cupped her butt to lift her up just slightly as his mouth closed over the swollen bud of her clitoris. His tongue worked the sensitive nub in a series of slow licks, suckling her clit as if he planned to keep it up for hours.

Then he released her clit and worked his tongue down the folds of her sex. He really was tasting her. Exploring her with his tongue. And then he slid his tongue inside her. He swirled it around. He licked and thrust with his tongue in alternating movements Willow could never predict or anticipate. Then he began alternating sliding his tongue in and out of her with long licks along her folds and suckling at her clit.

She never wanted it to end. She wanted him to stop driving her wild and just make her come. Torn between two wants, she trembled and moaned and opened her legs wider to let him do whatever he wanted.

He thrust his tongue into her one last time and then kissed his way up her pubic bone, along her belly, and up to her breasts. She was on the brink of orgasm, more aroused than she ever remembered being. Every nerve ending on fire. Shuddering with need. He was still fully clothed. She could feel the rough denim of his jeans against her bare skin.

"I'm going to take my pants off, Willow," Gabe told her. "But before I do, I'm going to do something else."

She was breathing fast but managed to ask, "What?"

"I'm going to tie you up." He bent his head and drew first one of her nipples into his mouth, then the other.

The added stimulation when she was already on the brink made her realize she might come if he did it again, without him even getting inside her. But then his next words pushed her even closer to the edge.

"You taste good everywhere, Willow, but I think you'll taste even better if your legs are spread wide for me and tied at the ankles. I'll tie your arms at the wrists. And you'll be spread-eagled for me. That's how I want you the first time I make you come."

Well. That was kinky. Unexpected. And it turned her on. The idea of letting him tie her up seduced her on more than one level. It was sexually exciting. It was also risky and Willow was sick of playing it safe. But it wasn't so risky that it was outside the bounds of rational behavior.

The two men Gabe had been with had been frequent visitors at Lemon Espresso recently. Laura liked them, and she had sound judgment. Her experiences as a nurse had given her a finely honed sense for who was likely to cause trouble. Jolie liked them, too, enough that she'd let the blond man carry her off. She had street smarts in addition to a law degree, and Willow knew Jolie wouldn't have picked him to play with if he wasn't a decent man.

So. His two friends had won the approval of two women who didn't give it lightly. It wasn't likely that Gabe's character didn't measure up to the standard of his friends.

Missoula also had a small-town environment, where gossip raged like wildfire on the wind. If a man had a bad reputation, everybody knew about it and the entire history behind it. There were a handful of men all the women avoided. She'd been warned about them by her landlady the first week she'd been in town. Gabe's name wasn't among those.

Willow thought of what she'd seen of Gabe so far. His careful handling of her. The way he'd driven. He hadn't given her any reason to suspect that he'd do anything she didn't want him to do, and his every word and action so far made her feel comfortable with him.

"What do you say, Willow? Will you let me do that?" he asked her.

He wouldn't insist if she said no. She didn't want to say no. It wasn't the safe thing to do. It was erotic as hell and she wanted to do it.

"Yes."

Gabe lifted himself off her and produced rope from somewhere. He must have brought it out along with the quilts. He wrapped it around her wrists and ankles and then tied the other end of each rope to a loop on the truck's sides. Two at the top on either side, two at the bottom.

"Do you get extra points for roping?" Willow asked, her voice husky with passion. She was so close. Her sex throbbed. Her nipples ached for more pressure. And the smooth rope he tied her with meant she couldn't touch herself. Couldn't do anything to bring him closer to gain any relief.

"The erotic rodeo?" He smiled at her in the starlight. "There's an idea with merit." He knelt beside her and undid his jeans. Then he stood to get them off, along with his boots. He stripped away his shirt, too, and then looked down at her. "Watch me, Willow."

She did. She watched, fascinated, as he slid his boxers down, freeing his thick, hard cock.

"See how hard you've made me?" he asked. "I'm going to let you taste for yourself. I'm going to kneel over you and slide my cock between your lips. I want your tongue gliding over the head of my cock and your mouth wrapped around me."

Torture. He really was taking his time. Making her crazy for him. And his graphic description of exactly how he wanted her to pleasure his cock heated her even further.

He suited actions to words, and Willow opened her mouth to take him in. She let her tongue explore him the way he'd explored her. As if they had all night and all the next night, too, if that wasn't enough time. She raised her head to take more of him into her mouth and savored the texture of his smooth, hard length gliding in and out of her lips, over her tongue.

He tasted so good. A tang of salt, a hint of musk, an earthy male taste she loved. He was so hard, so smooth. He was a stranger. She was naked, bound, and so excited, she was trembling, shivers running through her body. Sucking his cock made her even wilder for him.

"Suck me hard," Gabe instructed. She did, drawing him even farther into her mouth in the process. She wrapped her lips tightly around him and found herself wishing that he'd coat her tongue with semen, come down her throat. She wanted to swallow him and keep right on sucking his cock.

"That's enough." He pulled free, then reached over and retrieved a condom, tore open the packet, and rolled the condom down to the base of his cock.

He moved down to settle between her spread-eagled thighs. The thick head of his cock probed against her opening. "I'm going to come inside you, Willow, but not in your mouth. Not the first time. The first time I come inside you, I'll be balls-deep in your sweet, hot pussy. You're going to grip my cock and milk me dry because I'm going to make you come so hard, you won't have any other choice."

Gabe let the head of his cock press inside her and then he eased in farther, filling her by inches, until he'd worked his length all the way inside.

He was so leisurely about entering her that Willow let out a soft laugh when he came to a stop. "Done?"

He ground his pelvis against hers, letting her feel his cock probing even deeper inside her. "I'm just beginning."

4

Gabe was buried to his balls in Willow, feeling a satisfaction so complete that his orgasm would just be the icing on the cake.

A man did not get to be thirty-four without taking a few trips between the blankets. He enjoyed women. He enjoyed sex. The pure act of release was a basic need.

But he was old enough to know the difference between providing mutual relief and making love. Whether she knew it or not, Willow hadn't penned an invitation to a one-night stand. She didn't want a hurried, uncomplicated fuck. She wanted a lover. She was a romantic and it showed in her choice of words.

She wanted an erotic ride, and he was the man to take her on it, but after that she was going across the front of his saddle and they were riding off into the sunset together, so to speak.

One night wasn't going to be nearly enough time for either

of them. There was too much heat between them. Since she wasn't planning to stick around, that posed a challenge.

He'd decided to pursue her because she was worth pursuing. She'd agreed to be with him tonight easily, but Gabe had been willing to persist as long as it took.

He was taking his time with her because she was worth the time. Gaining Willow for his lover was worth an unrushed and thorough seduction. He wanted more from her than one night of mutual pleasure. Her body, her responses, her imagination and emotions, everything that was the key to the heart of this woman would not be won by a man who didn't take the time to understand her. Her full sexual response would belong to the man who took the time to awaken it.

Her poem had told him she wanted that. Wanted to be seduced utterly. Wanted a lover who could match her passion. He understood that very well. He'd waited a long time to find the lover who could match his.

He'd been willing to suspend judgment until they had a chance to try each other out, but now he was certain. Willow was the one for him. And by the end of the night, he'd make sure she knew he was the man for her.

He intended to lay claim to her and persuade her to stay, and he didn't expect it to be easy.

Being inside her was pure heaven. He loved the taste of her, the sensation of burying his cock in her, and he was going to enjoy the hell out of fucking her.

"I hope you're ready, Willow," he murmured as he trailed kisses along her cheek. "I'm going to ride you hard."

She quivered under him, and her inner walls clasped his cock like a hot silk glove. She was so ready for him, swollen and soft with need. His balls tightened in response.

He withdrew, then thrust back into her, again and again, a slow, steady rhythm. "I love fucking you," he told her as he continued to ride in and out of her. "I love how you feel under me. I love how you look, naked and ready for me, all spread out and tied up, just begging to be fucked long and hard."

He gave her a fast, deep thrust and instructed, "Bend your knees a bit more. I want your hips lifted up just a little."

Willow shifted under him, and the new angle made her moan in pleasure.

"Now it's time for you to come," he said. He kept up a steady rhythm, made each thrust harder, driving deep into her. He felt her inner muscles begin the fluttering that meant she was on the edge and he gave it to her a little harder. That did it. She shuddered under him and clamped down on his cock as she came.

"That's it," he murmured. "Now you're going to milk my cock until my balls are empty." He thrust deep into her and let his release sweep through him. Her little pussy muscles tightened as she continued to come, surrendering to the pleasure he gave her, squeezing his cock, and he pumped himself into her as she did, in fact, milk him of every drop.

She let out a long sigh of satisfaction and ground her pelvis against him, clearly enjoying the feel of him inside her and on top of her.

Gabe rested on top of her, careful to support his weight so he didn't crush her, savoring the feel of the woman he wanted naked underneath him, legs open to him, still quivering with the aftershocks of orgasm. She felt more his in this moment, with his cock still buried in her and both of them spent, than she had when he'd laid her out and tied her for his taking.

After a few minutes he moved off her and disposed of the condom, then settled beside her. He raised up on one elbow and let his free hand trail over her body, exploring the curve of her belly, her hips, the rise of her rib cage.

When she shifted her hips restlessly, he smiled and settled his hand between her legs. He slid two fingers into her, wanting to keep her penetrated by some part of himself, and she made a little sound of pleasure that indicated she shared his desire.

The feel of her silky skin under his hands, the way she responded to him, the heat between her thighs, and the snug clasp of her most vulnerable flesh made an irresistible temptation.

"You are more than hot enough to keep me inside you all night long," he told her. "Next time, though, I'm going to tie your hands behind your back and I'm going to have you on your knees. I'm going to fill my hands with your ass while I fill this—" He moved his fingers inside her in a graphic demonstration. "—with my cock and my come."

"*Yes,*" she said in fervent agreement.

"Right now, though, I like looking at you all relaxed with pleasure, on your back for me."

He continued to work her pussy with his fingers, and her hips started to move in rhythm with his hand.

"I love this," Willow sighed. "I'm naked in the back of a pickup truck under the stars. It's so beautiful out here. I can't remember the last time I felt this relaxed."

Gabe wiggled a finger inside her. "You don't feel relaxed," he teased. "You feel tight. Maybe a massage will help that."

She giggled. "You could be right. I might need an internal massage."

He toyed with her, enjoying the feel of her flesh and the pleasure she took from him. "You're some woman, Willow Daniels."

"You're some man, Gabe Wilson." She tilted her head to smile at him. "Are you going to make me come again?"

"Later," he told her. "This is called afterplay."

"Ah. Afterplay." She hummed in delight as he thrust his fingers deeper into her. "Your afterplay is better than most men's play. So is your foreplay, for that matter."

"That's because we suit each other." He let his fingers slide out of her and trail up to stroke her clit. "And I have to keep you warmed up. I'm not finished fucking you."

He gave her pussy a last petting and then rose up to undo the ropes. He removed the ropes tying her wrists and ankles and set them aside. "Roll over on your belly and put your hands behind your back."

She complied.

"Now cross your wrists." She did as he instructed, and Gabe bound her hands with expert speed. "Spread your knees apart and lift your ass for me. Keep your head and shoulders down."

Willow shifted into position. Her ass raised high, thighs spread, sex exposed to him, she invited his cock to plunge into her and take everything she offered.

"What a sight." He knelt behind her and ran his hands over the lush curves of her ass. The head of his cock seemed to seek out her slick folds, nudging against her.

Willow thrust back at him and his head pressed into her. With nothing between them, he could feel the full heat of her flesh waiting to enclose him. He wanted to press forward and let his cock slide all the way in, but it wasn't safe. Unless . . .

"You on the Pill, Willow?" he asked her. "Is there any reason why I should stop now?"

She made a sound of frustration. "I'm not on the Pill."

"Well, that makes it risky. I want you like this, but better safe than sorry." He reached for another condom and sheathed himself in it. Then he sheathed his cock in her flesh.

"I'm going to go hard and fast and deep this time," he warned her. "That ass of yours is too inviting and your sweet pussy is too hot for me to take it slow."

"You say that like it's a bad thing," Willow said. He could hear the smile in her voice, along with the sensual invitation.

She was softened from pleasure, relaxed enough to enjoy it

like this without him having to hold back for fear that he'd hurt her. He held her ass in his hands and then he gave his cock to her as hard and fast as she could take it. Slamming into her as deep as he could go. Taking her from behind until they both came in a lusty rush.

Gabe stayed buried inside her for a minute while his heart returned to normal. When he felt her knees tremble with the effort to hold the position, he withdrew, disposed of the second condom of the night, and lay down beside her.

He pulled her on top of him and shifted her until they were both comfortable. Her legs spread to rest on either side of his thighs and her head rested on his chest under his chin. He could feel the soft weight of her breasts pressing into him, the length of her hair spilling over his arm, her lips moving against his shoulder in a string of light kisses.

"I have a beautiful woman in my arms, and the night is young," he said. "I have to ask if you want to spend the entire night out here or if you want to go inside at some point."

"Dunno." She nuzzled his throat and cuddled into him. "Maybe later. I like being out here right now. It's like camping out. Or at least, I think it is. I've never camped out. If it's like this, I've really been missing something."

"You've been missing me," Gabe informed her. "Camping holds no thrills to compare to my manly form."

She let out a low, rippling laugh. "Roller coasters hold no thrills to compare to your manly form."

"You inspire me to new heights." Gabe squeezed her ass and Willow squirmed against him in response. "I'm going to lay here and recover awhile. You'd better rest up, too. Your legs were giving out on you. You're out of shape. You'll never last on a ranch if you can't even keep up with me in bed."

"I can keep up with you in bed." She nipped at his shoulder, grazing his skin with her teeth. "But I think I will just lay here for a minute."

Willow settled into him and in a few minutes Gabe heard her breathing settle into a rhythm that told him she'd fallen asleep in his arms. He watched the stars wheel overhead and held her close.

She was so comfortable. Mmm. Willow stretched and felt something hard prodding her belly. She shifted against it, an exploratory movement, and realized she'd dozed off and Gabe was clearly ready for her to wake up. His cock jutted into her, a silent demand for attention, and she felt a wide smile spreading over her face. What a way to wake up.

She wanted some more attention herself, now that she was awake again. Wanted more of him hard and hot inside her.

"Do I get to be on top this time?" she asked.

"If you like."

For an answer, she spread her legs farther apart and shifted up along his body until her sex pressed against his erect penis. She was still slick from the last time, ready to take him again. His erection opened her, preparing the way for him to slide inside.

"Hold on." Gabe lifted her hips slightly and reached between them to roll another condom on. "Good thing I bought a whole box of these at the drugstore while I was waiting for you to come out of that coffee shop. I'd hate to run out."

"You bought a whole box of condoms for me?" Willow asked. "Before you even spoke to me?"

"I spoke to you. I said yes when you asked me a question. I recited the world's most romantic poem to you. Then I bought a box of condoms."

"Oh. That changes everything," Willow agreed, rolling her eyes. "You buy boxes of condoms at the drop of a hat, then."

"I'll buy a new box every time you drop your hat. Especially if you drop your drawers next," Gabe promised. "Now stop talking. I'm trying to get laid."

She let her hips rise until she felt the head of his cock

nudge against her opening and then she sank down, taking him inside her.

"That's better." He reached down between their bodies and stroked her clit.

"God, that feels good," she sighed. He filled her, making her pussy stretch to accommodate him. The added stimulation from his hand made her melt into him. If it were possible to die of pleasure, she was in a lot of danger with this man.

"How are your arms?"

Now that he mentioned it, it was starting to feel a little uncomfortable, having them bound behind her. "I think they're starting to cramp," she answered.

He gave her clit a last stroke and then his hands went around her, working at the rope.

"Do you have to untie me? I like it."

Willow felt a curious reluctance to be freed. She'd never had a lover who wanted her bound for him before. She'd never thought to ask for it, either. Hadn't imagined it would make her feel like this, sexual and feminine. Intensely turned on.

"You're an impatient woman. There's plenty of time for me to tie you into all sorts of interesting positions, but you'll enjoy it a lot more if you don't get sore now."

Gabe finished undoing the knot and freed her hands. "Stretch those arms out. While you're at it, run them over my body. I want your hands on me." His voice was low and deep in the darkness, like a part of the night.

She stretched, luxuriating in the unrestricted movement. Then she let her hands explore the fascinating territory that was Gabe Wilson. His chest. His shoulders. His lean waist. She sat up higher and reached behind to feel the long muscles of his thighs and then she slipped one hand between them to stroke his balls. They tightened at her touch.

"What were you going to do with that box of condoms if I hadn't been interested?" Willow asked, curious.

"Give it to Reuben," he answered. He rocked his hips under her, thrusting up into her welcoming heat.

Willow arched her back and rose up and down, meeting his thrusts, sinking down onto his cock and then lifting up again. Slow. Delicious. She loved the sensation of him filling her inch by inch, drawing each stroke out.

"Reuben's your friend, the one who was inside waiting for Laura?" she asked.

"Yep." Gabe grasped her hips and held her down so he could thrust deeper. "If Laura's the brown-haired one who was behind the coffee counter."

"That's her. She owns Lemon Espresso." *Yes, just like that,* she thought, her body going liquid for him as she took the deeper penetration and wished she could take even more.

"She ever tell you why she named it that?"

His voice kept her anchored like his hands. He wasn't ready to let her come yet. She knew when she did, she'd come harder because he'd let it build and refused to let her rush.

"It's her philosophy. When life hands you lemons, make coffee and get to work." Willow bent forward and let her breasts press into him, loving the contact of his bare flesh against hers, his cock thick and hard inside her, his hands holding her hips in a firm grip while he fucked her at his unhurried pace.

"Practical. No wonder Reuben likes her."

"Um," Willow agreed. She was rapidly losing the thread of the conversation. Gabe had increased the tempo of his thrusts just a little and oh, God, it felt so good. . . .

"I'm going to make you come again," he told her. "I'm going to drive my cock into you as deep as you can take it and fuck you mindless."

He suited action to words, and in this position he could go very deep. Willow spread her thighs as wide as she could and positioned her hips to take him as deep as possible. His hands kept her right where he wanted her, and with each thrust Willow felt all rational thought slipping away. There was nothing but the solid reality of Gabe under her and inside her, filling her, fucking her.

"Gabe," she moaned, all but shaking with the need to come.

He let go of one hip and found her clit with his fingers and that extra stimulation sent her over the edge. She came hard and it seemed to go on and on as he fingered and fucked her into oblivion.

Willow collapsed into him and tried to breathe, tried to slow her racing heart as the last ripples of orgasm faded.

"Gabe," she said again when she could speak. And then she couldn't think of any more words.

"Willow." He rolled so that she was under him, his cock still buried inside her, his body covering hers. She wrapped her legs around him and her arms curled around his neck, hugging him close with all her limbs.

5

Long minutes later, Gabe stirred. "I'm squashing you."

"No, you're not."

"I need to move, anyway. The condom might slip off."

"Oh."

Willow loosened her hold on him and Gabe withdrew. He hated to pull out of her. Then again, now he could look forward to the next time he slid home into that sweet pussy of hers.

He disposed of the latest dead soldier of the night and wondered how many more brothers would fall before the sunrise. He smiled at the thought.

"You are a wild thing," he said, lying back down beside her. He shifted her so that they spooned together. His penis nestled in the soft curves of her ass, making a snug resting place, and his arms clasped her close. "We're going to need another box soon."

She let out a soft laugh. "I don't think we can use up a whole box of condoms in one night."

"Well, there's tomorrow. The next night. That box is living on borrowed time. We're going to need the industrial-sized box."

Gabe nuzzled the side of her neck and let his hands cup her breasts. They were just the right size, not too big, nicely shaped. And her nipples were pure temptation. He gave them each a gentle pinch and was rewarded when she shuddered in response.

"You sound like you're planning to do this again," she said.

"You're not?" He released one nipple and sent his hand down her body to nudge between her thighs and cup her sex. "I find it hard to believe that I've satisfied you so thoroughly you won't want any more of me. Also, there are many ways I have yet to tie you up."

"I should try them all," Willow agreed. Would it hurt anything if she let this one night stretch out, enjoy what he offered her as long as she could? They might be able to try all the variations before she had to leave. She shivered a little and cuddled closer to him.

"Getting cold?"

"A bit."

"Hold on." He moved away, rolled her onto her back, flipped the top quilt around her, piled their discarded clothes onto her belly, and tugged his boots on to protect his bare feet. Then he bent and scooped her up. "Time to move this party indoors. And maybe you'd like a shower. I'll wash you. You can wash me."

"Sounds good." Willow snuggled into him as he climbed out of the truck and carried her to the house.

Once inside, he set her on her feet and took the loose bundle of clothing from her. She held the quilt around herself and smiled at him. "I love your outfit."

"A man's never naked if he's got his boots on," Gabe informed her. He put their clothes on a low bench that stood by the door. He'd hung his hat on the rack above it earlier.

"I think you should leave them on the next time. So you don't feel naked." She gave him an innocent look.

"Well, now I know your secret. Cowboy boots make you hot."

"There is something about them." She eyed his boots, then the rest of him, with avid interest.

He stripped the quilt away from her, folded it, and set it next to their clothes.

"That's not fair," she complained. "Now I'm the only one naked."

"I'll buy you a pair of boots," Gabe promised.

She giggled. "So we can knock them together?"

"That's one good reason."

Gabe pulled his boots off and set them under the bench. Then he took her hand and pulled her into his arms. "Kiss me, Willow."

She did. She gave him her mouth, tilted her head back to give him better access, opened her lips for him, twined her tongue with his. Her naked breasts teased his chest, and his cock twitched against her belly.

It didn't matter that he'd just finished fucking her not ten minutes ago. She was so sensual and passionate, the depths of her response only beginning to be tapped. He knew already that he'd always want her again, no matter how many times he had her.

He lifted his head. "Keep kissing me like that and we won't make it to the bedroom, let alone the shower."

"We probably could use a shower," she said.

He led her along the hallway to the bathroom and turned the shower on. A cold shower wouldn't hurt him, but he doubted Willow would enjoy it, so he adjusted the temperature to something moderate. He looked over at the naked woman waiting beside him and felt his cock twitch again. She was turning him downright insatiable.

He took her by the hand and tugged her forward, into the shower and under the waiting spray. He joined her and let the shower curtain fall shut, closing them in, and then he took a minute to stand back and enjoy the view.

Willow stood facing him, her head tilted back slightly, the water pouring down her body, drops clinging to the rosy buds of her nipples and the small thatch of hair between her thighs.

He didn't think he'd ever in his life seen a more erotic sight, although Willow spread-eagled and tied on her back for his pleasure might top it. Willow with her hands bound behind her, on her knees, her ass and her sex offered up to him was definitely in the running, too.

She was easy on the eyes.

Gabe reached for the soap, wet it, and made a lather in his hands. Then he set the soap aside and pulled Willow forward, so the water just hit her back.

He soaped her shoulders, the delicate hollows of her collarbones, the slope of her breasts, the hard points of her nipples. He lathered her belly, her hips, her thighs. He worked his way down her body, then turned her around to face the water and let it rinse the suds away.

Getting more soap, he washed her back and then the full globes of her butt. He let his finger trail down between them and felt Willow shiver in response. He went down farther, until he probed at her anus with one soap-slick finger. She arched her back to open herself to his touch, silent encouragement. He toyed with the rosy little opening, running his finger over and around it, and she let out a moan.

It was a delicate, highly sensitive area. Some women found a little anal stimulation very pleasurable. Some found it orgasmic. Willow was definitely open to letting him touch her there. She didn't flinch away and responded to his light touch. He continued to caress her, exploring her, letting her reactions guide him.

Reaching around to the front of her, Gabe cupped her pussy in one hand and stroked her clit. He kept stroking it in a leisurely circular motion as he worked his finger, lubricated with the soap, into her tight ass.

She moaned again and moved her hips back and forth, rocking into his hands.

"I want to make you come like this," he said, moving his finger in and out of her ass in slow, gentle strokes.

"Yes." She leaned into him and shifted her feet to spread her legs wider apart.

He built a careful rhythm, not putting too much direct pressure on her sensitive clit, not using her ass too hard or too fast as the delicate tissue stretched for his penetration.

She moaned louder, shuddered, and came hard in his hands.

"I love making you come, Willow." He stroked his finger in and out of her ass a few more times, while his other hand cupped and squeezed her mound. "Now it's your turn. I want you to suck my cock until I come, and then I want you to swallow every drop of it I give you."

He slid his finger out of her and traded places with her, standing under the spray.

Willow took the soap and washed him first, his shoulders, back, chest, belly. Then she knelt in front of him and ran soap-slick hands over his cock, his balls, between his legs and along the crevice of his ass. He tilted back to let the water rinse away the lather, leaving his half-erect cock water slick and soap free.

She leaned forward and took him into her mouth. He wasn't fully engorged, so she was able to take him all the way to the base of his cock. She stroked his balls with one hand. With the other, she teased his anus with a soap-slick finger, but didn't try to go further.

She sucked the length of him, ran her tongue around him, flicked it over the head of his cock, and grazed him lightly with her teeth.

Gabe fisted his hands in her hair. "God, woman. You do that right."

She worked him with her mouth, up and down, around, until he was fully engorged and aching to come.

"Suck me hard, now," he instructed. "Fuck me with your mouth."

Willow did, increasing the pressure and moving her lips up and down his cock a little faster, and then he came, spurting into her mouth. She swallowed, then licked at the head of his cock as if greedy for every last taste of him. He was highly sensitized so soon after coming, and the light touch of her tongue made his balls go tight.

Fucking her mouth was an entirely different pleasure from sinking the thick length of his erection into her. Like making her come while he stimulated her anally was a different pleasure for her. He liked her openness to variety, her enthusiasm for enjoying her body and his.

"You sucked me so good, Willow," he told her, massaging his fingers along her scalp. "I think the next time I come down your throat I want you all tied up. Sitting, so your lips are level with my cock and I can stand in front of you and just rock back and forth, fucking your mouth."

He felt her shudder at his graphic words.

"Or maybe I'll position you so I can fuck you with my tongue while you swallow my cock."

"Gabe." She clutched at him. "If you keep saying things like that, I'm going to lose my balance."

"I won't let you." He pulled her upright and under the water with him, rinsing away the rest of the soap. He held her naked body close against him, bracing her. She leaned into him.

Relaxed. Trusting. His, if he had anything to say about it, and for more than tonight.

Gabe shut off the water before they ran out of hot and reached out to grab towels. He draped one around her and the other around himself. They stepped out of the shower and dried off in silence.

He took the damp towels and hung them up. Then he took Willow's hand and led her out of the bathroom and down the hall to his bedroom.

Gabe flipped the light switch on and walked to the bed, folded back the top sheet and the quilt, and made an inviting gesture. Willow climbed onto the bed. He studied the picture she made there, her body flushed and relaxed from pleasure, naked, a hint of pink flesh showing between her thighs and her nipples in hard buds.

Beauty.

"Spread your legs. I want you to show me all of you."

She opened her thighs and exposed herself to him. And that was even more beautiful. She was glistening with moisture from the shower, slightly swollen from fucking, rosy from arousal.

"I have to taste that sweet pussy of yours again."

Gabe knelt beside the bed and reached for Willow. He drew her forward, hooked her legs over his shoulders, and filled his hands with her heart-shaped ass. He ran his tongue along the length of her lips, and then buried it inside. Again and again he thrust his tongue into her pussy while she moaned and bucked her hips against him.

Gabe lapped at her and enjoyed the taste of her, the sensation of naked, wiggling woman in his arms, the sight of her on her back with her legs open. He slid his tongue out of her and licked the slick folds of her sex, teasing her.

"Are you going to fuck me again any time soon?" she asked, breathing hard.

"Yes." He'd left the box of condoms in the truck, but he had two packets left in his jeans. He thrust his tongue into her one last time while she squirmed in pleasure, then released her and stood up. "Be right back. Don't move."

He made the trip down the hall and back in record time, rolling the condom on as he worked his way back to Willow. She hadn't moved. He took his place between her spread thighs again and thrust his cock home.

It was fast and furious and ended quickly, Willow keening her pleasure when they both came again.

Gabe made a quick trip to the bathroom to lose the condom, turned the bedroom light off, then crawled into bed and nudged her hip with his knee on the way. "Get over here, woman."

She made an inarticulate sound and complied, moving up toward the pillows and the center of the bed, into his open arms. He held her against his chest and they were both asleep within minutes.

Gabe woke later in the night and went down the hall again, tugged on his boots, and retrieved the box of condoms from his truck. If either of them woke up wanting more—and given the degree of lust between them, the odds of that were good—they might deplete the supply on hand. He didn't want to have to interrupt things to take care of that little errand. Best do it now.

He left his boots under the bench by the door again and carried the box into the bedroom. He set it on the bedside table, peeled out of his jeans, and climbed back into bed naked. Willow snuggled into him as if she'd missed his warmth.

"I missed you, too," he told her.

Her breasts teased his chest, and she slid one leg over his until he could feel the softness of her pussy nestled up against his thigh.

He dropped a kiss on top of her silky hair and decided that

there was something to be said for the renegades of new Montana, after all.

Willow woke up to hear Gabe's voice in her ear. "Time to go take care of the horses."

Was that some sort of Western slang?

No, she realized a minute later as he left the bed and started to dress. She yawned and leaned up on one arm, watching him with bleary eyes. "Should I help you?"

"Do you know how?" he asked, pausing a moment midway through the task of tucking a plain white T-shirt into his jeans.

"No." Willow sat up all the way and swung her legs over the edge of the bed. "Is it hard?"

"It takes some muscle. How about if you make the coffee and bring a cup to me in the barn, instead?"

"Okay."

She lowered her feet to the hardwood floor. It felt cool in the early morning air. She stood up, naked and completely relaxed, and stretched while she watched Gabe put on a pair of thick cotton socks. Then they headed down the hall together. He pulled on his boots. She retrieved her discarded clothing from the night before and dressed.

"Coffeepot's on the counter in the kitchen. Coffee's in the can next to it. Mugs in the cupboard above. I take mine black, no sugar." Gabe leaned down and brushed his mouth across hers in a hard, quick kiss that curled her toes, and went out the door.

She grinned as she watched the door close behind him. Not a word about the wild wreck her hair had to be, or the fact that she probably had creases on her face from burying it in the pillow. She'd been right about his priorities.

Willow walked to the kitchen and realized as she took a

step that she'd adopted Gabe's lazy pace. Not that he was slow, he just didn't waste any movements. He conserved his strength. Efficiency experts were always saying that hurrying caused accidents and breakage and wasted time, making people less effective. She'd be willing to bet that Gabe was very effective. He certainly was in bed.

She found the coffeemaker and can of grounds where he'd told her they'd be. It didn't take long to start a pot brewing. She pulled out mugs and looked in his refrigerator for cream for hers. He didn't have any. She shrugged. Drinking her coffee black the morning after was a small price to pay for a night of world-class sex.

His kitchen looked rustic. Oak cabinets mellow with age. Countertops in an olive green shade that had been popular in the seventies and had come back into style as the retro look. Plain white walls. The wood floor looked like the same vintage as the cabinets and ran throughout the house. She'd seen a few scattered woven rag rugs, but no other floor coverings.

Gabe's bedroom was plain, too, what little she'd noticed of the decor. Gabe was by far the most interesting thing in it, and everything else had sort of faded into the background. She had noticed the bed's Hollywood frame covered with a bright quilt, a low oak dresser, and matching bedside table.

The furniture she'd seen in his living room was equally simple. All of it looked sturdy, as if it had lasted for a couple of generations already and would last a few more.

Willow leaned against the kitchen counter and watched the world outside the wide kitchen window come to life. Birds and squirrels were busily going about their tasks at the crack of dawn. The coffeemaker gurgled and hissed in the background. She had a dreamy smile on her face and a slight ache between her thighs.

God is in his heaven and all's right with the world, she thought.

She made a trip to the bathroom and rummaged around

for a brush to smooth out the tangles in her hair. She splashed water on her face and dried it off, then looked at the result.

She looked happy. Possibly even smug.

"You look like a very satisfied woman," Willow said to her reflection.

She'd taken a risk, spending the night with Gabe. She'd taken another risk in letting him tie her up, and that had led to the most satisfying sexual experience she could remember.

With risks came rewards.

She returned to the kitchen, poured two mugs full of coffee, and carried them down to the barn and Gabe.

6

Willow watched Gabe work while she sipped her coffee. It was stronger than she was used to, but she liked the way it woke her up. Although just watching him move could do that without caffeine. No wonder she'd jumped at his erotic offer. No wonder she'd jumped *him*. A woman would have to be dead from the waist down not to wake up and pay attention to a man like him.

She hid a smile behind her mug at that thought and took another drink of the hot, bitter brew.

It was easy to see where he'd gotten the strength in his arms, shoulders, and back. Swinging a pitchfork would do that. Not to mention lifting heavy bales of hay. She didn't know how much each bale weighed, but it had to be a lot. He worked quickly and easily, doing a task Willow was pretty sure would leave her dripping with sweat and trembling, and then he put the pitchfork and his gloves away and took the mug of coffee she'd brought him.

He wasn't even breathing hard.

"How about breakfast?" he asked her over the rim of his mug.

I think I might say yes to anything this man asked me, Willow thought. Which, come to think of it, was already an impressive list. *Yes, I'd like to go home with a total stranger and have sex. Yes, I'd like to be tied up. Yes, I want my ass fingered while I have an orgasm.* Was she forgetting anything? Oh, yeah, she'd given him head on her knees and loved every second of it. He'd asked her to do that, too.

"Breakfast sounds good." Her stomach growled as she answered and he smiled at her.

"I'd better feed you. You need to keep up your strength if you want to place in the erotic rodeo," he teased.

Willow laughed. "I thought I was already winning."

"That was just the trials." Gabe tweaked her nipple and she felt her sex quiver. "This is no time to lose focus."

He set his coffee mug down and ran his hands under her shirt to cup her breasts and stroke her nipples. "Ever done it in a hayloft?" he asked her.

Willow shook her head from side to side.

"That's a damn shame. It's an American tradition." He lowered his head to hers and kissed her, sliding his tongue into her mouth while he pinched her nipples between his fingers. "Breakfast may have to wait."

Heat curled through her belly and she felt her sex swelling with anticipation. God, he made her hot. The idea of lying back in a pile of hay, having sex in a barn . . . Why was that such a turn-on?

"Are you going to leave your boots on this time?" she asked him, breaking the kiss for a minute.

"Yes. I'm going to leave everything on. I'm just going to unfasten my jeans and take them down far enough to get my cock free."

She felt her sex clench as she imagined herself, naked from

the waist down, her shirt open, bare breasts exposed, her nipples hard from the cool morning air and arousal, her pussy glistening with her own lubrication, legs spread open. And Gabe kneeling between her spread thighs, fully dressed, with his hard cock in his hand.

It was hard to breathe. It was hard to stay standing. She put her coffee mug down before she dropped it and grasped his shirt with both hands. She leaned into his body and tilted her head back to meet his mouth. They kissed deeply, tongues tangling, hearts racing.

Gabe slid one hand down her belly and into her jeans. She moaned in pleasure and encouragement and thrust her pelvis up to give him a better angle. The tips of his fingers just barely brushed the top of her mound. The jeans didn't allow him to reach far enough to stroke the aching bud of her clit or to spread open her folds and thrust inside her.

Willow made a low sound of frustration and let go of his shirt to undo the snap and zipper.

That was better. His hand slid in farther, down inside her panties, until he was cupping her heat-slick flesh. His palm pressing into her mound felt so good, Willow thought that alone would be enough to make her come. Then one finger slid between her labia and penetrated her.

"Gabe." She moaned his name into his open mouth. She ran her hands over him, squeezing his ass, rubbing the denim-covered bulge of his erection. She wanted to touch him everywhere.

"I'm going to have you, Willow," he told her, lifting his head and looking down into her eyes. "I'm going to get you out of these pants and I'm going to get inside you. I'm going to give you my cock and you're going to love every inch of it."

She already did. She shuddered with want.

"And it's going to take a long time for me to come because

I've already filled this sweet pussy of yours so many times. I may have to fuck you for hours."

She felt her vaginal muscles clench around his finger as it teased her, thrusting in and out of her. He drew it out again, along the length of her lips, over her throbbing clit, and then pulled his hand out of her pants, leaving her aching for more.

"You'd better get moving while you can still climb the ladder," Gabe said.

Ladder? Her dazed mind tried to process that. Oh. Yes. They were heading for the hayloft. That would be up.

"This way." He turned her around and urged her forward with a light slap on her butt. "Get that luscious ass moving."

Willow saw the ladder and went toward it. She climbed up to the hayloft, vividly aware of Gabe behind her, hot and weak from his graphic words and the images they built in her mind.

She reached the top and sat down on a loose pile of hay next to the stacked bales. Gabe climbed up into the loft with her and stood over her.

"This is kinky," she informed him. "Sex in a barn. In broad daylight." It was also fun. He made her feel so good inside. Happy. Relaxed. Unhurried. Playful.

"Kinky would involve whips." Gabe grinned down at her.

"Some would say your rope fetish is pretty kinky." She tilted her head and gave him a considering look. "Tying up helpless women. Using them to satisfy your base urges."

"One woman," Gabe corrected. "Do you see a harem up here?"

"Just me." She lay back and unbuttoned her shirt, but didn't open it.

"Hey." He prodded her foot with one boot. "No hiding. I want to see those."

"These?" Willow gave him an innocent look and ran her hands over her fabric-draped breasts.

"Those."

She pulled the shirt open to expose her bared torso to him, her nipples hardened into tight pink buds.

"Touch them."

She grinned at him. "See? You are kinky."

"You started it. Touch your breasts for me, Willow. Pinch your nipples." Gabe's voice was low and husky with desire, his eyes hot as he watched her.

She did as he asked, moving her hands slowly over her breasts. Her palms slid over her swollen nipples and she pinched them between her fingers. The pressure felt good and created an answering need for pressure between her legs. "Like this?"

"Just like that." Gabe knelt beside her and tugged her jeans down her hips.

She'd left them unfastened so it was easy for him to strip her bare to the waist. It was so like the erotic image she'd pictured in the barn below. She was naked except for her unbuttoned, open shirt. He was fully clothed. There was something very exciting about that. It made her feel daring and naughty.

Although the hay wasn't as soft as she'd imagined. She grimaced when she felt it poke into her hip.

"Here." Gabe spread her pants out and lifted her onto them, keeping a protective barrier of cloth between her skin and the hay. She lay on her back, knees drawn up and just slightly apart, her head turned to one side to look at him. She gave her nipples another pinch and felt her sex throb with need.

"Open your legs."

Willow moved her feet farther apart and let her thighs fall open, exposing herself to him.

"Touch yourself there."

She stroked her fingertip lightly over her clit, massaging it.

"Beautiful." Gabe undid his jeans and worked them down his hips. His engorged penis jutted out toward her.

"Did you bring a condom?" Willow asked.

"In my pocket." He pulled out a packet, tore it open, and started to roll it on.

"Wait." She reached over and held his hand. "I want you in my mouth first."

"Well, now who's kinky." Gabe didn't sound like he objected. She could hear the amusement in his voice as he moved to a better angle to accommodate her, and guided his penis into her mouth.

She swirled her tongue around him, licking at him, tasting him, sucking him as far into her mouth as she could take him.

She let him slide out of her lips so she could speak, and sighed, "I am." She licked her tongue across the head and then took him into her mouth again.

"A kinky woman. The best kind." Gabe thrust in and out of her lips in a series of long strokes, and then pulled free and rolled the condom on. Then he lowered his head to her body and kissed his way down to her spread thighs. He blew across her exposed vulva, and Willow shivered in delight. He gave her a leisurely lick. "And you taste good, too."

His tongue moving over her clit made her moan. She'd come so many times already, how could he make her so hot, and so needy, so fast?

"I think I may be turning into a sex maniac," she warned him.

"Well, then, I'm a lucky man," Gabe said. He gave her a last kiss between her legs and moved around to position himself between her thighs. He took his cock in his hand and guided it to her opening. He paused there, looking at her. "What a picture."

"Stop talking," Willow said, returning his words from the previous night. "I'm trying to get laid."

He thrust slowly into her, inch by inch, until he filled her. He paused to ask, "Comfortable? Floor's not too hard?"

"Not as hard as you." Willow tightened around him, loving

the feeling of him on her, inside her, his clothes brushing against her bare skin.

He ground his pelvis against hers, driving even deeper inside. His cock throbbed and her inner muscles quivered in reaction. "I am very hard. If I hadn't been before, I would have been by the time I followed that ass of yours up the ladder. Now it's mine."

Gabe began to move inside her.

Willow wrapped her arms around him and raised her hips to offer herself more fully to him, taking him as far into her body as he could go.

The rhythmic slide of his cock filling her and receding and filling her again was blissful torture. The soft cotton of his T-shirt rubbed her nipples as he moved on her, and the denim of his jeans brushing her thighs heightened her senses, making her even more aware of him and what he was doing to her.

She wanted to tell him to hurry, go faster, make her come now.

She wanted it to last forever.

She closed her eyes and held on, saying nothing.

The barn smelled of fresh, sun-warmed hay and straw, and the horses made soft blowing sounds far below them. It was easy to imagine they inhabited a different place in time here in the hayloft, making love.

He'd said he would take a long time, and Gabe was a man of his word. She let him live up to it, and managed to remember not to scream when he finally made her come. She didn't want to scare the horses.

7

By the time they finally sat down to have breakfast, they were both starving. Willow sat across from Gabe and
dug into a plate full of eggs, bacon, and generously buttered
toast without a moment of hesitation over the fat content. She
must have burned a million calories in the last twenty-four
hours, and they were screaming to be replaced.

Keeping up with Gabe in bed was more physically demanding than anything she was used to doing. She was very
ready to refuel her depleted energy stores.

"You don't work weekends, do you?" he asked her.

"No." She took a bite of fluffy eggs and chewed. Bliss.

"Then I have to tell you it's my intention to keep you my
prisoner."

"Really." Willow grinned at him and picked up a piece of
toast. "You feed your prisoners well."

"It's all part of the fair-prisoner-treatment regulations," he
informed her. "In the spirit of which I should probably take

you home to get a few things. Clean clothes, clean underwear. Not that you'll need those. I've decided you should stop wearing them. It saves time."

"It doesn't save condoms. They're dying in record numbers around here." She hummed *Taps* and picked up her fork again.

"They don't help the landfill issue, either." Gabe gave her a look of grave concern. "Save the environment. Get on the Pill or get an IUD before the conservationists find out about us."

"You just don't want to keep using condoms." Willow gave him a knowing look and kept devouring her breakfast.

Everything tasted delicious. Everything look fresh and sparkling this morning, too. As if rediscovering sex had added zest to every other aspect of life. Made colors brighter, textures more detailed, flavors more distinctive.

"Tell me you don't want me inside you with nothing between us." He gave her a knowing look.

"Of course I want you inside me with nothing between us." She wanted to feel him come deep inside her, too, filling her with hot, liquid spurts. "But it's a big step."

It was a long-term-relationship step, something that didn't make sense given that they were going to be living in different states soon. She could always stay, but to drastically change her life around for a man she'd met only the night before . . . she'd have to be a total flake.

He lifted a hand to her cheek and smoothed back a strand of hair that had fallen forward. "I don't intend to rush you, Willow. But I do plan to have you every way possible."

She looked down at her plate. Somehow she'd eaten everything on it. She set her fork down and looked up into Gabe's eyes.

"If you're worried about diseases, I don't have any of them. I doubt you do, either."

"I don't." She bit her lower lip, tempted beyond reason to experience that with him, just once.

"Willow." Gabe gestured her to come toward him. She stood up and moved within reach. He scooted his chair back and pulled her onto his lap. "Don't worry about it now. I said I wouldn't rush you."

She leaned into him. "I want to."

"I think we both agree that we want to. There's no rush." He settled her more comfortably across his legs and cupped one hand over her breast, thumbing her nipple. "We have all the time in the world and unless the planet runs out of rubber trees, we won't run out of prophylactics."

She shifted to prompt him to pay attention to her other breast and he complied, stroking and caressing and squeezing them both. "We don't have all the time in the world," she reminded him.

"Why not?"

"The poet-in-residence program is sort of like a scholarship. Winning it meant I could take a six-month leave of absence from my job in Redmond and come here to write full-time. But it's ending soon and I'll have to go back to my job."

She thought about that, about her ongoing conflict and increasing resistance to the idea, and added, "Unless I quit. But that would be dumb."

"Why dumb?" Gabe kissed her forehead and settled his hands on her belly, cuddling her.

"Irresponsible, then. Good jobs are hard to come by. I shouldn't just quit the one I have because I don't want it anymore."

"What do you want instead?" he asked.

"I want to keep writing. But . . ." She broke off, feeling a cold knot of tension forming in her stomach.

"But what?"

She took a deep breath. "I used the residency time to write a novel."

"That's impressive." There was a note of genuine respect in his voice.

She shook her head. "No. It's a terrible book, Gabe. It's so bad, I can't even fix it with more drafts."

The feeling of defeat that had hit her when she realized how awful and unsalvageable a novel she'd written dragged at her. She'd finally been given months to do nothing but write, and she'd wasted them writing garbage.

She'd thought it would be easier. She knew how to write. Her poetry had been published in major national magazines and journals. Her two poetry volumes had done well. But there wasn't enough of a market for poetry to ever earn a living at it, which was why she'd decided to write a novel.

Willow had discovered that knowing how to write a poem was one thing. A novel was another thing altogether and might be beyond her reach.

It would be dumb to quit her job and give up a secure future to keep trying for a goal she might never be able to achieve.

"Well, it was your first, wasn't it?" He rubbed her belly in little circles, and Willow felt the knot inside her loosening at his touch.

"Yes."

"How's the second one coming along?"

She felt her jaw drop. "How's what? Did you hear what I said? I spent almost six months writing the first one and it's terrible."

"Firsts usually aren't very successful." Gabe sounded unconcerned. He let his hands move up over her breasts again. "The first time I rode a horse, I fell off. The first time I dug a fence post hole, I wasn't strong enough to do it right." He lowered one hand to her lap and nudged her thighs apart. She opened them enough for his hand to slide between them and cup her mound.

"The first time you had sex, was it terrific?"

Willow's mouth twitched. "No. It was awkward and uncomfortable and it didn't last long enough for me to, you know, get there."

"You didn't come," he stated.

"No." *Not even close.*

"Last night you came plenty. You came this morning in the barn, too. I bet I could make you come again right now if I tried."

She was starting to feel very warm and tingly with his hand between her legs. "You probably could," she agreed.

"So. Firsts are just firsts." He rubbed his hand on her mound in a subtle circle, stimulating her. "Try again."

She felt helpless tears forming against her will and struggled to hold them back. "It's not that easy. It took me almost six months, writing nearly full-time, to write the first one. I can't afford to keep wasting that much time."

"If it's what you want to do, it's not a waste of time," Gabe pointed out. "Another six months will pass, whether you write or don't write. What would it hurt if you spent the time writing another lousy book?"

That was the temptation she'd been fighting. Keep doing it, not give up. Quit her job, stay in Missoula, do something else less demanding to pay the bills and find out if she could do better on her second try.

And if she couldn't?

"How many lousy books should I write before I give up?" she asked.

"Do it until you don't want to anymore," Gabe advised. "How you spend your time is nobody's business but yours. If you want to spend it writing bad novels, why shouldn't you?"

She smiled. Gabe's brand of humor had a way of putting things into perspective. "I could become known as that crazy woman who writes the worst books ever put to paper, over and over."

Gabe shook his head. She could feel the movement against

her hair. "It'll never happen. It's not nearly as interesting to speculate about as your latex fetish is. We're going to go through a lot of boxes of condoms. People will notice. They'll talk. You'll be known as the shameless hussy from the big city who's trying to kill me with sex."

He paused and added thoughtfully, "Rumors may even begin to circulate about me importing low-cost Viagra from Canada. Whatever you scribble in your spare time won't even warrant a mention, unless it has to do with sex. That might get people talking."

Willow turned and straddled him on the chair. "Sex is a hot gossip topic," she agreed.

The way he talked about them as a couple made her wonder if it was really possible. If they might have something that could last. It was too soon to know, and two weeks wasn't long enough to find out.

Gabe wrapped his arms around her and brought her close for a brief kiss. She settled into the firm, steady pressure of his lips on hers, the strong clasp of his arms, the warmth of his body. She could spend hours kissing him. Touching and being touched by him. Exploring and sharing each other's bodies.

My lover, she thought. She'd just found him. She rebelled at the idea of giving him up as strongly as she rebelled against doing the responsible, familiar thing and going back to the job that didn't fit her anymore, if it ever had.

He lifted his head to break the kiss and continue the conversation. He looked into her eyes. "I think you should give serious thought to quitting your job and staying on. Forget the bad books. Think of the sex. Think of all the things I haven't had a chance to do to you yet."

His voice was light, teasing. But his face was serious.

Gabe slid his hands down her back and cupped her butt, pressing her closer so that his groin rubbed between her open legs. "I might inspire you to write better." He rocked his pelvis into her, adding emphasis to his words.

She let out a long sigh, dropping her head into the curve of his shoulder. "I could hardly write worse," she admitted.

"Your poem was good. And I should know. I teach English."

She raised her head and stared at him in shock. "You teach? All this time I've been having sex with a teacher, and you never mentioned it?"

"You didn't ask." He squeezed her ass. "Want to earn an A?"

"Yes." She grinned and laid her head on his shoulder. "I can be the naughty schoolgirl. I have an outfit that'll work for that, too."

"Does it include panties?"

"No. I'm a naughty schoolgirl. You'll be shocked to discover that my ass is bare under my skirt."

"I'm shocked now. What ideas you have." His voice told her he was anything but shocked.

"You have a few ideas of your own. You're getting hard again," Willow said.

"It's the thought of you in a skirt with no panties underneath," Gabe explained. "Also, you sat on my lap facing me and started rubbing your body all over mine. You do that and then mention no panties, you can expect to deal with the consequences."

"I can handle the consequences." She wiggled in his lap. "Although maybe not right now. You were very thorough in the barn."

"I was thorough in the truck, the shower, and the bed, too," he pointed out.

"Mmmm, yes, you were." She rubbed her cheek against his shoulder and felt utterly content, just sitting there cuddled up to Gabe, replete from breakfast and a marathon of sex, enjoying his presence and the sound of his voice.

"I'm going to be thorough again later," he informed her. "The next time I get you tied up, I'm going to use the opportunity to persuade you to stay in Montana forever."

She didn't know what to say to that, so she didn't say anything. Already she didn't want to leave. It wasn't just Gabe; it was the pace of life here, the beauty all around her, the eclectic cultural mix that was Missoula. She didn't want to go back to the fast-paced pressure of her old job. And now that she'd discovered him, she didn't want to leave Gabe, either.

What if she didn't go back? What if she had this to look forward to on weekends or maybe more, the two of them talking and laughing and having hot, lust-crazed sex?

What if she tried again and her next book wasn't awful? If she didn't try, she'd never know. Did she want to look back on her life and wonder if she'd given up too easily and long for what might have been, when it was too late?

"Walk with me." Gabe stood up with her in his arms and then set her onto her feet. "I'll show you around. I'd offer to take you riding, but I don't want to make you saddle sore. I have plans for you later that don't involve rubbing you with horse liniment."

Willow laughed. "That sounds like something that would smell terrible."

Although riding on a horse sounded fun. Feeling the sun on her face and the wind in her hair. As long as they didn't go too fast. The horses were tall. Falling off had to hurt.

As much as it had hurt to realize she'd written a horrible book nobody would ever read, much less publish? Maybe in a different way. But Gabe had fallen off, taken his bruises, and gotten back up to try again. She didn't even have to see him on a horse to know that he rode like an expert now.

Willow had a feeling Gabe was going to inspire her in many ways. Anticipating his brand of persuasion was only one of them.

"The smell is what makes it work." He took her hand and led her toward the door. "Come on, there's a beautiful day out there and we should go enjoy it."

"I'm already enjoying it." She followed him and watched the way his jeans clung to his butt, the relaxed strength in his movements. "A lot."

8

"What are we doing?" Willow asked.

She turned her head to look at Gabe. His arms were pillowed under his head. They were lying side by side, sprawled in the grass under a tree that shaded them from the direct sun.

"Communing with nature while you tell me what your next book will be about." His eyes were closed as he spoke. His chest rose and fell in a steady rhythm. He wasn't asleep, but the man really knew how to relax.

Willow let her breathing slow to match his, relaxing her muscles against the soft grass. Feeling the earth underneath her, imagining the tree roots going deep into the soil to find hidden sources of water to sustain it in the dark while the leaves transformed sunlight above. Light, dark. And in between, life.

"I haven't thought about it," she answered.

"Think about it now."

Emotions churned in her belly. Anger. Grief. Defeat. Hope. All that work, a wasted effort. Do it again?

Gabe rolled onto his side and placed a hand on her stomach. His touch soothed her and heated her at the same time. "Don't take it so seriously. Make it a game. Tell me anything. Doesn't mean you have to write it."

"A game." She looked at his hand, stroking the curve of her belly. She hadn't known him twenty-four hours earlier. Now he had the power to calm her with a touch, excite her with a kiss, bring her to a level of sexual awareness and satisfaction she'd never experienced before.

Okay. A game. Pretend she was going to stay. Pretend she'd try again. Write what? She could tell him anything; it could be ridiculous and it wouldn't matter.

"A book about a mysterious wave of condom disappearances."

She smiled. There. She'd said something.

"That sounds serious." Gabe's hand roamed down toward her mound, massaging her pelvis. "Somebody would have to investigate these disturbing disappearances. The criminal responsible couldn't be allowed to get off."

His hand rubbed over her clit as he said *get off,* and Willow let her legs fall open in case he wanted to see if any condom-destroying desperado in the area should get off.

"What if the criminal has already gotten off?" Willow asked him in a dramatic near-whisper. "What if the criminal has gotten off repeatedly and has no remorse?"

Gabe leaned over her and nipped at her breast, grazing the soft flesh with his teeth through the thin fabric of her shirt. "Criminals must be brought to justice."

"Criminals prefer to be brought to orgasm." Willow rocked her hips against his hand.

"How many condoms must die before you repent your

ways?" He drew her nipple into his mouth, then released it, leaving the fabric that covered it damp. Her breasts swelled and her nipples grew tighter.

"This really shouldn't be possible," she told him. "I'm losing track of how many times we've had sex, and already you're turning me on again."

"That's because I'm playing with your clit and your nipples. Very sensitive places." His hand moved in lazy circles along her mons, pressed lightly between her legs, traveled up again to rub across her clit.

"That helps," she sighed. "But that's not all. Watching you walk turns me on. I watched you use a pitchfork this morning and it turned me on. You could probably recite the dictionary and I'd go weak over the sound of your voice."

"You're infatuated with me." He hooked a leg over hers, trapping her close. As if she'd try to get away. "Soon I'll have you hopelessly addicted."

"Do you want me addicted?" She tilted her head to look into his eyes, and her breath caught. There was something almost unbearably intimate about meeting his eyes while his hand moved between her legs, cupping and stroking her sex.

"I want you, Willow." Gabe lowered his head to hers. His mouth took hers in a bruising kiss. His teeth scraped over her lower lip and she shivered. "Think of it like a pair of boots."

She laughed. "Boots?"

"Don't laugh about boots. Unless you're talking about sissy boots, then laugh away. But real boots are serious."

"Serious," Willow repeated, doubt clear in her voice.

"A good pair is important. You need the right fit. They can't rub or chafe. You don't want any flimsy, cheap pair that'll give out on you right when you need them."

While he talked, Gabe slid her zipper down and spread the fabric apart so he could slide his hand inside her panties. His fingertips brushed against her, and Willow tilted her hips up to meet him. It was so erotic, the barely there contact of his fingertips against the swollen lips.

He pressed a finger lightly between the slick folds, and she parted for him. "You find the right ones and you don't quibble about the price. The right fit is going to cost you, but far less than wasting your time on the wrong fit over and over would."

His hand moved down just a fraction of an inch, and his fingertip slid farther inside her. "Then you have to break them in. You have to take care of the leather. The right boots will last and last, as comfortable to slide into years later as they were the very first time."

He penetrated her fully as he spoke, thrusting his finger all the way into her core.

"I'm not sure it's flattering to be compared to a pair of cowboy boots. Your imagery needs work."

His technique, however, did not. Willow rolled onto her hip to face him, shifting one leg forward so he could keep touching her without her legs pressing closed and interfering.

"That's a metaphor," he corrected her.

"Yes, but it created this image of me all dusty and I'm sure it's anti-feminist or something to compare me to an object that gets walked on." Her complaint lacked conviction with her voice catching in her throat as he manipulated her with expert movements.

"Walked in. Not on." Gabe slid his hand out of her, out of her pants, and ran it over her hip, then down to cup her butt and pull her closer.

"Still." She pressed up against him and breathed in the scents of sun-warmed grass and virile male. "It sounds like something from another century."

"Sex existed in previous centuries," Gabe assured her. "We know this from written records and pictures that have survived through the ages. Along with the population explosion the world is currently experiencing."

Willow laughed. Sex. Boots. The two of them. Well, that last thought didn't make her laugh. It made her feel warm and happy inside and also wanton and needy to think of the two of them with their bodies locked together, moving in perfect rhythm.

They did fit. Gabe wasn't wrong about that.

"You still have doubts." He sounded unconcerned and almost amused. He massaged her ass, making her wiggle in pleasure, her pelvis tilting to cradle his. His cock pressed into her belly.

"That doesn't seem to bother you," she said into his shirt.

"It doesn't. I'm going to enjoy the hell out of persuading you."

The sensual promise in his voice nearly made her heart stop.

"How are you going to persuade me?" She managed to ask the question without stuttering.

"First I will strip you naked and get you into the shower again. I'll wash every inch of you. Then I'm going to dry you off and make sure I don't miss any spots." Gabe's voice sounded low and seductive as he spoke.

"Then I'm going to tie you up again. I'm going to blindfold you so you can't see a thing and you won't know what I'm going to do. And after that, Willow, I'll do anything I want with you."

His lips brushed across her forehead while he kneaded her ass with his hands. "By the time I finally sink my cock into you again, you'll be screaming for me."

She was almost ready to scream for him now. His erection pressed into her. Her sex throbbed from his touch. His hands on her butt made her want to move until he could reach other, more sensitive areas that were demanding attention.

"What if you don't persuade me?" she managed to ask, her voice almost a whisper. Her throat felt dry and tight. Speech was an effort.

"Then I'll have to keep trying until I do persuade you."

Gabe worked his hands up her back, smoothing out the muscles in her shoulders, then tangling in her hair to pull her head up for his kiss. His mouth devoured hers. His tongue penetrated her lips in slow, sensual thrusts.

Her breasts felt too tight, swollen, aching. Her entire body felt heated, and it had nothing to do with the temperature outside.

She could picture the scene Gabe described so easily. His hands, soap-slick, moving over her body from head to toe. Then she imagined herself naked and bound. Blindfolded. She'd never know what he was doing until she felt it happen. He might do anything. He might do everything.

Did she trust him enough to let him do that?

She did. He'd done nothing but give her pleasure and take his own, everything he did designed to enhance their mutual enjoyment of their bodies and each other. Gabe was a careful, deliberate man. He wouldn't hurt her. He wouldn't do anything that frightened her.

The blindfold, she knew, would intensify every physical sensation. Blocking out her sight would enhance her sensory awareness. The rope binding her would make her feel deliciously helpless and feminine and hot. A very physical reminder that a man had her bound for his sexual conquest.

Her breath sounded fast in her ears and her heartbeat was racing. She wanted him. She wanted him to tie her up, blindfold her, tantalize her, and fuck her.

His mouth possessed hers now the way he intended to possess her entire body. She shuddered with want, ached with need.

He broke the kiss to murmur against her cheek, "Will you let me do all that to you, Willow?"

"Yes." Her voice was a breath of sound.

She wanted him again. Now. Here. And she knew it wasn't going to happen, that he was going to draw it out until she really might scream for him by the time he let her have his cock inside her, where she already felt hollow and empty, needing him to fill her.

She shut her eyes and pressed closer to him, hooking one thigh over his hip to bring her sex into contact with him.

She felt his hand slide between her parted thighs to cup her through her jeans.

"You're going to have to wait for it," he told her. "You know that, don't you?"

"Yes." Willow rocked into his hand anyway. The pressure against her swollen sex gave her some relief.

He palmed her and gave her mons a light squeeze. "Think you can walk back to the house?"

"Not just yet." She tried to slow her breathing, to calm the lust that surged through her. The presence of his hand helped her come down a little.

"Do I have to carry you piggyback?" His voice was low and amused.

Willow shook her head. She didn't want to be carried with her aching nipples pressing into his back and her open legs locked around him, turning her on even more with every step he took. She'd come before they got to the shower.

"I can walk," she said out loud. "But I hope you're not planning to wait until tonight to persuade me."

His hand rubbed a slow circle against her mound. "I think you'll take a lot of persuading and that could take some time. We'd better start now."

Gabe removed his hand from between her legs and used it to reach around and deliver a sharp slap to her butt. Her muscles contracted sharply, making her sex squeeze in anticipation. God, was this why women got into spanking with their lovers? Was he planning to spank her when she was bound? If he did, would she like it?

He took her hands in his and they stood up together. Gabe

helped her, supporting her weight until she had her feet firmly underneath her.

"All right?" he asked her.

"I'm all right." She looked into his eyes. They were full of heat and sexual intent and tenderness. His hands kept a firm grasp on hers, making her feel protected by his strength.

"I'm going to make love to you, Willow," Gabe told her. "I'm going to make you mine. I'm going to learn every inch of your body and make it respond to me. I'll make you want me with every fiber of your being. And then I will satisfy your every want. Every need."

She swallowed with an effort. There were no words to say in response to that. Or if there were, she was too lost in desire to think of them.

Instead, she simply followed as he turned and began walking back to the house, letting him lead her by the hand to the stage of her final seduction.

9

The shower was torture. Gabe stripped her slowly, unbuttoning her shirt one button at a time, uncovering her inch by inch, pausing to kiss every new bit of exposed flesh until her shirt was open. He pulled it off her shoulders and down but not off, trapping her in the fabric while he lowered his mouth to her breasts and devoured them.

The pull of his lips on the hard, aching buds of her swollen nipples made Willow groan out loud. She would have reached up to grab his head and hold it there, but her hands were effectively bound by her shirt.

When he was finally finished exploring every curve of her breasts, the points of her nipples, the rise of her rib cage and the hollow of her belly with his mouth and tongue, Gabe stripped her shirt away and worked her jeans down her hips.

He left her panties on while he bared her legs. Her shoes and socks had been left by the door, discarded by her as soon as they came inside, so there was no barrier to slow him when he got her jeans down to her ankles.

Then his hands explored the new territory he'd uncovered. He stroked her calves and thighs. His fingertips teased the sensitive backs of her knees, and worked their way up to the edge of her panties.

Willow planted her feet apart for balance and to give him better access as his mouth followed his hands. He bit gently at the insides of her thighs, kissed points around her hips and thighs she never would have guessed could be so full of nerve endings, teased her by sliding the tips of his fingers under the leg bands of her panties and barely touching the beginning curve of her ass.

By the time he slid his hands into her panties and rolled them down her legs, her body was on fire with need, and she knew it wouldn't be quenched anytime soon.

Gabe stood up without touching her swollen sex with his hands or his mouth. He turned the shower on, adjusted the temperature, and then stripped his own clothes away before stepping under the water and pulling her in with him.

"I like seeing you naked," he told her. "Such lovely breasts. Such hard little nipples. Your pussy, all dewy and plump for me. That luscious ass of yours, curvy and round and tempting me to take it. Beautiful to look at. Even better to touch."

Gabe pulled her body against his. Her nipples pressed into the hard muscles of his chest. His cock rubbed against the soft skin of her belly. The water poured over her back and it felt like a thousand little points of contact, making every nerve react.

He soaped her back first, and the feeling of his hands and the slickness of the soap gliding over her back and down the curves of her ass were unbearably erotic. She'd never thought of her back as an erogenous zone, and having a man's hands on her butt had never felt so pleasurable.

Willow wanted him to fill his hands with her ass and her pussy with his cock. For now, she had to be content with his hands smoothing their way along the rounded globes of her butt, a fingertip gliding between them, teasing the rosy opening they protected.

She'd never imagined she had so many nerve endings there, or that they could be so responsive to a lover's touch. Until Gabe had caressed her and slid his finger into her the night before, she'd never experimented with anal play. It had felt so good, better than she'd guessed it could feel, having his finger sliding in and out of her ass while his other hand stimulated her clit.

Would he penetrate her like that again now? She waited, anticipation and uncertainty building, as he stroked over and around the opening. He paused and probed her with his fingertip, sliding it partway in.

"Are you sore there, Willow?" he asked her. "Do you want me to stop touching you like this?"

"Don't stop," she begged him. She moved her hips against him so that his fingertip penetrated her ass farther. "It feels so good."

His finger slid all the way in, stretching her. Then he pulled back before gliding back in, fingering her ass so carefully but making her intent on the erotic possibilities. She'd never considered letting a man slide himself into her like that. If she'd been asked, she would have refused. It sounded uncomfortable. Painful. A world apart from the sensual feeling of fullness as Gabe penetrated her tight ass with his finger.

If Gabe wanted to fuck her ass, would she let him?

She licked her lips. "Gabe."

"Yes, Willow?" He kept up a slow, steady rhythm. He used his other hand to cup and stroke her folds.

"Could I take you like this?"

"Not without taking a lot of time and preparing you." He

kissed her and slid two fingers up into her pussy, penetrating her from both sides with his hands. "If you want to explore that later, we can. We'll need to take it very slow and make you ready for it. You've never even had a man finger your ass before, have you?"

Willow shook her head.

"Then don't rush ahead. When two fingers feels good to you, we can explore other options. You might never be ready for my cock filling you here." He wiggled the finger in her ass gently to demonstrate. "But there's no reason you can't enjoy a little extra stimulation, even if you never want more than this."

Willow felt stretched and unbelievably excited from the sensation of having his hands working her, penetrating her in two places at once. What would it be like to have his cock filling her mouth while he banged her ass and her pussy, all at the same time?

"It feels so good," she sighed. "I love your hands on me and in me."

"That's because your body knows you're mine." He kissed her again, thrusting his tongue into her mouth to match the rhythm of his fingers thrusting into her.

She melted into him, wanting him closer, giving him her mouth, her pussy, any part of her he wanted. He ended the kiss and slid his fingers out of her. She immediately missed the feeling of being penetrated.

"Time to wash the rest of you." Gabe soaped his hands again and then soaped the rest of her in slow circles and strokes, moving his hands over her shoulders, her breasts, paying attention to her nipples by pinching them between his fingers. He made good on his promise to wash every inch of her. His hands explored her legs, her feet, her hips, her waist.

She loved his hands moving over her body. She loved the way he touched her, his hands firm but gentle, not rushing, learning all of her.

When he finally stopped and let the water rinse away the last bit of soap from her skin, Willow realized that she'd never had a lover take so much time to get acquainted with her body and her responses. It had been only a day and already he knew her more intimately than any other man she'd ever had sex with. He really was making her his in a way she'd never experienced.

Gabe patted her dry while she stood and let him. The soft fabric teased her everywhere, rubbing her nipples, her ass, her belly, her thighs. The texture of the towel was such a contrast to the slick sensation of soap or the liquid glide of water on her skin. She felt sensitized and aware in every pore, every nerve stimulated, every bit of her eager for his next touch.

When he'd dried them both off, Gabe led her to his bedroom and wrapped a blindfold around her eyes. Then he bound her wrists together in front of her and her legs together at the ankles.

"How will that work?" Willow protested as she felt what he was doing near her feet.

"You'll find out," Gabe said. "There are many ways I can take you. When your legs are together you'll feel even fuller when I slide my cock inside your tight pussy."

His words made her quiver and made her sex clench. Willow imagined him penetrating her without parting her legs, making her pussy feel stretched and stuffed.

"Don't worry, Willow. When I fuck you again, it'll be so good, you won't care what position you're in." He gave the rope a final tug. "Onto the bed with you."

Gabe picked her up in his arms. She felt his body against hers, solid and strong, his arms around her supporting her. Then she felt him lowering her until her back rested on the soft fabric of the quilt.

She felt the mattress dip as he joined her on the bed.

"Beautiful Willow. Naked. Blindfolded. All tied up. What will I do with you first?"

What, indeed? Willow waited, not even able to guess what to anticipate.

Cool air touched her bare skin, still slightly damp from the shower. The bed underneath her felt firm, the fabric of the quilt soft with age and repeated washings.

The rope on her wrists and ankles felt smooth and snug. Gabe had tied her tightly enough so that she couldn't slip free, but the restraints didn't pinch the delicate skin of her wrists or ankles, or interfere with her circulation. She wasn't uncomfortable in any way.

Maybe a little uncomfortable, needing his hands on her breasts. Or between her legs. Willow shifted restlessly on the bed.

Something tickled her collarbone.

"What's that?" Willow asked.

"What does it feel like?" Gabe countered.

She felt it brush over her nipples, one by one, then tease her belly, her hips.

She smiled as she identified it. "A feather. You've got me all tied up so you can tickle me."

"Does this tickle?"

Gabe shifted to kneel over her. Something smooth and hard and warm rubbed between her breasts.

"No."

She imagined how it must look, his hard cock lying in the valley between her breasts, moving back and forth. His hands pressed the outsides of her breasts, squeezing them together, making a tighter fit for his erect penis.

She felt him working back and forth and moved her head down to brush her mouth over the velvety head as it reached the end of his upward stroke.

"So you want a taste?" Gabe asked her.

"Yes." Her voice sounded strange to her own ears. Lower, softer. Sexy.

His cock stroked back and forth between her breasts a few more times. Then she felt Gabe move forward and that hard, smooth flesh pressed against her lips.

She opened them for him and took him inside her mouth. She swirled her tongue around him and sucked as he rocked in and out, fucking her mouth.

"I love your mouth around my cock, Willow," he told her. His fingers found her nipples and pinched them, gradually adding pressure until it was on the edge of what she could tolerate without the pleasure slipping into pain. "I love it when you suck me."

She opened wider, taking more of him on the next stroke. He was so hard, so male. He made her so very focused on her soft female flesh, designed to accommodate his penetration.

He pulled out of her mouth and Willow made a faint sound of protest.

"That feels too good," he said. "I'm not going to come again until I'm inside your hot, tight pussy."

She felt very hot and tight. Needing him. Gabe moved down her and she felt the feather teasing her hips again. When she moved her hips in reaction, his finger found her clit.

"Oh." She gasped at the sensation. He was tickling her hips. Working a finger into the slick folds of her sex. Making her wild.

The feather danced over her belly, around her breasts, the hollow of her throat. His finger slid farther down and then penetrated her, just barely, no more than a fingertip inside her.

"Gabe," she protested. "I can't take this."

"You can take it."

His mouth came down over her mound and closed on her clit, sucking at it. Then he released her and she felt bereft.

"Time to turn you over, Willow."

She felt his hands lift and turn her so that she was on her belly with her bound arms stretched out above her head. Willow wiggled, feeling the quilt rubbing against her nipples. Her ass was bare to him. What would he do, tickle it?

He did. The feather teased the curves of her ass, stroked the sensitive valley between the twin globes, then moved along her side.

She felt Gabe shift until he was straddling her again. His cock rested between her ass cheeks. He moved back and forth in tiny strokes.

"Mmmmm." Willow let out a sigh of pleasure and wiggled her hips, loving the feel of his cock against her.

Long before she was ready for him to, Gabe lifted up and shifted position, lying beside her. He reached for something and she heard a sound she couldn't quite identify. Then she felt cool liquid drops falling onto her back, her butt, the backs of her thighs.

"Oh!" She breathed in sharply. "What is that?"

"Lotion." Gabe's hands smoothed out the drops he'd squeezed onto her back, massaging his way downward along her spine, then up to her shoulders. He stroked her arms, down to her hands, rubbed her fingertips between his palms, not neglecting any part of her.

It would have been blissfully relaxing if she wasn't so excited, a throbbing ache between her legs that was begging for his attention.

When he worked his way back down her body and kneaded the curves of her ass, Willow let out a low moan. His hands moved down her hips, rubbing, stroking, kneading. He paid attention to her legs, her thighs, calves, the bottoms of her feet, and then massaged his way back up the insides of her legs.

By the time his fingertips brushed the sensitive skin between her thighs, just below her pussy, she needed him to touch her there so badly, she wanted to scream.

"Gabe," she pleaded. "Touch me. I need you to touch me."

"Where? Here?" He toyed with the backs of her thighs.

She rose up on her knees, arching her back, moving her thighs apart with her ankles still bound together. She rested her chest on the bed since her hands couldn't easily support her the way she was tied, but the position made her sex visible and accessible to him.

"What a beautiful pussy." Gabe's voice sounded low and husky. He stroked her, trailing a finger along her folds, parting her but not touching the bud of her clit or plunging inside her.

"Please, Gabe," Willow gasped. She moved her hips back, echoing the plea with her body.

"You need my cock inside you, right there, don't you, Willow?" Gabe teased her opening with the tip of his finger.

"*Yes.*" She could feel how soft and slick she was for him. He'd slide in so easily, filling her with his thick length.

"My cock is going to fit so perfectly here, Willow." He toyed with her pussy, making her want to shout in frustration. "I'm going to fill you with it. One day soon I'm going to fill you with my come, too."

Yes. She felt her sex clench, muscles squeezing together in anticipation. Oh, God, yes, how she wanted that. Wanted him hot and deep inside her, spurting liquid jets of come into her, no barriers, nothing but their flesh coming together.

He stopped touching her pussy and she heard the tearing sound that told her another condom was about to die. There was a short pause while he rolled it on.

Then Gabe's hands took her hips in a firm grip and he guided her down, onto her side. He pushed her bent knees up so that when he spooned behind her, his engorged cock met her slick, exposed sex. He pushed into her an inch at a time, stretching her, filling her.

She could feel the head of his cock butting up against her

G-spot. "Yes. Gabe, oh, God, yes, right there. Harder," she pleaded.

In, out. Short, hard strokes. Willow felt the pressure building, the intense pleasure each time he made contact against that sensitive place deep inside her, the incredible sensation of fullness as he buried his cock in her. She was breathing faster, trembling with the need to come.

As if sensing she needed something more to push her over the edge, Gabe reached around her and stroked her clit. The next thrust into her made her scream. And she was clenching around him as she came harder than she'd ever come before, the intensity of her orgasm almost more than she could take.

"Gabe."

"I've got you." His hands stroked and soothed her as he continued to thrust into her. "I'm going to come inside you now, Willow. Feel me coming inside you."

He thrust into her one last time, and she could feel his cock throbbing as he came, her muscles gripping him, still tightening rhythmically in the aftershocks of her orgasm.

"I think you killed me," she gasped out when she could finally talk.

"It's called the little death for a reason." Gabe pulled out of her and she heard rustling sounds that told her he was taking care of the condom. Then he spooned back up against her, cuddling her. "Are you all right?"

"Yes. Sort of. I think." She felt dazed, limp, spent. And off center, as if the balance of her world had shifted and she hadn't adjusted.

"You're not going back to Redmond." It wasn't a question but a statement. Gabe stroked her belly in a gentle circle.

"No."

She was going to do what she wanted to do. Take the risks she wanted to take before she was too old and it was too late.

Even if she never wrote a decent book, she could find something else she wanted to do that fit her better than her old job.

She'd wanted to stay in Missoula before she met Gabe, and he gave her another compelling reason not to leave. If she stayed, she could find out what the future might hold for them, as well as for her career options.

"Good." He kissed the nape of her neck, and she sighed in bliss at the brush of his lips against that sensitive skin. "I'll untie you."

"Okay."

But neither of them moved for a long time.

10

Willow made the long walk from the mailbox up the drive toward the house in easy strides. Her boots made a rhythmic crunching sound as they met the gravel. She glanced down at her feet and smiled at the sight.

Gabe had proved that in the West, a man's word was his bond. Within a week of the day he'd vowed to buy her boots so they could knock them together, a box had arrived at her house with MONTANA BOOT WAREHOUSE on the shipping label.

She'd opened the package to find a card that said only, "Walk in beauty."

The boots were beautiful. Black leather, with an intricate lacy design decorating them. According to the box, the style was called Leather and Lace.

They'd fit her perfectly.

She'd gone on the Pill a month after she started wearing them.

Gabe had been right about boots. She'd walked a lot of

miles in hers since then, and they never rubbed or chafed. He'd been right about a lot of things, including his belief that she could do better the next time she tried to write a book.

She'd finished the second one by Christmas. It wasn't good, but she could see enough improvement over her first effort to feel encouraged. By then she was living at the ranch with Gabe. She'd started off staying in her own rented house, but as the trees changed color and the nights got cold, she'd gradually found herself spending all her nights with him.

When the autumn leaves had all fallen and the ground frosted, Gabe had persuaded her to stop wasting money renting a place she used only for storage.

Willow smiled at the memory of Gabe's brand of persuasion.

With the second book finished, instead of starting the third, she'd studied the first two to see where she'd gone wrong. What hadn't worked. What she'd done right.

She'd discovered strengths she hadn't realized she had and thought of a way to use them for her third attempt.

Willow had worked steadily on that manuscript in her spare time through the winter months and the early spring. When she wasn't working as Laura's new assistant at Lemon Espresso or giving a poetry workshop, she was writing.

She and Gabe had settled into an easy routine at the ranch, tending the horses together and going to work, coming home and eating dinner together, Gabe grading papers in the evening while she worked on her book, then going to bed to make love and sleep tangled together.

With the third manuscript completed, Willow spent more time reworking it. Then she'd started to send out query letters. This one she'd believed had a chance of succeeding.

The results of all that work she now carried in her hand, nearly a full year from the day she'd decided to keep trying.

Willow quickened her stride. Gabe was in the barn, and she had plans for him.

"You look like you're up to something."

Gabe stepped up onto the porch and smiled at Willow. She was sitting on the front porch swing she'd insisted he buy and install, pushing herself back and forth with one booted foot. The other was drawn up onto the seat.

She wore a long, loose skirt that pooled around her legs and the filmy white shirt she'd worn the first night he'd seen her, the top few buttons undone so that it was open at her throat and showed a hint of cleavage.

Her eyes sparkled and her answering smile was full of mischief. "I am. Come and join me."

"Am I about to get laid?"

"Yes. Right here, on this swing. In broad daylight." Willow patted the empty space beside her invitingly. As if her lush body weren't invitation enough.

"You're not wearing a bra, are you?" Gabe asked. He sat beside her and began undoing the buttons on her shirt.

"No. There's nothing but me under this shirt."

"I'm a lucky man." He finished unbuttoning and spread the fabric open to enjoy the sight of her bare breasts, her nipples forming tight pink buds that tempted his hands. His cock swelled, forcing him to shift to try to make more room inside his jeans.

"There's more," she said.

"Do tell." Gabe filled his hands with her breasts, cupping them, squeezing gently.

"I'm not wearing any panties."

He felt his cock growing even harder. "I'm shocked."

Gabe freed one hand and used it to gather the fabric of her skirt, drawing it up enough to let him slide his hand underneath it and explore the bare skin it covered. His fingers followed the line her thighs made, all the way up, until he touched her there, naked and open to him under the skirt.

Willow parted her thighs to invite his touch and he stroked her, petting the soft thatch of hair, rubbing her clit, trailing a finger along her slick folds.

"I want to see you," he told her.

She pulled her skirt up and spread her thighs wider, exposing her to his view. Plump with arousal, pink flesh glistening with her natural lubrication, her sex was an intoxicating sight. Her boots, open shirt, and hiked-up skirt added to the erotic picture she made, making her bared breasts and pussy look even more naked in contrast than if she'd worn nothing at all.

"Beautiful." Gabe thrust two fingers into her and moved them inside her.

"That feels so good," she sighed.

"It looks good, too," he said, watching his fingers penetrating her, her slick flesh opening and parting for him. With his other hand he pinched her nipples, shifting from one breast to the other. He watched the flush of arousal spread over her pale skin and the buds of her nipples grow even harder.

"Where do you want me to fuck you?" Gabe asked. "Inside? Outside? Sitting? Standing?"

"Here, on the swing." Willow leaned back and closed her eyes. "I want you to unzip your jeans enough to take your cock out but leave your clothes on. Then I want to sit on your lap, facing you. I want you to fuck me like that, with my skirt covering us, while you play with my nipples and we rock back and forth in the swing."

"You've been giving this some thought, haven't you?" Gabe smiled at her and rubbed his thumb over her clit while he worked his fingers in and out of her.

"Yes. I fantasized about it the first time you brought me here to have sex with you. I imagined us like that and I wanted to do it one day."

"No wonder you wanted a porch swing." Gabe felt his cock growing so engorged, he knew he'd have to open his jeans or risk injury. He let go of Willow and undid his pants, freeing his erect penis. "You could have mentioned this sooner. The swing's been up for months."

"I was saving it for a special occasion." Willow opened her eyes to smile at him, then dropped her eyes to his thick cock, bared for her.

"I'm not saving this for a special occasion." Gabe wrapped a hand around the base of his penis and stroked up and down while Willow watched him. "I intend to use it right now. On your mouth, first. Wrap your lips around me, Willow."

She leaned down and scooted back so that her head lay in his lap and took his head into her mouth, sucking him while he worked his shaft with his own hand.

"Your mouth feels so good on me."

He felt her lips tighten around him, her tongue flicking at the sensitive spot on his shaft below the head of his cock, and groaned. "I want to get inside that hot pussy of yours now. I want to fill you with my cock. I want to fuck you. And then I'm going to pump you full of come."

Gabe pulled out of her mouth and reached down to help her onto his lap. She straddled him. He lifted her skirt out of the way, savoring the sight of her naked underneath it. Her knees rested on either side of his thighs as she rose up, found the head of his cock with her slick opening, and sank down, taking him inside the hot clasp of her snug sheath.

He reached under the skirt to fill his hands with her ass. His fingertip grazed her second opening and stroked over it. "Do you want more?" he asked her.

"Yes. I want to feel you in my ass while you fuck my pussy," Willow answered.

Gabe reached farther down to coat his fingertip with her slick moisture and then penetrated her tight ass while she rode up and down on his cock.

He used his booted feet to rock the swing back and forth,

making a countermotion and adding momentum to his thrusts as he moved his hips in rhythm with hers.

Her breasts bounced as she moved with him. Her hot, slick flesh enclosed him with nothing between them, and the sensation brought him close to coming within minutes.

"I can't hold back long," he told her. He slid his fingertip out of her anus and gripped her hips with both hands. "I have to fuck you hard now."

"Yes." She threw her head back. "Fuck me hard, Gabe."

He did, using deep, fast strokes, pulling her down as he thrust up into her. He felt her pussy muscles quivering and then tightening around him as she started to come. As she did, he let go and came with her, pumping her full of his come.

"Hell," Chet's disappointed voice behind them said, "If I'd gotten here sooner, I could have watched."

Willow started at the sound, and Gabe held her securely so she didn't pull free of him. He wasn't finished coming. He kept his cock buried deep in her pussy and continued to spurt inside her and she stared at him, her face showing her shock at the interruption. At the same time he felt her muscles tighten around him and realized she was coming again, as if their unexpected discovery had pushed her to the peak of orgasm one last time.

"Don't you have a woman of your own?" Gabe asked the source of Willow's consternation. He pulled her shirt closed so Chet wouldn't see her bared breasts.

"She's busy," Chet answered. "I thought I'd come and see how you were doing. Guess I don't have to ask what you're up to."

Willow sank forward and buried her face against his chest. Gabe stroked her hair and wrapped his arms around her. "Go down to the barn. You're embarrassing Willow."

"Well, if you're going to do it on the front porch in broad daylight, you can't expect privacy," Chet complained. But he moved off. Gabe listened to the sounds of his booted feet receding.

"Oh, God," Willow moaned into his shirt. "I'm going to die. I'll never be able to face him again. I've had that fantasy for months, and I never once imagined it ending with an audience."

"Life is unpredictable." Gabe hugged her closer, enjoying the feel of her in his arms, on his lap, his penis still planted deep inside her. "Was there a reason you waited all this time to try out the swing?"

"Yes." She lifted her head and met his eyes. "I sold the book."

"Really." Gabe felt pride in her accomplishment swelling his chest. "I told you. Firsts are just firsts. Which one is it?"

"The third."

"The one you wouldn't tell me about? What'd you write?" he asked, curious.

"A book of short stories." She bit her lip and blushed. "Erotic short stories. There's one about the naughty schoolgirl and her favorite teacher. One about the woman who gets seduced by a cowboy in a hayloft."

She waited for his reaction, visibly unsure about what he'd think.

"Is there one about a woman who seduces a man on a front porch swing and gets caught in the act?" Gabe asked, unable to resist teasing her.

"No, but maybe I'll write that next," Willow sighed. "Do you think he saw anything?"

"No. Your skirt covered everything, and he came up from the back so he couldn't see your pretty bare breasts bouncing up and down." Gabe tweaked one of her nipples. "Nothing compromised but your dignity."

"Well, that's enough." Willow dropped her head into his shoulder.

He ground his cock deeper into her. "It'll never be enough," he said. "It's coming up on a year. Are you going to marry me now?"

Willow laughed. "You can't propose like that. Right after we got caught having sex outside in broad daylight."

"I'll ask you again in the morning," he said. "You can start thinking over how you'll answer."

"There's only one answer," Willow said. "Yes."

"Well, then. Time for us to ride off into the sunset." Gabe stood up with her still wrapped around him and carried her into the house.

"This is riding?" Willow asked as he walked.

"Yes. You're going to save a horse and ride a cowboy."

The door banged shut behind them.

READY TO play

11

Jolie McIntyre punched up the volume on her car's CD player and sang along with the Dixie Chicks. It was a song about a woman who'd been good for too long and was ready to be bad, and it perfectly described Jolie's mood.

After years of effort, working her way through college followed by the grueling pace of law school, she was done. Graduated, finished. Nothing left but the bar exam, which she fully intended to pass on her first attempt.

Her twenties were nearly spent, a blur of work and study. The years when most people her age were most carefree, gone. No dancing the night away, no string of dates, no relationships. Few relationships survived the strain of law school, anyway. Most of the classmates she'd graduated with had come through with breakups or a divorce as part of the price they'd paid to meet the commitment a law degree demanded.

She'd made the sacrifice willingly. She'd known it wouldn't be easy to achieve her goal. But she was free now. She had some time off before she had to buckle down and study for the bar with nothing more strenuous than her job at Lemon Espresso to occupy her, and she was ready for some long overdue recreation.

Jolie was ready to play.

The first thing she'd done to celebrate was now between her and her Calvin Kleins. A butterfly tattoo decorated her backside, bright and colorful. Jolie felt like she'd spent years in a chrysalis, and the butterfly seemed symbolic of the new life she was ready to start.

After the tattoo, she'd decided to find a less permanent emblem of her freedom. She wanted a playmate. A man who knew how to have fun and who was looking for the same thing she was—some no-strings sex. No boring missionary position sex. No polite pretending to have an orgasm. Just hot, sweaty, wild, wicked sex and plenty of satisfaction.

A relationship would be nice, but Jolie had seen too many men back away when they realized the extent of the demands on her time she'd committed to with her career choice. She didn't kid herself: Sex was possible. A man who'd wait while she studied for the bar, then wait some more while she worked long hours was maybe possible, but not so likely.

It took time to build a relationship. Time she didn't really have after this short period of reprieve ended, and she knew very well how unfair it was to expect a man to understand that. Still, that was no reason to deprive herself of male companionship altogether. She was long overdue for some consensual sheet-tangling fun.

Singing along to the CD with less than perfect pitch but a whole lot of feeling, Jolie barreled along the highway back toward Missoula. She'd left home well before she needed to head to work to enjoy a little thinking and driving time. Some days she just needed to drive, and Montana highways made her feel free. The horizon was so broad. There was a reason it was called Big Sky country—the sky really did seem bigger in Montana, so close you could almost touch it, so blue it didn't seem real.

She heard a horn behind her and checked her rearview mirror. A blond-haired, blue-eyed cowboy who had become a familiar fixture in her world was scowling at her and gesturing for her to slow down.

Like hell I will, thought Jolie. Full speed ahead. She wasn't going to waste any of the precious minutes she had before playtime was over and it was back to the books, the bar, and the beginning of her legal career that was going to take as many long hours as law school had required of her just to get it off the ground.

He was just trying to annoy her, anyway. Pushing her buttons and trading verbal volleys with her seemed to be his new favorite hobby. She didn't mind. In fact, she looked forward to his daily stops at Lemon Espresso for coffee and harassment. Arguing with him was stimulating.

Jolie blew him a kiss in the rearview mirror and gave the car some more gas. She wasn't driving at anywhere near a reckless speed, and she didn't see any reason to drive like her grandmother just because Chet Andrews thought she should be more cautious.

She'd spent the last several years of her life living like the poster child for cautious. She'd have plenty of time to practice caution and restraint as an attorney. Right now she wanted to be anything but. Even though it was Saturday and she was on her way to work. Hardly the epitome of a reckless woman on the loose. Still, people needed coffee and she needed to pay the bills.

Tonight there was an event scheduled, a poetry reading. Willow Daniels would be there, and that made Jolie brighten. She liked the woman who'd come to Missoula from Redmond for a poet-in-residence program.

Willow was easy to talk to, and the three of them—Willow, herself, and Laura, Lemon Espresso's owner—had formed a bond as newcomers among the old-guard Montana traditionalists. It should be a good time at work, and Lemon Espresso closed at ten. The night would still be young.

The last time she'd seen Willow, Jolie had told her she intended to find a playmate to get horizontal with, but had she done anything about her desire yet? No. Instead, she'd made a stop on the way to work to get more batteries for her favorite mechanical playmate. Fun, but no substitute for the real thing. It was time to take action. After work tonight, Jolie was going to go find herself a man.

Chet was a man.

The thought made her frown. Yes, he was a man. And not exactly the settled-down kind of man, either. He was pretty much the classic example of a rodeo cowboy, a handsome heartbreaker who showed no signs of settling down with any woman. He'd quit the rodeo circuit and used his earnings to fund his own horse-breeding operation, but there weren't any indications that he was in the market for a wife.

So, he wouldn't be looking for a relationship.

Jolie thought about her impressions of Chet. He was a regular customer at Lemon Espresso, and always came in with his friend, Reuben. The two men seemed as opposite as their hair color. While blond Chet looked like a man who'd be at home performing for the bright lights, dark-haired Reuben Black looked like a gunslinger who'd ride into town some moonless night to exterminate the outlaws. She was pretty sure Reuben had his eye on Laura and planned to ask her for something hotter than an Americano any day now.

Laura, for her part, was harder to read. She wasn't a flirt. She didn't date. She kept her mind and her energies focused on her business. But she always waited on Chet's friend Reuben personally, and Jolie thought that was very telling.

Reuben didn't say much, but he gave off a sort of John Wayne vibe. He seemed like the sort of man who was capable of handling any trouble that came up but not the type to start it. Jolie liked him, and she thought Laura was a good foil for his personality. If the two of them got together, she didn't think it would be short-term.

Chet had more of a daredevil attitude—except, apparently, when it came to women drivers. He broke horses to supplement his ranch income and had probably broken more than a few bones in the process. He'd certainly broken a few hearts.

Since he'd chosen ranching as a profession, that told her something about his character. It wasn't an easy life, which meant that under the daredevil exterior was a man who had staying power and a sense of responsbility.

She wasn't sure of his exact age, but Jolie guessed he was around thirty. She knew he'd managed to dodge any marital lassos thrown in his direction. If he'd ever been married, she would have heard the whole story by now from at least a hundred different coffee shop regulars.

So, he was single and attractive and, judging by the signals he gave off, interested in sex. Definitely interested in women. And unless he pestered everybody in her chromosome group the way he pestered Jolie, he was interested in her. He was energetic and Jolie suspected he'd be an enthusiastic bed partner. The air fairly crackled around him from the force of his personality and his lust for life.

He was strong, healthy, muscular without being overly bulky. She liked the look of his body and the way he seemed at home in it. He had a good sense of humor and loved to tease. Outgoing, not exactly the stereotypical strong, silent man of the West. That was good; she didn't want to have sex in silence.

Really, aside from his disapproval of her tendency to go five miles over the posted speed limit, Chet seemed like an ideal candidate. He knew how to have fun, and of all the lady-killer stories Jolie had heard circulating about him, none of them implied he had a problem leaving a woman satisfied. The only complaint any woman ever had about him was that he left.

Not a problem for her. Perfect, in fact. He wouldn't want or expect a relationship, so she wouldn't disappoint him when playtime ended and she had to buckle down again.

Chet Andrews. Why not? If he came in tonight, she'd see if the idea seemed as good with him standing in front of her as it did with him looming in her imagination. If it did . . . well, he'd have his boots under her bed before midnight if she had anything to say about it.

Unless he wanted to start off in a more interesting location.

Chet shook his head as a certain blonde sped away from him. That woman was trouble. He'd known it the first time he locked eyes with her. Direct brown eyes that made him feel like she'd see through any bullshit and he'd better not try to pass any off on her.

She had blond hair streaked all shades and cut in a sexy shag that made him want to run his fingers through it and also led him to wonder if it looked exactly the same first thing in the morning. Every time he saw her, he pictured her all tousle-haired and sleepy-eyed, naked and tangled in his sheets.

Jolie McIntyre had a wicked mouth, a body built for sin, and a razor-sharp brain. The combination had him tied up in knots.

The woman got under his skin like a burr under a saddle blanket, maddening and impossible to ignore.

This was Reuben's fault.

If Reuben hadn't gotten it into his head that they had to start buying coffee from that damn fancy Seattle-style coffee shop where everything came in too many flavors and sizes and variations to keep track of when all a man needed was good, strong, black coffee and maybe some sugar, Chet would never have seen Jolie.

He wouldn't be sitting here right now, imagining her lithe body twisted in the wreckage of her sporty car because she'd been driving too fast and had an accident.

Not that she was concerned. He swore under his breath, remembering the airy kiss she'd blown his way.

And he was destined to spend the evening with the source of his aggravation drawing his eyes with every movement she made, because Reuben was dragging him to Lemon Espresso for some idiotic poetry reading. Since she was the owner's assistant, Jolie would be working.

On the bright side, he wasn't going to suffer alone. He'd roped Gabe into joining them for the evening. Chet, Gabe, and Reuben had been friends since childhood. If Reuben was going to drag him to poetry hell, Gabe could show some solidarity and come along for the ride.

Chet grinned just imagining the suffering on Gabe's face. Maybe the evening would turn out to be more entertaining than he'd thought.

A few hours later, he wasn't grinning. He was scowling.

Reuben's mysterious fascination with designer coffee had finally been made clear. The coffee wasn't the attraction. It was the owner Reuben had fixed his interest on. He was making a play for her now, under the pretext of helping her get a bag of coffee beans that was too high for her to reach, while Chet watched.

As far as he knew, Reuben hadn't even had a one-night stand since he'd left the army and come back home. If life as an Army Ranger didn't exactly create opportunities for romantic relationships, running a ranch made finding time for romance even more difficult. Reuben had been working like a demon to make his sheep operation profitable, so if he was taking time out for a woman now, it was significant.

Chet knew what it meant. It meant Reuben was about to take the big fall. Their bachelor trio was about to get split up.

Well, one of them had to do it first. Marriage wasn't a certainty, but it did happen to most people sooner or later. And if Reuben had decided to get hitched, a calm, steady woman like Laura, who struck Chet as pretty much shock proof, was a good choice.

A woman who was easily shocked wouldn't be able to handle Reuben. Chet could just picture Reuben's approach to courtship, laid out like a military strategy. The poor woman did not know what she was in for.

Yes, Reuben was a lost cause and so was the woman he'd set his sights on, whether she knew it or not. And then there was Gabe. Chet wanted to roll his eyes and resisted the urge. Gabe couldn't seem to take his eyes off the lovely dark-haired poet who was the main attraction for tonight's event.

One bachelor about to take the fall. Another showing every sign that he'd been smitten. And himself in between them, watching Jolie swing her hips to the beat of the music that played behind the counter while she worked the espresso machine, the curve of her ass displayed to advantage by the snug fit of her low-rise jeans.

He might not be ready to take the big fall himself, but that didn't mean he wasn't interested in having some fun.

Chet could see the beginning of a colorful tattoo just above the waistband that disappeared into the denim and couldn't stop trying to complete the picture of Jolie's bare backside in his mind. What did her tattoo look like? What did the inviting shape of her bare tush look like, forget the tattoo?

"Is there a problem, cowboy?"

Jolie had apparently noticed him watching her and had walked up to confront him. Chet scowled at her.

He did not need a woman like her in his life. He didn't need a woman, period. Especially not this one, with her direct eyes and her sharp mouth and her body that had him thinking of creative ways to use the counter space at Lemon Espresso, if only the place wasn't full of other people.

He didn't need her, but he sure as hell wanted her and already he knew she was going to be difficult. Then again, if he just wanted somebody who gazed adoringly at him, he could date rodeo groupies. Of course, those weren't the kind of women who understood why he wanted to stay home and raise horses now. Time to face facts. The only woman he wanted right now was the one who liked to argue with him and who was giving him gray hair.

Chet knew it wasn't reasonable for him to worry about her. Jolie handled her car with confidence and competence. She was perfectly capable of taking care of herself. But for some reason, whenever he saw her, he didn't feel very reasonable. Like now.

"You were speeding on the highway again," he said. "I saw you."

She gave him a long look. "Montana had fewer fatalities when there was no highway speed limit."

"Doesn't mean you can drive like you're trying to put your foot through the floor. Cattle get loose and wander onto the highway. You hit one, your sweet little tattooed ass is in a sling."

"My ass isn't your business and neither is my driving," Jolie answered. Her stance, every line of her body, her expression, and her voice all seemed to challenge him.

Chet was up to the challenge. Time to get this woman out of his system. "How about if I make it mine?"

She leaned forward, putting her cleavage at his eye level, lifted his Stetson off, and trailed a long-nailed, red-tipped finger through his hair. "You think you're up to my speed?"

Her voice was low, seductive, teasing. Daring him.

He imagined those long red nails digging into his back while he drove into her. Up to her speed? *Oh, yeah.*

"Think you're up to mine?" Chet countered. He stood, came around the table, and planted his hat on her head.

Jolie tilted her head back and gave him a look that spelled sex. "I'm ready to cowboy up and ride."

"You off work now?" he asked her.

"Yes."

"Good." Chet scooped her up into his arms and headed for the door. "Night, Gabe, Rube," he called over his shoulder.

He wondered how long it would take her to give him hell for carrying her off and whether or not he could get her outside before she did. He knew it was an outrageous thing to do, but then, she inspired him that way. They'd been playing off each other for weeks, and now that she'd given him an opening, he was taking it.

He was finally going to satisfy his desire for this woman, and he didn't doubt she'd be worth any trouble she caused him. While he was at it, he'd satisfy his curiosity and find out what her hair looked like in the morning. He didn't intend to let her speed away from him again tonight.

12

Well, that wasn't hard, Jolie thought. But she was willing to bet Chet Andrews was. She imagined Chet naked with a hard-on, his body sprawled out like an invitation for her to come and play, and felt heat flash through her.

He held her against his chest, the look in his eyes daring her to protest or argue, while he carried her off. Since he expected it, she decided to be contrary and say nothing. Where did he plan to take her? She couldn't guess, but she knew it would be someplace where they could both fully enjoy themselves.

A hard man is good to find, she thought, and put one hand on his cowboy hat to keep it from tilting down over her eyes.

"Where are you taking me?" she asked.

"Right now? My truck. I've seen the way you drive—I'm going to be the one behind the wheel," Chet answered.

Jolie rolled her eyes. "You are such a hypocrite. If you weren't speeding, how'd you catch up to me?"

He scowled at her. "That's not the point."

Jolie laughed. "You can't win, so you want to change the subject." She ran one nail down the front of his shirt. "You think I should drive slower than you do. That's called a double standard, cowboy."

"Chet."

Jolie blinked at his tone. "I know what your name is."

"Say it." He stopped and looked into her eyes, and she saw a degree of intensity there that would have made her knees go weak if she'd been standing up.

"Chet." She said it with a smile, then shifted so she could graze his earlobe with her teeth. "I know whose name to scream when the time comes."

He slid one of his hands down to cup her ass while he held her against his chest. "And when will that be?"

"The next time you harass me about my driving." Jolie gave him a wicked smile.

"Bet I can make you scream my name under more interesting circumstances." Chet squeezed her butt, then set her on her feet. He unlocked the truck door and opened it for her.

"I can do that myself," Jolie informed him.

"I'm sure you can do a lot of things for yourself." Chet shifted so that his body hid hers from view of anybody who might be passing by and cupped his hand over her crotch. He squeezed and she sucked in a breath at the intimate contact and the firm pressure against her mons. The jeans she wore weren't much of a barrier to the sensation. "Some things are more fun to let somebody else do for you."

"Are you offering to do something for me, Chet?" Jolie asked him, her voice low and teasing.

"Challenging you." He squeezed her between her legs again, his fingers stroking her sex in the process, then released her and helped her into the truck. "You get yourself off. Then let me get you off. See which you like better." He gave her a cocky grin.

She pulled the door shut with a solid sound, leaving him on the other side of it, and wanted to laugh. Oh, this was perfect. He was perfect. He knew how to play and she didn't doubt he'd play hard, but if he thought he could play her, he had a few surprises ahead.

Chet joined her in the truck and put the key in the ignition before he turned to look at her. He hooked one arm along the back of her seat. "I have a feeling you don't think I'm going to win."

"I have a feeling I can't lose," she said. "One game, two orgasms. Really, I'm not seeing a downside here."

She didn't doubt the two orgasms. If Chet couldn't make her come, she'd eat his hat. Now which one would be more satisfying, that would be very interesting to find out.

"So you don't mind getting yourself off for me while I watch?" Chet tilted his head and considered her.

"Not in the least." Jolie sat back and fastened her seat belt, relaxed and confident, savoring the rush of anticipation. "If you expected me to blush and get all flustered, you haven't been paying attention. I don't embarrass easily."

"I've been paying attention." He touched the back of her neck lightly. "I want something from you if I win."

"What?"

His hand cupped the base of her head just below the hat while his fingers speared into her hair. "I want you to spend the night with me."

"Did you think I was just planning to kiss you good night and go my merry way after I had my fun?" Jolie asked.

"No, but I didn't assume you'd stay the night. I want you to stay the night, Jolie."

"Don't want the inconvenience of getting up to drive me back to my car after I've exhausted you?" She sighed in mock sympathy. "Okay. You win, and you'll get my elbow in your back for the night."

"I'll win and you'll get something in your back," he said with a slow smile. "But it won't be my elbow."

He let go of her and started up the truck, then placed both hands on the wheel, assured and so sexy, she wanted to attack him right there, on the street, with people and cars all around them. Although something niggled at her, a question she had to know the answer to.

"Why?" Jolie asked as the truck moved onto the street and forward.

"Why am I driving? We've already been over that."

Jolie rolled her eyes. "Yes, we've established your double standard. Why do you want me to spend the night with you if you win?"

Chet glanced at her, then plucked his hat off her head and resettled it on his. "Because if we're going to do this, I want to do it right."

"And that involves me spending the night."

He shook his head and heaved a mock sigh. "Already you're giving me a hard time. Instead of claiming some other prize, I'm very generously offering to give you a night in my bed, because I know perfectly well once is not going to be enough and we'll probably need a rematch in the morning, too. Are you grateful? No. Questions, complaints, demands. You're high maintenance."

Jolie laughed out loud. "You criticize my driving and now you want grateful?"

"Oh, I'll get grateful." He gave her a knowing smile. "Right about the time I win."

Jolie liked his confidence. She liked even better that Chet was determined to satisfy her. She liked that he wanted to do it right, too. If she was going to seek out a man for sex, she didn't want the experience to turn out to be a frustrating waste of time. She was goal oriented, driven, focused on achievement. She understood why he called her high maintenance, but it was built into her personality. Anything worth doing was worth overdoing in Jolie's opinion. That included hot, grinding sex.

"Make me come hard enough, and I'll be very grateful," Jolie said. She reached over to lightly scrape one long-tipped nail down his arm.

"You'll claw the hell out of me, that's how grateful you'll be," Chet said. "I hope you'll apply antibiotic ointment to all the gouges you leave in my back. Those hard-to-reach places are a bitch to treat."

"Am I going to leave gouges in your back?" Jolie asked.

"Yep. You won't be able to help yourself when I ride you through the mattress and make you come screaming." He winked at her. "I'm willing to endure the pain, though."

"Brave man. But who says you're going to be on top?"

He shook his head. "There, see, I'm willing to do the hard work, but you—you can't just lay back and enjoy it. Tell you what, after I win the first round, we'll come up with a new challenge. The winner gets to be on top."

"And who gets to pick our location?" Jolie noted the direction he was heading, then smiled. "You're going to the river, aren't you?"

The Clark Fork River ran through Missoula on its way to Idaho, and although most of the fishing enthusiasts stuck to the area from Milltown Dam to Thompson Falls, the river attracted all types along its path. It was a good place to find privacy and a peaceful place to think. Jolie spent a lot of her free time enjoying the scenic spot.

"Yep. Good place to go parking, and if you're a screamer, it won't matter at this time of night. Nobody's out fishing, so you won't end up breaking anybody's concentration while they're casting, or scare the fish away."

"You think I'm going to be loud." That made her want to laugh, and she wasn't sure why. Maybe because he so obviously didn't mind if she was.

"I think you're going to be harder to ride than a wild mustang." He rubbed his jaw and glanced at her. "Although you probably won't bite or kick."

"I won't kick," Jolie said. "But I may bite."

"That's okay. I'll bite back." Chet maneuvered the truck into a private spot underneath spreading trees and parked. He lowered the windows enough to let the night air circulate through the cab, and the sound of the river running was audible even before he turned off the engine. "Here we are."

"So we're just going to get right to it here? No kiss? No foreplay? Just drop my jeans and masturbate while you watch?" Jolie unbuckled her seat belt and wiggled out of the harness while she talked.

"Well, here's the problem." Chet unbuckled himself and turned to face her. "If I start kissing you and getting into foreplay, I'll end up getting you off before you get your turn. Then you might accuse me of not playing fair. Can't have that."

For some reason, the idea of making herself come while Chet watched her was an incredible turn-on. It wasn't something she'd ever done before, pleasuring herself while a partner watched. The idea of showing off, teasing him with her body, performing for him sexually, made her hot.

"Well, since you're all about playing fair, let's be clear on the rules." Jolie unsnapped her jeans and lowered the zipper, then shimmied out of them, kicking her shoes off in the process. "You can look, but you can't touch. Not until I say."

She lifted her hips and slid her panties down, then handed them to Chet. The fabric seat cover rubbed against her bare ass, making her fully aware of where she was and what she was doing. She turned toward him and settled one bare foot on the seat, knee bent, her pussy exposed to his view in the moonlight.

He was looking at her, the brim of his hat shadowing his

face and making his expression hard to read, but there was no doubt where his attention was fixed.

They probably weren't the only ones out looking for a private place to park on a Saturday night. Somebody else could come along. Fortunately she wouldn't be identifiable in the dark. They were just another couple in a pickup truck, perfect Montana camouflage. As anonymous as they could get. But what she was doing would be obvious if anybody saw them parked here, and that made her even hotter.

Anticipation and sexual excitement had her feeling slick and wet before she even got started.

And how to get started? Jolie leaned her back against the door and cupped her hand over her sex, hiding herself from view.

"Tease," Chet said.

"Uh-huh." She rubbed her hand in a circle, enjoying the indirect pressure on her clit. "Maybe I won't let you see."

"I can see your face. I can see how you react."

"Hmm." Jolie smiled and closed her eyes, moving her hand harder. "How am I reacting?"

"You're enjoying this. You like me watching you. And I'm guessing you like sex."

Her eyes opened to meet his. "Doesn't everybody like it? Sex is a basic need."

"Yes, but not everybody accepts that. You look like you're at home with your body the same way you're at home making espresso. You know what you're doing and you know you're good at it. I like that about you. You're confident, you know what you like, and you're not going to feel guilty tomorrow."

"I might feel a little guilty for leaving claw marks in your back," Jolie teased. She drew her hand up, then slid a finger inside herself, making sure Chet had an unobstructed view.

She felt hot and liquid, but tight. It had been a while since she'd had anybody to play with. Okay, more than a while. But tonight, she would have Chet's hand where hers was now. Jolie imagined Chet touching her, circling her clit, parting her folds, and penetrating her. She opened her eyes and watched him watching her and felt a rush of anticipation.

"Like what you see?" she asked him, her voice low and inviting.

"Very much. I hope you're not planning to keep the look-but-don't-touch rule for long."

"What if I do?" Jolie teased herself and him both with her hand, showing him what she liked.

"Then I'm likely to break the rules. I want to touch you, Jolie."

"Like this?" she thrust two fingers inside herself with one hand and used the tip of one finger from her other hand to stroke her clit.

"Yes, I want to touch you like that. First with my hands. Then my mouth. And then I want to bury my cock inside you and feel you hot and slick and tight around me."

His intent expression, his heated words, and the intimate tone of his voice sent a buzz of pleasurable expectancy through her. "How is your cock right now?" Jolie asked. She stroked her clit in leisurely motions, up, down, circling around, pinching it between her thumb and forefingers.

"How do you think my cock is?" Chet shifted on the seat beside her. "I've got you sitting right there with no pants on, showing me your pretty little pussy while you pet and stroke yourself off. My cock is turning into a California redwood. If it gets any bigger, my jeans are going to rupture."

"Maybe you should loosen those jeans before you damage something," Jolie suggested. She stroked her clit faster, harder, imagining Chet taking his cock out, gripping it, and stroking his hand up and down the shaft while he watched her masturbate.

"I don't want to distract you." He grinned at her in the

semidarkness. "I want you to concentrate on coming. Are you getting close, baby?"

The term should have annoyed her, but for some reason in this setting it was endearing. Intimate. "Yes." She could feel her inner muscles tightening, clenching, liquid heat building.

"Show me. Show me how good it feels when you come."

His words pushed her over the edge, and Jolie felt the orgasm shoot from almost there to *there*, yes, right there. She let her head fall back while she moaned and panted and came with a lot more intensity than she'd ever experienced in her solo sessions. There were definite benefits to having an audience.

"Did that feel good, baby?" Chet's voice was low and warm in the close confines of the truck cab. She heard him slide closer.

"Yes." Her voice sounded satisfied even to her.

"Tell me I can touch you now."

"You can touch me now." She gave him permission and waited to see what he would do first. He pulled her toward him, turned her sideways onto his lap with her back to the driver's-side door, and settled her bare butt between his thighs. His arm behind her back braced her, and she rested her head against his shoulder.

"I like you with no pants on. I need to flip you over and admire your tattoo later." Chet took his hat off and tossed it behind the seat, into the extended-cab area. "That was a pretty nice show you gave me, but you forgot something. You left your shirt on."

"I didn't want to distract you." Jolie grinned, relaxed from the combination of physical release and the fun of bantering with a man who didn't seem to have any trouble keeping up with her. On any level. The unmistakable shape of his erection pressing into her hip let her know that his libido was in fine shape along with his verbal skills.

"You distract me by breathing." Chet tugged the hem of her shirt up, baring her belly, then her bra, before pulling it over her head. She lifted her arms and let the fabric slide free as he took her shirt off and dropped it onto the passenger-side seat. "Take your bra off for me."

Jolie leaned forward and reached up to undo the hooks, then stripped the bra away with slow, deliberately teasing motions, keeping the cups over her nipples until the last minute. "You want to see these?" she asked, rubbing one hand across the bare upper curves of her breasts.

"Yes. Show me."

She tossed the bra away and arched her back, displaying herself for him.

Chet looked for a long minute, then covered one bare breast with his hand, cupping the slight weight of it while he rubbed his palm over her nipple. "Very nice. Now I get to touch."

"Mmm. Please do." Jolie settled back, enjoying the sensation of his hand on her breast and very interested in finding out what else he planned to do now that he wasn't limited to looking.

13

"Spread your legs a little," Chet said. Jolie shifted on his lap and let her thighs part. Her feet were resting flat on the seat, knees bent. "Yeah, just like that. Is your pussy all soft and wet for me?"

"Why don't you find out?" Jolie asked, her voice as lazy and provocative as her pose.

"Not so fast." He moved so that the hand behind her could toy with her nipple while his other hand splayed over her belly. "I have you naked and you're not giving me hell for once. I'm enjoying this."

"I don't give you hell," Jolie said. "I'm polite. I make your coffee exactly the way you ask for it. I give you cup sleeves so you don't burn your hand."

"You're provoking about it." He stroked the outline of her rib cage and the curve of her belly.

"Am not."

"Provocative, then."

Jolie considered that. "Maybe."

Maybe she'd been provoking Chet, because he provoked her. And it wasn't anything she could put her finger on, precisely. It was his attitude, the way he tilted his head, his smile, his teasing manner. She always got the feeling he was trying to get a rise out of her, and maybe she'd wanted to get a rise out of him, too. Like the one presently bumping into her hip.

Maybe the decision to play with Chet hadn't been as spontaneous as she thought. Maybe it had been lurking under the surface for a while. That thought made her uncomfortable for some reason, so she edged away from it.

Okay, fine, they had a mutual attraction. They were both unattached and consenting adults, and they were acting on it. That was all. And given how good Chet's hand felt just exploring her ribs, that was enough. Jolie pushed the idea that they'd been dancing around each other from the beginning aside, and focused on the pleasurable sensation of his hands on her bare skin.

"You're very good at that," she told him.

"It gets better." He grinned at her and let his hands travel over her in leisurely, wandering paths of discovery. "Are you ticklish?"

"No."

"Are you sure? I bet I can find a ticklish spot."

"Bet you can't."

"That'll be two bets I'm winning tonight." He prodded her hip. "Turn over. I want to see your tattoo. It's been driving me crazy, trying to imagine what the whole thing looks like and how far down it goes."

Jolie rolled to her side, scooted down slightly, then onto her belly across his lap. "Good thing there's lots of room in here," she told Chet.

"Extended cab. A man needs his space." He reached up and flipped on the interior light. "Damn."

She grinned and wiggled her hips. "Like it?"

"I like it." His hands traced the outline of the butterfly, the spread upper wings, and then followed the curve of the lower wing pair. "Damn," he said again, this time in a completely different tone. "Tell me a woman did this. I can kind of enjoy thinking about that. If a big bald guy with a lot of muscles was touching you there, I may have to go hit him."

"You're talking about Lloyd." Jolie stretched on Chet's lap. "So what if Lloyd had his hand there? He's a tattoo artist. And it's not like getting a tattoo can be mistaken for foreplay, unless you're into needles and pain."

"He probably is," Chet grumbled.

"He's a sweetheart. And what he's into hardly matters. I'm not into that. And it's none of your business anyway."

He flipped off the light. "It's none of my business who touches your ass. It's none of my business how fast you drive. I know this logically, and yet I want to go punch Lloyd in the gut and fix your car so it won't go over fifty-five."

Jolie sat up. "This isn't going to work, is it?"

"Yes, it is." Chet wrapped his arms around her and pulled her back against his chest. "I have something called self-control, which is why I'm going to win the first bet. I have something else called persistence, which is why I'll win the second. And I have a huge hard-on, which you will kick yourself for missing out on if you get dressed now."

She shifted on his lap. "You do have a huge hard-on. It'd be a shame to waste that."

His hands closed over her breasts. "That hard-on is probably why I get idiotic ideas around you. All the blood leaves my brain and goes straight to my groin."

"Poor man." Her tone was completely unsympathetic.

"Yes, it's sad." He sighed. "But you're sitting naked on my lap and I'm about to make you come screaming, after which you will be mine for the night. Then I'll put that hard-on to good use and the blood will go back to my brain. I'll be a sane, reasonable man again."

"Sane and reasonable aren't the first words people use to describe you," Jolie said. She closed her eyes, rested her head against his chest, and savored the sensation of his hands cupping and squeezing her breasts.

"Those must not be the qualities you look for in a lover, then." Chet tugged at her nipples, pinched them lightly between his fingers, then rubbed his thumbs over them. "Since it's my lap you're sitting naked on."

She wiggled on his lap, feeling a distinct throbbing sensation between her legs and a rush of impatience. "You do remember that naked means I'm not wearing pants, don't you?"

"The blood loss from my brain hasn't damaged my short-term memory, although I do appreciate your concern. Spread your legs wide for me. Put your thighs on the outsides of mine."

She did, making her sex easily accessible to him, but still he didn't touch her there. His hands worked her breasts, building heat and a clenching need low in her belly, until she couldn't stand it. "Chet. Touch me."

"I am."

"Lower."

"Here?" His hand moved down her belly.

"Lower," Jolie gritted out, twisting in his lap. His arms gripped her and held her still.

"You're so hot," he whispered, kissing the side of her neck. "You're going to come so hard."

Sensation shot from the sensitive skin his lips touched, down to her breasts, which felt heavy and full. He rubbed one thumb across her nipples and Jolie groaned as her sex throbbed in response.

Keeping her firmly in place with one arm, Chet settled his

palm over her mons. "Soft," he said. He rubbed his palm against her. "Wet."

"Chet. Please." She rocked her pelvis forward, trying to get more pressure on her clit, or to urge his fingers inside her.

"I'll please you, baby." He separated her swollen, slick folds and slid two fingers inside her. His other hand moved down to circle her clit, then rub it while he penetrated her with his fingers. In and out, he started a slow, steady rhythm, countered by the shorter strokes stimulating her clit.

She moved her head from side to side, restless and needing to move, to do something. Her hips moved to meet his fingers, and the rocking motion ground his cock into her ass. Chet's body, under and around hers, his hands working her pussy, his lips kissing the curve of her neck all combined to overwhelm her senses with his presence and his sexual intent.

He was going to make her come, right here, in the front seat of his truck. Parked out of sight and private, but where somebody could come along and see enough to know what was happening. Her breathing sped up at the thought.

And then, after he made her come, Chet was going to fuck her. Oh, god. The reality of that hit her, his fingers thrust deep into her, and Jolie bucked and writhed in his lap while she came. Chet thrust into her faster while he increased the pressure on her clit, drawing it out, and she came so hard, she couldn't breathe for a split second.

When she managed to fill her lungs, she made a strangled sound.

"It's okay. More intense than you expected. I've got you." He slowed the rhythmic stroking but didn't stop, gradually slowing even further by degrees while she shuddered and gasped. He gave her clit a last gentle touch and then slid his hand back up to cup her breast while keeping the fingers of his first hand buried in her. "You came so hard for me, I almost shot off in my shorts."

The thought of turning him on to the point that he lost control made her inner muscles clench hard against his fingers.

"Do that to my dick, and I'll last about two seconds," he teased.

She shuddered, overcome with the need to feel him filling her, feel him throbbing and spurting inside her.

"Jolie?" He worked a third finger inside her, testing, and she moaned and rocked into his hand, frantic to take more. "You're so ready for me. You want me inside you, don't you?"

"Yes." She needed more than his hand between her legs, and she needed it right now. When he took his hand away, she bit her lip and tried not to groan out loud.

"Hang on." Chet scooted her forward on his thighs, then jerked at his jeans, fighting to get the zipper down with one hand while he held her around the waist with the other. "Damn. Need both hands."

"Hurry," Jolie urged, her voice thick, still struggling to breathe let alone talk. She felt robbed of his touch and wondered if he felt the same, if he'd tried to keep one hand on her because he didn't want to let go even for the short time it would take to get his pants open. Touching and being touched had shot from enjoyable to essential.

"I'm hurrying." She heard material rustle and felt him move under her as he worked his jeans far enough out of the way to accommodate her and then a distinctive tearing sound. Good, he was putting a condom on. That meant any second now . . .

"Brace your hands on the dashboard and lean forward."

She did, and Chet lifted her hips, positioned her over his cock, and thrust into her.

She was so turned on, it was unbelievable. She'd come twice already, and it was as if the temporary pleasure of each release had only been building toward something bigger. She was literally trembling, breathing as hard as if she'd been running. Chet filled her, stretched her, so hot and hard inside her.

"Jolie, baby, you feel so good. So wet, so tight." He rocked into her, and she moaned. "You need me to fuck you, don't you? Fast and hard."

"*Yes.*"

He used his grip on her hips to hold her where he wanted her and pull her into his thrusts. He made it fast and hard, and Jolie screamed when she felt the orgasm breaking over her. The sheer intensity made it almost a pleasure-pain as his cock drove into her, deeper, then deeper still. He kept up a driving rhythm while she shuddered and spasmed, her inner muscles squeezing him and milking his balls dry as he emptied himself into her.

Chet's arms wrapped around her, holding her close in the aftermath, his cock still buried in her depths, her sex quivering around the length and width of him, while their breathing slowed and their heartbeats steadied.

His thighs were hard under her, the denim fabric that covered them rasping slightly against her bare skin. Her legs splayed open and hung over either side of his. A breeze from the open gap at the tops of the windows hit the sheen of sweat on her skin and made her nipples tighten.

She felt his lips move along her cheek. "Told you I'd last about two seconds if you squeezed my dick like that," he told her, his voice rough. "We'll do better on the next round."

Jolie let out a shaky breath. "If you can do better than that, you'll need to keep a team of paramedics on speed dial because I could have a heart attack."

"Well, that's more like it." He tightened his arms around her. "Give you a couple of good orgasms and you start showing some respect. I should have bent you over the coffee counter a month ago and saved myself some aggravation."

Jolie laughed softly. "That would certainly have livened up the workday." She could easily picture herself naked and bent over the counter, her legs spread apart and her bared butterfly tattoo raised in an erotic invitation.

"Yes, and that could lead to all sorts of unfortunate Pavlovian associations. As a matter of fact, I've already been affected. Next time you ask me if I want cream, I'm not going to think about dairy products."

"No?"

"No." He moved his hand down between her legs to lightly brush her clit. "I'm going to think about your pretty pussy creaming for me. I'll think about your beautiful naked body, your legs spread for me, the way you touch yourself while I watch you, my fingers inside you, and your cream spilling for me until you're so wet and I'm so hard, I have to fuck you."

He circled her clit, his touch gentle, careful of her oversensitive state. "I'm going to start getting a monstrous hard-on every time you even ask me if I want coffee, and if you offer me cream, I'm going to have to haul you into the supply room to get some."

"You'll be happy to know that the supply room has a lock." Jolie clenched around him at the thought of a midmorning quickie after the early-morning coffee rush ended. She'd have to bite her lip to keep from moaning out loud in case anybody came into the shop. Sounds like *ohhh* and *ahhhh* coming from the supply room would be a dead giveaway that she wasn't back there stocking the shelves.

Jolie blinked her eyes to clear away the vivid imaginary scenario and turned her attention back to the conversation and their usual light banter. Teasing him was a much better idea than torturing herself with fantasies that were probably going to spring back up the next time she went into the supply room.

"So now you have an espresso fetish. Sexually aroused by coffee with cream. How degenerate."

"You're a fine one to call me degenerate. You're the one who peeled out of her pants and turned masturbation into performance art. You got off on me watching you."

"Okay, we're both degenerates." Jolie felt liquid and relaxed and realized that it was going to require monumental effort to climb off Chet and wiggle back into her clothes. More effort than she felt capable of summoning just then. A yawn escaped her.

"Yes, degenerates. Both of us. Don't let it keep you awake at night," Chet said.

"I won't." She closed her eyes, just for a minute. Her breathing settled into a steady pattern. She was so warm, so comfortable.

"Hey." Chet gave her a gentle shake. "Don't go to sleep on me here. I can't drive you back to my place naked. Think how it would look if I got pulled over. Caught with a naked unconscious woman in my truck."

Jolie yawned again. "Don't speed and you won't get pulled over."

He lifted her off his lap, pulling out of her in the process. "You're a heartless woman." He retrieved the scattered pieces of her clothing and started dressing her.

"You're pretty good at that," Jolie informed him, impressed by his dexterity in the dark. He'd even found her panties.

"I'm a man of many talents." He worked her jeans up to her thighs and stopped. "Lift."

Jolie obediently raised her hips, and then batted his hands away, taking over. "I'll finish."

"Leave them unzipped—it'll save time later," he suggested.

Jolie laughed. "What about how it'll look if you get pulled over? Caught with a woman who has her pants unzipped."

"It'll look like I'm about to get lucky, but we can probably explain it away by saying you ate too much dinner and felt uncomfortable."

She gave him a dirty look and he laughed at her reaction.

The river murmured outside the truck windows and a light breeze teased her hair. She couldn't remember the last time she'd felt so thoroughly relaxed, so spent. She had a smile on her face, and it wasn't just from the world-class orgasms. She'd made a good choice with Chet. Playing with him was going to work out perfectly, after all.

Then he leaned over and kissed her, and there was nothing playful about it.

14

Chet's lips claimed hers in a kiss so hot and hard, she could almost imagine his brand burning into her lips. He cupped the back of her head with one hand to hold her still while he took her mouth with bruising force.

Jolie put her hands against his chest, feeling the warmth of his body and the rhythm of his heart under her palms as she fell into the intensity of his kiss. When it ended, she twisted her fingers into the fabric of his shirt and clung, feeling like she'd been swept away by a current as strong as the river they'd parked beside.

"What was that about?" she asked when she found her voice again.

"I thought it was time we kissed," Chet answered. He tugged at her hair. "I've seen you naked. I've touched you and watched you touch yourself. I've buried myself inside you and emptied my balls into you, and while the position worked for our location, it meant I couldn't kiss you. Car sex does limit the options. Next time we'll be in a bed and we'll be facing each other so I can kiss you while I slide inside you."

Next time. Jolie closed her eyes and could almost feel it, their bodies tangling together, Chet thrusting into her, kissing her, taking her mouth and her sex at the same time, stealing her breath, filling her, thrilling her.

"Not chickening out, are you?" Chet traced the curve of her cheek with one finger, his other hand still cupping the back of her head. "You, me, my place, round two. And then I'm going to find your ticklish spot. In fact, I should probably find your ticklish spot first so I can be on top."

"I'm not chickening out. And I'm not ticklish. You are so going to lose that one," Jolie said.

"Well, even if I lose, I'll still have you naked in my bed. I'm not seeing a downside, here." Chet tousled her hair and sat back. "I'm going to step out for a minute. Want to wait in the truck, or come with me?"

Oh. Right. He'd have to get rid of the condom. The cool, fresh air would probably wake her all the way up, and help overcome the postcoital lethargy that weighted her down. Probably a good idea, unless she wanted round two to happen after a nap. "I'll get out with you."

They climbed out their separate doors and by the time Jolie came around, Chet's jeans were zipped again and he was tapping dirt down with his boot. She felt a smile tug at the corners of her mouth.

"What'd you do, bury the evidence?"

"Yep. Can't leave something like that just laying around." Chet walked toward her and took her by the shoulders. "It's not like you can put them back into the little foil packets they come in to toss in the next handy trash can, but nobody wants to stumble over a used rubber on the way to a fishing hole. Disturbs the concentration."

He bent and kissed her, a slow, warm, lazy kiss that curled

her toes. Jolie leaned into it and kissed him back, liking the firm pressure of his lips and the easy way their mouths fit together. He was a practiced kisser. Jolie found very few things sexier than a man who knew how to kiss a woman breathless, and in her experience it was a rare talent.

Chet had many other talents, too. She knew firsthand that he was equally practiced at foreplay and afterplay. She thought of his hands wandering over her, learning her, his fingers sliding into her, and then her bare butt bouncing on his lap while he impaled her with his cock, and she shuddered.

Chet broke off the kiss. "Cold, baby?"

"No, just excited. And is that nickname payback for calling you cowboy?"

"I like excited." He drew her closer until their bodies brushed against each other—light, barely-there contact. "I like the nickname, too. I think it suits you. But don't worry, baby. I know whose name to yell when the time comes." He feathered kisses across her forehead.

"When what time comes?" she asked, taking his setup line.

"When you use up all the hot water tomorrow morning and leave me with a cold shower."

"That would be rude of me," Jolie said. She slipped her arms around him and let her hands cup his ass. "But since I'm not familiar enough to gauge your hot-water supply, maybe the best way to prevent a problem is to shower together."

"Put your hands on me like that and you can do anything you want." Chet spanned her waist with his hands and swung her off her feet, turning them in a dizzying circle. "Hell, just let me get my hands on you and you can do anything you want."

"Didn't think you'd be satisfied to stop with your hands," Jolie teased.

"You would be right." He lowered her to the ground again, sliding her down his body and giving her a contact rush in the process. "Now that I know what it feels like to be inside you, I don't just want my hands to have access to your body. Judging by your reaction, I don't think you'd be satisfied if I stopped there, either."

"Well, I wouldn't want to waste another perfectly good hard-on if it happened to come up," Jolie said, moving into him. "And I wouldn't want to leave you suffering from lack of blood to your brain, either. I'm not heartless."

"Damn good of you." He wrapped his arms around her and nuzzled her neck. "I'll make it worth your while, baby."

She clutched at him, remembering the raw intensity of their bodies coming together. Chet had definitely made sex worthwhile. If she'd come any harder, she might have burst a blood vessel.

She wouldn't have guessed the two of them together would be like that. She'd expected the sex to be satisfying and enjoyable. She hadn't expected it to be so passionate or powerful.

Then again, she had never before realized she got a kinky thrill from being watched or from the possibility of discovery. Not that it had been all that possible. Enough of a risk to add excitement, but if they'd really been likely to be discovered, she would've called for a change of venue.

Chet nibbled at the curve of her neck and she quit thinking, tilting her head back to make it easier for him. "Mmm, that's nice."

"Nice? I must be doing it all wrong." He scraped his teeth lightly over her skin, and the unexpected sensation made her blink.

"There is nothing wrong with how you do that," Jolie informed him. "But if you think you need more practice, go right ahead."

He nipped at the spot where her neck and shoulder came together, homing in on a pressure point Jolie had had stimulated in therapeutic massage but never by a love bite. It felt exquisite.

His hands moved up her sides, stopping just below the curve of her breasts. "I shouldn't have put your shirt back on you."

"You were worried about public indecency," Jolie reminded him.

"There's nothing indecent about you topless," Chet informed her, backtracking to slip his hands under her tank top. "Although it's probably time we moved to a more private setting." He kissed the line of her shoulder, then down to the hollow of her throat and into the valley between her breasts. "Yep. Definitely time. These clothes are getting in my way."

Jolie could easily imagine his mouth moving lower, closing over her nipples by turns, then moving lower still, his progress unimpeded by shirt, bra, jeans, or panties. "Definitely time," she agreed.

He swung her up into his arms again before she guessed his intent and carried her back to the truck. "Those clothes of yours need to come off. I have another bet to win," Chet told her.

"You're not going to win."

"I win." Chet grinned at her in triumph and continued to tickle the sensitive spot behind her knees while she yelped, squealed, and attempted to roll away from him. "Don't be a sore loser, baby."

"I'm not a sore loser. Stop it," Jolie giggled, squirming under him when he attempted to pin her with his arms and legs. Cool, smooth cotton sheets rustled as she moved and his bare skin slid against hers.

"You're ticklish. I know your secret now." Chet stopped tickling and abandoned half measures. He rolled on top of her, settling his weight over hers, effectively trapping her. The sensation of his naked, hard-muscled body against hers with no barriers between them made her breath catch.

"You know one secret." Jolie gave him an arch look.

"I know a lot more than one." He wedged one thigh between hers, nudging them apart. When she shifted, he settled into the cradle of her hips. "But never underestimate the importance of knowing where to tickle. I can bring you low with that secret."

Jolie laughed out loud. "How do you think you could do that?"

He nuzzled her neck. "It's the perfect threat. I can get you to do anything if I play the tickle card."   -

The broad head of his erection pressed against her mons. Jolie lowered her lids and said, "That doesn't tickle."

"It's not supposed to." Chet flexed his hips, sliding himself along her labia in a teasing thrust. "Question time."

"Ask."

"I want to taste you, but I also want to kiss you while I take my turn on top. Will it bother you if I kiss you after going down on you?"

Jolie blinked. "Well, that's direct."

"Direct questions now can prevent future problems." His lips brushed against hers, first lightly, then harder, and then he slipped his tongue between her lips to deepen the kiss. The penetrating thrusts of his tongue were echoed by the movement of his hips rocking into hers, a teasing prelude of the act to come.

Chet lifted his head and looked into her eyes. "I love kissing you. I want to go down on you. I don't want to make you uncomfortable. So you tell me, will it bother you if I kiss you after?"

It wasn't the kind of question she'd expected, and she didn't know the answer. It had been so long since she'd had sex at all, let alone oral sex. Would it bother her if she tasted herself on Chet's tongue?

"Not sure?" He looked surprised as he read the confusion on her face. "Have you been sleeping with somebody who didn't want to put his mouth between your legs? Or don't you like oral?"

"I haven't been sleeping with anybody," Jolie admitted. "And it's been so long since I've had oral, I can't remember if I like it or not."

"Baby. Why not?" He looked astounded. "You're not a virgin. You're sexy as hell, and you're certainly not shy about your body."

"I've been busy," she said, feeling a little defensive.

"Too busy to have sex?" Chet stared at her, then rolled with her so they lay tangled together on their sides, facing each other.

"Yes, I've been too busy to have sex. Well, not so much too busy. I mean, with vibrators and so on, of course," Jolie said, and realized she was floundering. She took a deep breath and let it out slowly. "That's not coming out right. I mean, I have the usual needs and I don't pretend otherwise. But I've been too busy for a relationship, and that pretty much meant no sex. Okay?"

"Okay." Chet accepted her answer but gave her a searching look. "We'll talk about this some more later. For now, just tell me if you have any interest in letting me go down on you."

"I'm interested." Jolie licked her lips. "I'm interested in going down on you, too."

"You want to sixty-nine?" He grinned at her, his eyes warm with teasing humor. "Nope, don't think so. Not the first time. You'll distract me, and that could make me do a lousy job. If I don't give you a good oral experience, you might not let me do it again."

"I thought I distracted you by breathing."

"Not nearly as much as you'll distract me with your mouth around my dick. Get your lips and tongue on me, and I'll lose all concentration. That mouth of yours is like kryptonite on Superman. You'll make me weak." Chet shook his head. "You want to go down on me, you'll have to wait."

Jolie laughed at the idea that she had sexual superpowers capable of laying this cowboy low.

He stopped the laugh with another kiss, hot and slow, moving his mouth on hers while drawing her body closer to his until her breasts were crushed into his chest and his hard-on was pressed into her belly. His kiss was the real kryptonite, Jolie thought, weakening her until she clung to him, limp and trembling.

"I want to taste you," he whispered against her lips. "I want my mouth between your legs and I want to slide my tongue into you. Lay back and spread your thighs for me, Jolie."

She sank back on the bed and parted her thighs while Chet moved over her and between them. He kissed the valley between her breasts and worked his way down until his lips brushed her clit. He lifted his head to look at her. "Tell me if I do anything you don't like."

"You haven't so far," she said, her voice husky. She could feel the flush of heat spreading over her skin. The mattress was firm underneath her, his hands were strong and sure on her, and his mouth closed over her clit. Jolie watched him through half-lidded eyes.

A single lamp from the bedside table illuminated Chet's bedroom with soft, indirect light. Enough light to let her admire the breadth of his shoulders, the sculpted muscles of his arms, the way his head dipped between her thighs while he explored her folds and sensitive inner flesh with his lips and tongue.

He licked and sucked at her, tasting her, teasing her, making her squirm. Then he thrust his tongue into her, a slow in-and-out rhythm that demonstrated graphically what he wanted to do to her with a different organ.

Jolie let her eyes drift shut and gave herself up to the moment, to the pleasure of his mouth on her, and felt the heat build.

"You taste so good, baby." Chet raised his head and looked at her, lying back with her eyes closed, naked, caught in his sensual thrall, open to him. On more than one level?

Jolie was as complicated as he'd known she would be. But at least in the realm of the physical, things between them were very simple. Although even there, complications lurked. It shocked him that she hadn't been with any man in recent memory, almost as much as it pleased him. He felt distinctly territorial, as if he were laying claim to her body.

He tasted her on his tongue, and his cock throbbed with the need to be inside her. He lowered his head and sucked hard at her clit, making her moan. Her nipples stiffened in reaction.

She was hot and wet and ready, urging him with her body to take the next step. He was more than willing to accommodate her. Chet reached for the bedside table drawer, fumbled inside, found a foil-wrapped packet, and tore it open. He rolled the condom down his shaft and imagined Jolie's lips encasing him instead. His cock swelled, his balls ached, and he knew he was going to come too fast unless he slowed down.

He wanted slow. He wanted to savor her body under his, the sensation of his cock pushing into her, her nipples brushing against his chest, her mouth against his, tongues tangling while he fucked her.

"Jolie." Her eyes fluttered opened when he said her name. "Watch me, baby."

She watched as he settled between her thighs and wrapped one hand around his engorged shaft, stroking himself the way he wanted to stroke into her velvet sheath. Slowly. He used his hand to guide his cock down to her opening and pressed forward, letting the head enter her.

He looked into her eyes first, then admired the line of her

body, the tight buds of her nipples, the soft flesh between her thighs all pink and plump from his mouth's attention. He slid another inch of his shaft into her and then lowered himself down to settle his weight on her. "Spread wider, baby. Wrap your legs around my waist."

She did, and the shift in position left her even more open for him. Chet groaned and thrust all the way inside her, burying himself in her slick heat. "That feels so damn good." He brushed his lips against hers in a light kiss. "Try not to move. I want to go slow, and if you move, I'm going to lose it."

He felt her shudder under him at his words, felt her inner muscles clamp down on his cock, and groaned again. "Work with me here, Jolie. I want this to last."

Her breath was coming fast and her muscles kept squeezing him. "Can't help it," she muttered in a thick voice.

She was too close to the edge, Chet realized, both of them on the verge of coming. That's what he got for spending too much time stripping off her clothes and his, kissing, touching, exploring, making them both ready before he licked between her legs and kicked the need to be inside her from aching to bursting.

"Slow," he said, bracing his hands on either side of her to keep his weight from growing too much for her. "We can do slow."

It didn't convince either of them, but he had to try.

He withdrew by inches, then thrust back into her, rocking in and out of her in leisurely measured strokes. He might have been able to hold the pace down longer, but she shuddered under him, clawed at him, and sank her teeth into his shoulder.

"Chet." Half shriek, half plea, all need. Jolie moved under him, tilting her pelvis to take him deeper. "Fuck me."

"Hell, yes." Control shattered. Her need drove him harder, deeper. Her body gave under his, taking him, opening for him. His.

That single thought gripped him as he rode her to orgasm and pumped himself into her. He stayed on top of her, inside her, holding her close as they collapsed together. *Mine*.

She was his only temporarily, but he took far too much pleasure for comfort in the thought that she was his for tonight.

15

"I can't move."

"That's because you lost the bet, baby. You're on the bottom," Chet pointed out.

"Ack. It's wet. There's a wet spot." Jolie squirmed underneath him and shoved at his shoulder. "No wonder you wanted to be on top. Move it, cowboy. You're crushing me."

"You weren't complaining about the wet spot a while ago. You were too busy coming and clawing my back to shreds." He kissed her shoulder and stayed put.

She prodded him more firmly. "I mean it. Move."

"Nope. Don't want to. I'm comfortable."

Jolie let out a strangled sound, then tickled his ribs.

"Hey!" He raised his head and frowned at her, a mock-hurt expression on his face. "No need to go that far. That's just cruel."

"I'm a cruel woman." She smirked at him.

"I know it. You've been torturing me for weeks. I shouldn't

have let you come so fast, but I felt sorry for you when you started begging me."

Jolie narrowed her eyes at him. "You did not feel sorry for me."

"I did." He rocked on top of her, settling himself deeper between her thighs. "You were so wet and hot and sweet. I wanted to go slow, but you wanted me to make you come. You looked like you were in pain. I couldn't let you suffer." He gave her a noble look.

She snorted.

"Am I really crushing you?" Chet asked, raising himself up on his arms. "I can move if you need me to."

"Not crushing, exactly, but I need the little girls' room." Jolie wiggled under him again to prompt him to shift.

"Oh." He rolled over onto his back, taking her with him so that she ended up sprawled on top. He waved a hand in the general direction of the hall beyond the bedroom door. "First door on the left. Washcloths and towels in the cupboard under the sink if you want to clean up a little."

She started to slide off him and he caught her, pulling her into a brief, hard kiss before he let her go. "Hurry back, baby."

Jolie kissed him back and then crawled backwards off the bed, turned when her feet hit the floor, and started walking away. When she reached the door, he called after her, "Damn, I love that tattoo."

He was watching her ass. A grin spread over her face as she padded naked and barefoot down the hall, in search of the bathroom.

A few minutes later she was rummaging underneath the cupboard for a washcloth when a pair of hands cupped and shaped her bare butt. "Really. The tattoo is amazing. Especially when you bend over like that."

She stood up and arched her brow at him. "So it's the tattoo you were looking at?"

"No, I was staring at your ass and thinking about keeping you bent over so I could fuck you again. Did you plan that tattoo to make a man insane every time you bent over?"

She blinked.

Chet shook his head at her expression and pulled her into his arms. "Never mind, don't answer that. But the next time you bend over in front of me, don't be surprised if you get your little pussy stuffed full of my cock."

It wasn't likely that Chet was going to find her naked and bent over on any other occasion, but the idea of him coming up behind her and immediately giving in to lust made her feel tingly between her legs. And after all the orgasms she'd already had, she should have been tingled out.

Chet dropped a brief kiss on her mouth and nudged her hip, prompting her to move to the side. He retrieved a washcloth for her and placed it in her hand, closing her fingers around it. "There you go, baby. Now you have something to scrub my back with."

"I'm scrubbing your back?"

"Yep. It's your job to clean those scratches you made before they get infected. You're a hellcat."

She rolled her eyes. "You're exaggerating. If there are any scratch marks visible at all, which I don't believe for a minute, I'll probably need glasses to see them."

"I'm sorry to hear that your eyesight's already started to go." He gave her a sad look and fondled her breast. "Didn't you know about the dangers of relying on yourself and your vibrator all this time? Good thing you found me before you went blind."

Before she could say anything to that, he turned away and started the shower, giving her a stunning view of his bare assets.

She leaned against the bathroom counter and admired six-foot-plus of naked Chet. He looked good from any angle, but from the back she could see the muscled planes and angles of his back, legs, and butt.

"Do you lift weights?" she asked.

"Hell, no. Waste of time." He looked back at her over his shoulder and gave her a crooked smile. "Think my ass needs a tattoo?"

"Maybe."

He stepped into the shower and held his hand out to her. "Come here."

"In a minute. I need to get something." Jolie backtracked to the bedroom, found her purse amid the tangle of her discarded clothes, and pulled her favorite bathtub toy out, trying not to giggle as she imagined Chet's reaction.

"Okay, I'm ready," she said with an innocent smile.

Jolie placed her free hand in Chet's and let him pull her under the spray with him. She closed her eyes and tilted her head back as the water streamed over her face and hair before stepping back so the water could hit the rest of her body.

"Do you always carry your rubber duck around with you?"

"No." Jolie gave him a wicked smile. "Only when I need to remind myself to buy new batteries."

"Batteries," he repeated.

"Uh-huh." Jolie turned it on and rubbed the waterproof toy along his shoulder, letting him feel the massaging vibration.

He let out a low whistle. "You're a very bad girl."

"I know." She trailed the duck down his stomach and laughed when he pulled back.

"An X-rated rubber ducky. Bathtub toys have changed a lot since I was a kid."

"Mm, they have," Jolie agreed. "The same company makes a penguin and a caterpillar, but I'm a sucker for the classics."

"A classic vibrator." He shook his head at her. "I think we'll keep this for later."

Chet took the duck and found the off switch, then set it aside. He reached for a bottle that sat on a ledge in the shower stall and squirted some liquid into his hand. "Turn around—I'll do your back first."

"What is that?" she asked, sniffing and failing to identify the scent.

"Peppermint." He started with her head, massaging it into her scalp, then moved down over her shoulders, back, butt, legs, coating her with the liquid herbal soap. "Turn."

When she turned back to him, he had more soap lathered in his hands. He washed her upper body, grinning at her as he slid his hands over her breasts several more times than hygiene required. He slid his hand between her legs last and kept his touch quick and light.

"Rinse off," he advised, moving to the side and pulling her forward so the water hit her. "It's got a real tingle to it if you're not used to it."

Jolie stood under the spray, turning in a slow circle to rinse herself completely, then tipped her head back under the water again to rinse her hair.

"I can't believe you put soap in my hair," she complained. "It'll be full of tangles."

"It's castile soap. Pretty much straight peppermint oil. You won't have tangles, and it'll make you feel relaxed and rejuvenated both. Peppermint's very soothing."

She finished rinsing, brushed water away from her eyes, and blinked at Chet. "Hello? When did you get into aromatherapy?"

"It's not aromatherapy. It's folk medicine." He gave her an insulted look and lathered himself up. "Home remedies that get rediscovered by New Age types are not new. Among other properties, peppermint oil keeps insects away. Natural mosquito repellent."

She ran a nail through the lather on his chest. "If you say so. Aromatherapy man." She smirked at him. "Now I know your secret. Wonder what the other cowboys would think of you and your 'mint is soothing' line?"

"Other cowboys know the value of peppermint castile soap already, you lippy woman." Chet hauled her into his arms, smearing lather over her breasts in the process. "But if you think you're going to ruin my manly reputation by telling other men what I keep in my shower, you're not thinking it through. They'll all know I've had *you* in my shower."

He turned with her so that he was under the water, and the spray washed over them both. He was right: the mint did feel soothing. It left her cool and tingly all over, too. Refreshing and rejuvenating was an accurate description.

"All rinsed?" he asked her.

"Uh-huh." She made a lazy gesture with the washcloth she'd brought into the shower. "Didn't you want me to do your back?"

"Please."

Chet turned and Jolie lathered up the washcloth, then applied it to his back. There was something oddly soothing about the intimate task, stroking the soapy cloth up and down his back. She noted that there weren't any visible marks on the skin. When she pointed that fact out, he whistled as if unable to hear her, then shot her a grin over his shoulder before turning around to face her.

The smile alone would have told her he was up to something, even without the toy in his hands. "Let's see how this works," he said. Chet stroked the vibrating duck over the upper curve of her breasts, teasing her.

Jolie closed her eyes, enjoying the light massage and the way her nipples tightened in anticipation. "I think you're getting the hang of it."

"Bet you spend a lot of time in the tub." Chet rubbed the duck slowly over her nipples and then let it move down her belly before moving it over her mons.

"Nothing like a long bath after a long day," Jolie agreed, giving him an innocent look.

"Relaxing." Chet stroked the toy between her legs. The vibration combined with the stimulation of peppermint oil tightening her skin, making her feel awake to every sensation, had Jolie anything but relaxed.

Her breathing quickened, and Chet's eyes darkened as he took in her response. He massaged her mons in a series of circles and lines, pressed the duck hard between her legs, moved it up and around her nipples, then back down to rub over her clit.

"Fun toy," Chet said, leaning down to lick a drop of water off her nipple as he shut off the vibration. His finger slid along her swollen slit as he withdrew the toy from between her legs. Jolie made a strangled sound of agreement.

He turned the water off and pushed her out of the shower with one hand on her butt. "Towels." Chet stepped past her, retrieved two from beneath the sink, and passed one to her. She used it to dry her hair first, then wrapped it around her while he did the same.

"That outfit suits you," he said.

"Yours, too." She grinned and waved in the general direction of the towel now slung around his hips. Hers covered her breasts and just barely came low enough to cover her butt.

He snagged her hand and pulled her close enough to kiss. His mouth moved against hers, firm, heated, thorough. When he finished, he folded his arms around her, keeping her close. "How're you doing, baby?" he asked.

"Fine."

She felt him shake his head. "Well, that's informative. Okay, I'll be more direct. You haven't had sex in a long time. Are you feeling sore? Do you need me to keep my hands off you for the rest of the night? Stick to the duck instead of what it rhymes with?"

"Oh." She leaned into his chest and rubbed her cheek against him. "No. I really am fine."

"Glad to hear it, baby." Chet kissed her forehead and squeezed her butt.

She relaxed against him, enjoying the feel of his hands on her, his arms around her, the fit of their bodies. Then her stomach growled audibly.

Chet laughed. "Come on, let's head to the kitchen before hunger makes you cranky."

"I don't get cranky."

"Bet you do. But we're not going to find out." He scooped her up and carried her into the hallway.

"I can walk, you know," Jolie said, tapping him with a red-tipped nail.

"I know. I like having you in my arms. Besides, this way I can put you where I want you." He tilted his head. "I have a nice view of your cleavage, too."

"Pervert," she said, but without any heat.

"If I was a pervert, I wouldn't have waited so long to get a look at more than your cleavage."

"True." She dropped her head back onto his shoulder and cuddled into him. "And now you've seen everything."

"Worth the wait." Chet deposited her on a wooden stool next to his kitchen counter. "Sit there and behave."

"You make me sound like a troublemaker." Jolie curled one leg underneath her and let her other leg swing while she watched him walk to the fridge.

"I knew you were trouble the first time I laid eyes on you." He smirked at her; then his head disappeared as he rummaged around behind the door. He reappeared with his hands full of grapes and cheese, and stepped back to close the door.

Chet set everything on the counter, opened a cupboard to pull out a plate, then a different cupboard for a box of crackers.

Crackers and grapes went on the plate; then he found a knife, added several slices of cheese, and put everything away. Plate in hand, he turned to her and offered her his free hand. "Come on. We'll have a bed picnic."

"Aren't you afraid I'll leave crumbs on the sheets?" she asked as she slid her hand into his.

"Nope. I just hope they don't catch fire." He dropped a kiss on her open mouth, and Jolie felt a little spark flare in response.

They walked hand in hand back to bed. Jolie sprawled with her back against the pillows, and Chet fed her a grape. "Time to talk," he said.

She lifted a brow in inquiry, since her mouth was full.

"I want to know more about why you've been too busy to have a man in your life."

Jolie swallowed, then answered. "I just graduated from law school."

"Job market's worse than I thought if a lawyer has to get a job working in a coffee shop," Chet said.

She snagged another grape off the plate. "The job market's fine. I have a real job with a law firm, but it doesn't start until late in the fall, and I had to have something else to fill in. I also need to take the Montana bar exam, and I wanted a flexible job that would leave me plenty of time to prepare."

"So you plan to stick around." Chet frowned at the grape in her hand and fed her a bite of cheese. "You need to eat more. No wonder your stomach's growling."

"Yes, I plan to stick around." She followed the cheese with a cracker, waving it at Chet before she popped it in her mouth. "See? I'm eating."

"Back to our main subject: you just graduated. Explain why this meant no men."

"Most men aren't interested in women who spend every free minute in class, working, or studying. They like women who are available."

Chet lounged beside her and slid an arm behind her, shifting her so that instead of leaning on the pillows, she was leaning on him. "Okay, so you were a very dedicated student and all the men you met were impatient."

"No. They were normal." Jolie ate another cracker.

"Impatient," Chet repeated. He fed her grapes, one by one, and then somehow the plate was empty. "Better?"

"Yes." The snack had been just what she needed. The shower had soothed her, and Chet had very thoroughly satisfied her. She felt him move as he picked up the plate and set it on the bedside table. He settled back with her and tugged at the end of the towel she'd tucked between her breasts. "Get naked with me again, Jolie."

"Smooth talker." She smiled and unwrapped the towel, letting it fall open.

"I like you naked." He tugged on it, and she lifted up so he could pull it out from under her and toss it away. His towel followed and then he pulled her into his arms and scooted so they lay on their sides facing each other. "Let's recap. You like men. You like sex. You like me."

"I didn't say I liked you," Jolie teased.

"Not every little thing has to be said." Chet slipped his hand between her legs. "I don't see you in some other man's bed. My hand is between your thighs. I think I can assume you like me a little bit."

"Can I assume you plan to do something with that hand?"

He squeezed her mons. "Hush, woman, I'm talking."

"What about?"

"I forget. My hand's between your legs." He stroked her sex, and Jolie shifted to make it easier for him.

"So it is." She batted her lashes at him. "And I know for a fact that isn't a pistol in your pocket."

"No, but I am happy to see you." He smiled at her. "Did I mention how much I like you naked?"

"You mentioned it." Jolie let her eyes drift closed and concentrated on the very pleasurable sensation of his fingers stroking and caressing her folds, teasing her clit, toying with her.

"Think you could take me again?" he asked, inserting one finger into her. "I'll let you be on top."

"I'm not some fragile flower," she said, moving against his hand. "I can take you, cowboy."

Jolie reached out and closed her hand around his thick shaft. She stroked up and down in tandem with the rhythm of his hand between her legs.

"That feels so good, baby," he told her. "I love your hand on me."

That was mutual, Jolie decided. He knew just how to touch her, how to vary the pressure and rhythm to make her squirm in pleasure and burn for more. He felt solid and warm in her hand, the skin velvety smooth. She ran her fingertip over the head of his cock and found it slick. "Somebody's getting excited."

"Want a taste?"

Heat coiled low in her belly as she imagined licking a salty drop from his head before closing her lips around his shaft and taking him deep into her mouth. "Yes."

Jolie scooted down to put her head level with his erection. It meant Chet couldn't keep his hand between her legs, but she wanted to explore him with her mouth. It seemed only fair. She closed her eyes at the memory of his mouth devouring her while his tongue thrust into her. She wanted to return the favor.

Chet slid his fingers into her hair and urged her head lower. "Taste me, Jolie."

16

Her sudden paralyzing attack of self-conscious-ness took her by surprise.

What if she was awkward? Chet was an accomplished lover, and she was badly out of practice. Jolie hesitated there, her hand wrapped around his shaft, mouth hovering just over the head of him, tense and unsure.

"Sorry, baby." Chet withdrew his hands from her hair. "I wouldn't hold you down on me—I just like playing with your hair. It looks like dandelion fluff."

"I hope you're not calling me a fluffy blonde," Jolie said, but she couldn't manage a flippant tone. It came out all stiff and wrong.

"Baby? What's the matter?" He touched her hair again, lightly, stroking it back from her forehead. "You don't have to do this. I thought you wanted to."

"No, I do. I just—" She broke off and tried to regroup. *Come on, Jolie, be a woman. It's a blow job, how can you do it wrong?*

"Hey." Chet pulled her back up to eye level. "I wanted to go down on you. I'm not going to demand you return the favor. If this makes you uncomfortable, forget about it. We can do other things. You could kiss me some more." He touched his finger to her lower lip as he made the suggestion.

"I want to return the favor." She spoke against his finger. "I just want to, you know, *return* the favor."

He frowned at her. "English is your first language, right?"

Jolie felt herself relaxing again as he tried to get a rise out of her. This was familiar territory. "Yes, it's my first language. Look, it's no big deal. I was ready to go, and then I realized how long it's been and I didn't know what to do next. I froze."

"Is that all?" Chet gave her a slow, sexy smile. "I'll talk you through it if you want."

"You will, huh?"

"Oh, yeah." He cupped her jaw and held her still for his kiss. Long, sweet, and hot, his mouth moved over hers until she melted into him, not noticing until she did that he'd moved closer and closer. He slid one leg over the top of hers and hooked her more securely into a full-body embrace, then kissed her some more.

When he finally lifted his head, her lips felt swollen. "Better now?"

"Yes." She felt a whole lot better, in fact, hot and lazy and liquid.

"Good." He touched his finger to her lower lip again. "Put your mouth on me, baby. Just a kiss."

Jolie slid down him and he moved up, making it easy for her. *Just a kiss.* She closed her eyes and touched her lips to the head of his penis.

"Mmm, that's nice," Chet said. He stroked her hair, his touch gentle and slow. "Now run your tongue around the ridge."

She licked the underside of the head that stood out slightly from the rest of his shaft, exploring with her tongue. After making a circle, she flicked her tongue over the top of his head, lapping up a salty drop of liquid that had seeped out.

"That feels good. I like your tongue, baby. Now take the head in your mouth."

Jolie fitted her lips over his head and slowly drew it into her mouth, until her lips met the thick shaft. She moved down a little farther, then back up until just the head remained in her mouth.

"Oh, yeah, baby. Just like that. Suck me," Chet encouraged.

She added suction to the fit of her mouth around him and slid up and down in lazy strokes, taking him as deep into her mouth as she could before letting him slide back out inch by inch. She swirled her tongue around him as she sucked and he groaned.

Jolie reached down to cup his balls while she drew his cock farther into her mouth. They felt warm and firm in her hand, the skin unbelievably soft. She stroked his balls while she sucked him and he groaned again. "Careful, baby, you'll make me come."

She repeated the movement three more times, and he put a hand down to lift her chin and stop her. She let his cock slide out of her mouth with regret. She liked the feel of him sliding between her lips and the salty taste of him.

"Jolie, not this time. I don't want to come down your throat. I want to be inside you."

She licked her lips. "Inside my mouth doesn't count?"

He pulled her back up into his arms. "It all counts, but it's not what I want right now."

Chet looked into the eyes of the woman he held and wondered if he was an idiot. But he'd had to stop her. Her mouth felt too damn good, and he didn't have nearly as much control as he should have had after coming twice already.

If he came in her mouth tonight, she might lap it up and

swallow and smile at him like the cat that got the cream. Or she might choke and decide blow jobs weren't for her. He enjoyed oral sex too much to risk putting her off it because he lost control and came before she was ready to deal with it. He already knew one night with her wasn't going to be enough, and he didn't want to discourage her from going down on him in the future.

He also suspected that if he did come in her mouth, it wouldn't satisfy him. He wanted her under him. He wanted to bury his cock inside her. He wanted to look into her eyes while he stroked in and out of her body, and he wanted to kiss her while he emptied his aching balls into her hot, tight sheath.

Chet took her mouth again, seducing her with his lips and tongue while he searched out her clit with his finger. She shuddered when he stroked it. She was so responsive to his touch. Was she ready for him? He stroked lower, encountering slick, swollen flesh, and felt a surge of triumph. Jolie wanted him again.

He thrust a finger into her, partly to open her and make it easier for her to take his cock, partly just because he could. She rocked her pelvis into his hand, soundlessly urging him to give her more penetration.

He put his free hand against her belly and pressed her lightly in the direction he wanted her to go, and she followed his signal, rolling from her side to lie on her back. "Spread your legs wide for me," Chet said, and when she complied he couldn't resist leaning down to lick her clit.

"You're so wet and sweet," he said, pushing another finger inside her. He suckled her clit, loving the taste and feel of her, the way she squirmed and bucked against him.

The need to drive his cock into her and feel her stretching to take him became urgent. It took a bare second to locate another foil packet in the bedside drawer and protect her. Then

Chet was settling between her thighs, his cock heavy and engorged, nudging at her opening.

Jolie's eyes were wide open, her face flushed with arousal, her lips swollen from his kisses. She'd never looked more beautiful to him than she did in that moment. He looked into her eyes, felt the softness of her body under his, the slick heat of her sex around the head of his cock as he eased into her.

"Jolie." He held her gaze as he thrust slowly home, filling her. He said nothing else, just her name. What else was there to say?

Their lips touched, softly at first, then harder. His tongue thrust into her mouth as he thrust his cock into her, again and again, slow, deep, drawing it out as long as he could stand it.

When he felt her body tightening under his, felt her inner muscles begin to squeeze him, he increased the tempo, thrusting faster, harder. She stiffened under him and cried out, and Chet let go, pouring himself into her, clutching her hips in his hands, pulling her into his thrusts to make them go deeper while he pumped his balls dry.

Spent, he collapsed on top of her and buried his face in her hair. He breathed in the scent of peppermint and woman mingled with the fragrance of cotton sheets dried in the sun, and felt something unfamiliar clutch in his chest.

"Remember, you lost the bet," he muttered as he felt the urge to sleep closing over him. "Have to stay the night."

It seemed vitally important to be assured that she would be there when he woke up.

"I remember," she answered. He felt her tuck her head under his chin and realized she'd be squashed if he fell asleep on top of her.

Chet rolled onto his back, coming out of her in the process, but that was okay. He had his arms around her. He arranged her on top of himself, her head resting on his chest, his chin touching the dandelion fluff of her hair. *Jolie.*

Not sure if he'd said her name out loud, he gave in to sleep.

———

A soft, unfamiliar noise woke him up a short time later. He came fully awake before he realized what it was. Jolie was muttering in her sleep. Chet smiled at the sleeping woman in his arms and wondered if she was giving him hell even in her dreams.

Then a sense of discomfort made him realize he'd neglected to perform a necessary little chore before dozing off. He'd left the condom on.

Chet eased Jolie off him, settling her head on the pillow. She immediately rolled onto her side and curled into a ball, her back to him. He slid out of bed and padded down the hall to clean up, shaking his head at himself. "Get your rocks off and pass out, way to impress the woman."

Although she'd nearly fallen asleep on him the first time, so she couldn't really complain.

There was something about deeply satisfying sex that made a nap range from inviting to imperative. Making love to Jolie satisfied him on every level, so it wasn't surprising that he'd passed out. The big surprise was that he hadn't lapsed into a coma right after the first time he'd come inside her.

Good thing she planned to stick around. He wasn't about to let her go just yet. For one thing, her taste in bathtub toys had given him ideas.

Mission accomplished, Chet crawled back into bed and spooned up behind her, wrapping his arms around her. She muttered in her sleep some more and snuggled into him, then sighed as if content. He closed his eyes and slid back into sleep with a smile on his face. Just like he'd told her, Jolie had something poking into her back, and it wasn't his elbow.

When she opened her eyes the next morning, the first thing she saw was Chet's bare chest. Her head was resting on his shoulder, and she had one knee hooked over his legs and one arm around his waist. She was using him like a body pillow. Jolie blinked away sleep and lifted her head, looking to see if he was awake. He wasn't.

Relaxed in sleep, Chet looked sexy and inviting. A faint shadow of beard clung to his chin, his fair hair was mussed, and the sheet twisted over his hips didn't hide the bulge at his groin. His skin was tanned a light golden color down as far as she could see. Had he had a tanline at his waist? She couldn't remember from the shower and wondered if he liked to sunbathe naked.

There was certainly plenty of space and privacy around his ranch house if he wanted to stretch out in the sun minus his shorts. He'd pointed out the property line last night on the way in, and it extended quite a ways in all directions. That much space created a sense of freedom, although he'd told her his friend Gabe's property bordered his on one side. So it wasn't exactly isolated. Just . . . private.

Jolie twisted to look for a clock, wondering what time it was. She relaxed when she saw the early hour. Plenty of time before she needed to be back at Lemon Espresso. Enough time to kiss Chet awake and see if her oral skills had improved?

She pushed the sheet back to expose his tumescent penis and touched her mouth to it, kissing her way up the shaft from base to head. She stroked her tongue over and around the head before sucking it into her mouth.

"Damn, that's a nice way to wake up." Chet's voice was low and husky from sleep. She felt his hand stroke her back. "Swing your hips around—let me kiss you awake, too."

Oh. He wanted to sixty-nine. Jolie smiled and let his cock slide out of her mouth while she adjusted her position, putting her knees on either side of his head, her upper torso brushing his, her mouth aligned with his groin. "Like that?"

"Just like that." Chet smoothed his hands along her bare

ass, then cupped her hips and drew her down to his mouth. The first touch of his tongue, tracing the folds of her sex, made her shudder.

She drew him back into her mouth, taking him as deep as she could, then letting him slide out inch by slow inch before drawing him back in while he explored her with his tongue. He really liked oral sex, Jolie decided. Fine with her. His mouth drew on her, softening her, coaxing her natural lubrication to release and her sex to swell in readiness. He sucked at her clit, and Jolie felt heat and need surge through her.

"Turn around, baby. I want inside you."

Jolie gave him a last hard suck before releasing his cock, then shifted around so that she was still over him, but straddling his hips. She brushed her sex along his shaft, and watched his blue eyes darken. He reached a hand into the drawer, pulled out a packet, tore it open, and rolled the condom on.

"Ride me."

Jolie rose up, positioned herself so that his head nudged her opening, and slowly sank down onto him, taking him in stages. When she was fully seated on him and he was all the way inside her, she closed her eyes and stretched out on top of him, rubbing her naked breasts against his chest.

Just being joined like that felt so good, she wanted to draw it out and make the moment last. Chet's arms wrapped around her, his hands moving over her.

"Feeling shy this morning?" he asked.

"No. I just wanted to be closer." She moved back and forth, dragging her nipples across his skin.

"I like you closer. I liked waking up with your mouth on me, too."

"I thought it was traditional to wake somebody with a kiss," Jolie said, smiling against his bare skin.

"I thought it was the guy who was supposed to do the kissing."

"Well, you did," Jolie pointed out. She shivered at the visceral memory of his tongue circling her clit, tracing her labia, spearing inside.

"You were already awake then." Chet squeezed her ass, pulling her down to take him even deeper.

"Mmmm." He was moving inside her, and it was getting hard to hold on to the thread of the conversation. Jolie melted into him and rocked with him, loving the feel of him thrusting into her.

"I want on top again," Chet said.

"I would never have guessed you loved missionary so much," Jolie teased.

"I like the control." He rolled over with her, staying buried inside her. He lifted his torso to deepen the angle of penetration and look down at her. "I like seeing you under me. I like being able to control the pace and the position."

He started thrusting harder. "I like knowing you're mine to fuck, that you're all soft and wet for me, your legs spread for me."

His words painted an erotic picture in her head. It made her feel intensely sexual, desirable. Feminine to his masculine. Where she was soft, he was hard, and his weight pushed his strokes deeper, giving her more pressure against a sweet spot deep inside. She thought of herself the way he saw her, naked, open, willing, letting him take her, and felt herself clench around him.

"Oh, yeah. That's it." Chet increased the tempo, the pressure, and Jolie felt the pleasure break over her, heard him groan and felt him shudder as he came with her.

17

Chet slid his arms under her to hold her tight while he rolled them onto their sides. "Don't want to crush you, baby." He kissed the top of her head and cuddled her close.

Jolie hugged him back, holding him to herself just as tightly. She could still feel him, thick and semierect inside her, her slick flesh encasing him. She tightened around him and he arched his pelvis into hers in response.

Chet. The man who lived to torment her, who seemed to feel no day was complete without ribbing her about something. Who would have thought it would feel so natural to wake up in his bed? She thought about the night before, how comfortable and easy it had been, how gentle he'd been with her when she froze up, how pleased he seemed with her sexually even though she'd all but forgotten how to be with a partner.

He'd had a chance to really hit a sore nerve, more than one, and he hadn't taken the shot. He'd done nothing to undermine her sexual confidence or make her feel awkward. He'd gone out of his way to check her comfort level and her re-actions, asking directly when he wasn't sure what she liked or would accept.

No wonder women hated it when he left. Chet was going to be a very hard act to follow. She realized this could well be the last time she had him inside her, the last time he'd smile down at her while he pulled her underneath him and thrust into her, and it made her feel cold.

She didn't realize she'd actually shivered until Chet stirred and tugged the sheet and blanket up over them. "There you go, baby," he murmured into her hair. "Gotta keep you warm."

But the cold feeling wasn't anything blankets could fix. It spread through her as she realized she'd made a terrible mistake. She hadn't picked Chet as her playmate at random. He'd been the first man who came to mind because he was the man she no-ticed, who got under her skin, who commanded her attention.

And now she was in bed with him. Probably for the last time. Even if it wasn't the last, the end would come soon. He'd kiss her and pat her on the butt and say, "Thanks, baby," and drop her off before he moved on to the next thing, the next woman, and forgot about her.

Even if he didn't, if he wanted more, she didn't have more to give. He'd lose patience with the long hours she spent study-ing for the bar, the stress of the exam itself, the nights she was too tired for sex even when she could pay attention to him.

Jolie huddled into his warmth while the icy feeling crept over her.

"You're all stiff," Chet murmured. His hands dug into her back and shoulders, massaging her. "I know what you need. Stay right here."

The bed dipped as he rolled away and stood. He leaned down and tucked the covers around her, dropped a kiss on her head, and gave her a lazy grin. "Be right back, baby."

His smile struck her like a punch in the gut.

Don't make this more than it is, she told herself sternly. *This is sex. Great sex. Phenomenal sex. The kind of sex you want to remember when you're old and looking back on your youth.*

She hadn't had any sex worth reminiscing over before now. Which made it a really good thing that she was experiencing some finally. So she should just be grateful for what she had.

Jolie rolled onto her back, looked up at the ceiling, and thought about how it felt when Chet touched her, beginning with his "I dare you to say something" way of carrying her off for the night. His arms were solid and strong, his hands were sure, and his mouth . . . If she hadn't been lying down already, the memory of his mouth would have toppled her.

He kissed with a degree of feeling and a level of skill that amazed her. Even if they hadn't been having phenomenal sex, kissing Chet would have been worth reminiscing over.

A series of noises from the general direction of the kitchen interrupted her thoughts. What was he doing? Footsteps. Cupboard doors banging. A door opened and closed with a solid sound. Then footsteps coming closer as Chet returned.

He stopped in the doorway and looked at her for a long minute. Jolie realized she was still lying on her back in his bed, the covers a tangle around her. Her hair had to be wild, and she probably looked like a man had just climbed off her.

It didn't seem to bother him. He kept looking. Then he smiled at her. "Lose the covers. I want to see all of you."

What the hell, the rest of her had to look better than her hair. Jolie pulled the covers off and pushed them to one side.

"Damn." Chet shook his head, walked over to her, and sat beside her. He took her hand and laced his fingers through hers. "I have to stop looking at you naked. You distract me."

"Then you shouldn't tell me to flash you," Jolie said.

Although showing him her body did make her feel tight and tingly. She'd certainly enjoyed touching herself while he watched, and then letting him touch her, knowing he was watching his hands on her body and her reaction to him. Maybe she had exhibitionist tendencies that she'd never had the chance to indulge before. Having Chet for an audience had inspired her.

"Thinking about last night?"

"Yes." She tilted her head to look at him. "Why do you ask?"

"Your nipples got all hard and tight and your face got all flushed and pouty." Chet used their joined hands to pull her up to a sitting position. "Bet that's not the only part of you all flushed and pouty."

"I'm not taking that bet," Jolie said.

He stood up and tugged at her. "Didn't think you would. I'll come up with one you can't resist later. For now, come with me."

She stood up and grimaced when her thigh muscle twinged.

"Don't worry, we'll fix your stiff muscles." Chet drew her along with him, through the doorway, down the hall, back to the kitchen, and then out the door that opened onto the backyard.

They were naked, Jolie realized. Outside. Sure, there was a lot of privacy, but . . . but nothing. It excited her to be outside and naked. Nobody was going to come along and see them; the odds were astronomical against it. But the possibility did exist, and that was what sent a little thrill through her.

I am turning into an exhibitionist, she thought. That, or she was rebelling against the strict code of conduct and careful public behavior she'd adopted to protect her budding legal career. But there was no doubt that last night's play in Chet's truck by the river had gained an erotic edge from knowing the possibility of discovery, however remote and unlikely, was there.

Okay, so she was a safe and sane exhibitionist, one who

wasn't going to take any chances that could genuinely lead to the destruction of everything she'd worked for. But here on Chet's private property, alone with him, she could enjoy walking around knowing her body was on display and also be sure that it wasn't going to be seen by anybody but Chet.

And if he wanted to look at her nipples, or her tattoo, or any other part of her, it wasn't exactly a turnoff to her.

She was so distracted by the setting and their au naturel state that she almost ran into Chet when he stopped. Jolie managed to check herself, then saw where he'd led her.

"Oh. Nice." That was an understatement. A hot tub was built into a stone patio, with steps leading down into it. A faint mist was visible above it as the heat rising from the water mixed with the cooler morning air. A thermos sat on the stone surface in easy reach from the hot tub, and two large mugs sat on either side of it. And her rubber duck floated on top of the water. Jolie grinned at the sight.

"Thought you'd like to soak while you had some coffee." Chet led her down the steps and they settled onto a ledge, side by side. He handed her a mug and she wrapped her hands around it, taking a grateful swallow.

"Thank you."

"You're welcome." Chet drank from his mug, then set it on the ledge. "Come sit between my legs."

"Okay." She moved around to sit in the cradle of his thighs. The ledge was wide enough to hold them both like that. His chest made a resting place for her head and supported her back.

The water was warm enough to feel relaxing but not too hot. She wondered what it would be like to sit out here in the winter with the heat turned up. She closed her eyes and imagined the two of them dashing naked and barefoot through a light dusting of snow to the kitchen door, wet and dripping, then rubbing each other dry with towels before racing to the bed.

Stop thinking like that, Jolie told herself. She drank some more coffee and hoped it would sober her up. Something needed to. She was on a sexual bender.

Chet's hands moved over her shoulders, traced the hollows of her collarbone, stroked the upper slope of her breasts. "I like to sit out here in the mornings," he said.

"I can see why."

It was a beautiful place to start the day, and there was something very peaceful about being in water, drinking coffee, watching the sun come fully up.

It was all too easy to picture a parade of naked women who had sat here between his legs the morning after. It depressed the hell out of her, which was ridiculous, because she didn't have any sort of claim on Chet Andrews now, let alone at any time in the past. He was a grown man, a single man, and what he did and with whom weren't any of her business.

"This is supposed to make you feel better, baby." Chet cupped his hands over her breasts and squeezed lightly. "You're still stiff. You can't be too cold. What's the matter?"

Her throat felt tight. "Nothing."

"Overdid it, didn't we?" Chet hugged her from behind, his hands moving down to splay over her belly. "I shouldn't have jumped you this morning. My fault. Well, partly your fault, now that I think about it. I warned you about your mouth, and you went and wrapped it around my cock."

"Oh. So it's my fault." She grinned at his logic.

"Since that's the version least likely to make me sleep alone tonight, I'm going with it." Chet rubbed his chin on the top of her head. "If you feel real guilty, you might even let me be on top again."

When she didn't say anything, he added, "If you're not too sore. If we really overdid it, we'll just have to be creative." He prodded her in the ribs. "This is where you tell me that creative

is fine with you, in fact you have some ideas, or that everything is fine and I can be on top. But tell me something."

I think I'm falling in love with you was probably the wrong
response. So was *I may have started falling the first time we sharp-
ened our wits on each other.*

"Everything is fine. You can be on top," Jolie said.

He blew out a breath. "Damn, baby, I was starting to worry
that I'd gotten too carried away and hurt you."

Chet turned her until she sat sideways across his legs so he
could look down at her. "I'm not a sex fiend," he said. "You
don't have to worry that anytime you spend the night I'm going to be on you all night long. I might want to fuck you until
the sun comes up, but I do have self-control."

She blinked at him.

He frowned at her. "You didn't think this was a one-
nighter, did you?"

"I didn't think," Jolie admitted. She hadn't gotten past *have
sex with Chet* in her mind to think about how many times it
might be possible.

"Well, for the record, I don't do one-nighters, and even if I
did, last night would have changed my mind." Chet touched
the side of her face. "I know you don't exactly sleep around, either. And I know you had a good time with me."

"Pretty good." Jolie gave him a considering look.

"Damn good." He gave her a cocky smile. "Baby, I made
you come your brains out."

"Your point?" Jolie tapped his bare chest with one nail.

"My point is that it seems reasonable to think that if two
consenting adults enjoy each other's company once, they will
want to do it again. Like tonight."

Jolie placed her palm against his skin, enjoying the feel of
him. Even the smallest contact sent a pleasurable buzz
through her.

It was reasonable for him to think that she'd be willing to have sex with him again. Especially since she was. Very willing.

She turned it over in her mind, weighing the pros and cons. On the pro side, Chet was an incredible lover. He made her laugh. He got under her skin. He challenged her. She was herself with him, and that realization took her a little aback. The sensual, playful side of herself that had no place in her life of study and work and career goals came alive with him.

On the con side, if she was falling for him, continuing to sleep with him was likely to make her fall harder.

Jolie remembered the icy sensation that had invaded her bones earlier and realized that if she thought backing away from him sooner rather than later would protect her from getting hurt, it was already too late.

When it ended between them, it was going to hurt. And it was going to end eventually. So why rush to make it happen sooner? Why couldn't she enjoy what they had, live for the moment, savor the pleasure of having Chet for a lover as long as it lasted?

"Tonight," she said, letting her hand slide down his chest.

"Is that yes?"

"Yes."

"I'm going to win another bet," he said, smiling at her.

"Don't get overconfident, cowboy."

He was far from overconfident, Chet thought. He teased her, dunked them both under the water, got her relaxed and at ease with him again. When he turned on the rubber duck and the toy began bumping into her breasts as it floated and vibrated, she giggled. Knowing he'd succeeded in lightening her mood eased something inside him. But he was pretty sure he'd had a very near miss when he brought up plans for tonight.

Maybe Jolie felt a little uncomfortable the morning after. She hadn't been with anybody for a while. She was used to spending her mornings alone.

More likely she was just skittish. He got the feeling from what she'd said about her lack of relationships that she didn't expect a typical man to understand her commitment to her career.

Good thing he wasn't typical. Nobody understood the hours it took to make it better than a farmer or rancher did. Work wasn't something you did nine to five with an hour off for lunch and weekends and holidays free. He'd spent Christmas Eve walking a colicky horse, gone sleepless in foaling season, and then put in a full day's work the next day because chores did not do themselves.

Mother Nature had a way of drilling patience, persistence, and self-control into anybody who worked with her on a regular basis.

It occurred to Chet that Jolie wasn't likely ever to complain about the hours he put in to keep his little operation in the black, because she had the same work ethic. She would understand when a horse needed him just as he would understand when she had a big court case pending.

Of course, he was probably going to have to prove that to her.

He'd known from the beginning that Jolie was different, but he hadn't fully understood why until that morning, when he'd woken up to find her still there, her hair sleep-tousled, her body soft and inviting, making love to him with her mouth. The sense of rightness had sunk in, and he'd understood why he couldn't stay away from her, why he wanted her, and why he didn't intend to let her go.

Somewhere, somehow, she'd slipped under his skin and into his heart. He'd fallen for her, and last night had sealed the deal. She might not realize it yet, but Jolie was his.

She'd told him enough about her future plans for him to

understand that they were dealing with a very small window of opportunity, when she had free time and playtime, before she'd have to study for an incredibly difficult exam and begin her job. Not enough time for a conventional dating relationship to progress to commitment. Which left him with unconventional ways to persuade her that he wasn't going to get impatient when she couldn't drop everything to be with him, that he would support her in her goals.

While he refilled their coffee mugs, cuddled with Jolie, and kept the conversation light, Chet plotted his strategy. A bet she couldn't resist with the rest of their lives at stake.

18

Laura was as distracted as she was, Jolie decided. Good thing it wasn't busy, because she could only imagine how many mistakes they'd make if a rush hit.

"Did you have a good time last night?" Jolie finally asked.

Laura turned red and touched the high collar of the yellow turtleneck tank top she wore. "Um. Yes."

Jolie struggled to keep from laughing at the giveaway gesture. That collar was hiding something. Hickeys, probably. Who would have thought sober-faced Reuben would leave love bites? Of course, who would have thought that daredevil Chet would be such a sweetheart between the sheets?

Well, maybe *sweetheart* was the wrong word. But it was sweet, the way he called her baby and cuddled her in between bouts of heated sex. Vibrators were all well and good, but they didn't cuddle.

Jolie realized she was drifting off again and shook her head to clear it. *Focus,* she told herself. *Think about Laura.*

Laura is your friend. She might want to talk about her new guy.

Then again, she might not. Jolie didn't really want to be cross-examined about the events of the night before right now. She could just imagine: *"Sure, Laura, I know Chet's a regular here, but I thought it'd be a great idea to have sex with him."*

Laura might be having similar thoughts, actually. Reuben was a regular. Although Jolie didn't believe for a minute that his interest in Laura had come up after he'd started coming into Lemon Espresso. Reuben did not strike her as the designer coffee type, and he never ordered anything but an Americano, the closest an espresso shop came to plain brewed coffee. The evidence indicated that Reuben had spotted her first and become a regular to get to know her.

Good strategy. Chet was probably part of the strategy in the form of camouflage. He was so outgoing and dramatic that attention would be focused on him while Reuben quietly went about his version of courtship.

At least, she was assuming it was some kind of courtship. Dammit, she was curious.

Jolie stopped and put down the parts of the espresso machine she'd been cleaning and turned to face Laura. "Okay, I can't stand it. What's with the turtleneck? Did that big guy give you a hickey?"

Laura flushed even darker. "No."

"No? Laura, he didn't hurt you or anything like that, did he?"

If he had, Jolie vowed, she would pursue him to the full extent of the law on Laura's behalf and then even further just to be a litigious bitch and make his life a legal nightmare.

"No." Laura sighed. "This is so embarrassing. You can't tell anybody."

Jolie blinked. What could have self-possessed I've-seen-everything Laura embarrassed? She would have sworn the woman was unshockable and unflappable.

"Well, now you have to tell me before curiosity kills me.

Your secret is safe with me." *Unless you tell me something that ought to be reported to the authorities,* Jolie added silently.

"I'm wearing a collar," Laura muttered, her voice so low, Jolie had to strain to hear.

It took a while for the meaning to penetrate.

Holy cow, Laura and the badass cowboy were playing leather games. Jolie wanted to laugh and worked hard to swallow it and keep her face straight instead. Nobody wanted to have their sex life ridiculed.

"Oh. Wow. He, uh, didn't seem the type," Jolie said. She left unspoken, *Neither did you.*

Who would have thought Laura wanted to play sexual submissive? Of course, the fantasy was popular for a reason. Jolie thought she could especially see the appeal for Laura, who shouldered all the responsibility for her own business.

It made sense that when she finally let her hair down, so to speak, she'd do it with a vengeance. And the bedroom roleplay of surrendering control was probably as close as her boss was going to get to actually taking a vacation.

"He's the type," Laura said, still blushing. "Very dominant."

"Sexy," Jolie volunteered. "I mean, if you like the type. Which you obviously do." Personally, she would probably have run like hell if Reuben had made a move on her, but she knew her limits. Chet she could handle.

The thought straightened her spine. She could handle him. She had so far. Okay, he'd also handled her. In fact, now that she thought about it, it was a toss-up which one of them was handling whom now.

She pictured Chet's hands on her, herself seated naked on his lap in his truck while he got her off, and felt dizzy.

"The collar thing," Jolie said, making an effort to keep her mind off a grinning blond cowboy who kissed like a god and fucked like a demon. "Is that permanent? Should I get a matching tank so we blend?"

"It's, um, he'll take it off tonight. Maybe."

"Uh-huh," Jolie said, unconvinced. Whatever game the two of them were playing, she found it difficult to believe the collar wouldn't be making more appearances in the future. "I'll buy some matching tanks."

Laura touched her throat. "That's probably wise."

"You really like this guy, don't you?" Jolie asked. It was a rhetorical question, but it took a little mental readjustment to grasp that Laura was now part of a couple. A leather couple. Go figure. In BDSM terms, the collar was probably a near equivalent to a wedding ring.

"Yes." Laura traced the outline of the collar underneath the concealing turtleneck.

Well, really, they were just symbols of the same thing, Jolie thought. Rings, collars, brands on cattle. All ways of saying "taken."

And all she had to show for her life so far was a law degree and a tattoo on her butt. For some reason, that depressed her.

"I need a mocha," Jolie said. She went back to cleaning and reassembling the espresso machine. When life got you down, caffeine, sugar, and chocolate could pick you back up.

"Me, too," Laura said. "Oh. And if Reuben comes in before closing time, I might need to take a little break."

Jolie flashed on the stockroom conversation she'd had with Chet. Sex in the back of the coffee shop definitely fell into the safe category, but with an edge of the forbidden to it. That had real possibilities for satisfying her naughty side. "I'll cover for you if you'll cover for me. Maybe we should put a futon in the stockroom. Good thing the door locks."

The two of them looked at each other and burst out laughing.

"We're wild, wild women," Laura said.

"Damn straight."

By closing time they'd made a lot of coffee but without any

clandestine encounters. Probably for the best, Jolie decided. She wasn't sure she was really brazen enough to Do It in the workplace, although according to some statistics she'd read, it was far from unusual.

Two men in cowboy hats showed up just as Laura flipped the sign on the door from OPEN to CLOSED.

"Hope you're not here for coffee. I've shut everything down," Jolie told Chet.

"I'm not here for coffee, baby." He waited for her to come around the counter to him, scooped her up in his arms, and nuzzled her neck while he whispered for her ears alone, "I'm here for the cream."

It was ridiculous to feel her heart stutter at the sight of him, to feel hot and weak when he held her, to get turned on by a whisper. Ridiculous, but there it was.

She closed her eyes and imagined him lapping up the cream he wanted and shuddered, feeling dizzy with heat and a tangle of emotions.

"Night," he added more audibly, with a nod to Reuben and Laura.

Jolie mouthed "Be good" to Laura and gave her a saucy wink over Chet's shoulder. She saw that Reuben had his hand on the small of Laura's back, a possessive gesture, and he was looking down at her with the softest expression she'd ever seen on his face.

Satisfied that Laura was in good hands, even if they were likely to hold leather restraints, Jolie set her teeth on either side of Chet's earlobe. "I've got your cream, cowboy."

"And I've got something for you, baby." Chet squeezed her in an affectionate hug. "Did you miss me today?"

She rolled her eyes. "Yes, I pined away."

"I bet you missed me a little."

"Only when I had to go into the stockroom."

"Did you touch yourself and think about me?"

She trailed a nail down the front of his T-shirt. "And make you miss the show? No."

"Good answer." He grinned at her and set her on her feet next to his truck. "Hop in. I have something to say to you."

Jolie felt her brows shoot up. "Something that can't be said in a public place?"

"You'll find out." Chet opened her door and went around to his side, leaving her curiosity to drive her to go along with him.

She jumped in and turned to him. "Okay, cowboy, let's hear it."

"First things first." Chet leaned over and kissed her. He took his time about it, and when he finally raised his head, she felt flushed and out of breath. "I missed you, baby."

"You saw me eight hours ago," Jolie pointed out.

"Time is relative. Einstein said so."

Jolie snorted.

"I've been thinking," Chet continued.

"Poor baby. I hope it doesn't hurt." She gave him her most sympathetic look.

He frowned at her. "I have ways of keeping your mouth busy."

"I'm tempted to find out what they are, but I'll cooperate and listen."

"Thank you. I've been thinking." He shot her a sideways look. "About this morning. About last night. About you. Us." He reached out and took her hand in one of his, twining his fingers with hers. "You said you haven't had time for a rela-tionship and that you've got the bar coming up."

Jolie nodded, her mouth suddenly too dry to speak.

"Be mine until the bar."

She opened her mouth to say something, but no sound came out.

He laid a finger over her lips. "No, just listen. I understand what you're up against better than you might think. I know you'll have work and you'll have to study and the closer it gets to exam time, the less time you'll have. Stay with me. Sleep with me. Until you take the bar. I won't make it hard for you—I'll do everything I can to help you pass. But I want you with me."

Jolie found her voice and spoke against his finger. "This is a bet?"

He shook his head. "The prize. If you agree."

"And what's the bet?"

Chet's mouth tilted in a half smile. "You like having an audience. It makes you hot. But you won't do anything too risky, because the repercussions would be devastating." He leaned forward and kissed the corner of her mouth. "I bet I can take you into a public place and make you come in the middle of a crowd without anybody besides us knowing."

Heat washed over her. He was offering her a chance to experience an erotic fantasy. And the stakes pretty well ensured that he wouldn't do anything that could lead to getting caught, because he wanted to win. If he gave them away, if anybody suspected, he lost.

He was offering her something more than that, too. Jolie wanted the prize as much as he did, even though she knew it was temporary. She'd known from the beginning it wouldn't last. He didn't stay. He might not do one-night stands, but he didn't do long-term relationships, either. She suspected he never would have asked her to share a roof with him if they didn't both know they had no future.

But in its own way, the prize was a fantasy more seductive than the bet. For a little while, she could pretend that this cowboy was hers. That she could have a relationship that would last and that would survive the demands of her career. That he could love her.

Jolie closed her eyes and admitted to herself, if not to him, that Chet already held a piece of her heart. The longer she was with him, the more times he laid claim to her body, the harder it would be when it was over.

Jolie was finally going to get everything she'd ever worked for, everything she wanted. And when she did, she'd lose the man she loved.

So what did she want to do? She breathed in and out, and opened her eyes. She found herself looking directly into his. He was still, watching her, waiting for her answer. She knew what it had to be.

"If you win, I get an incredible sexual experience and then I get to use your hot tub every morning until I take the bar." She arched her back in a slow stretch, displaying the curves of her breasts. "I can't lose."

Unless she counted her heart, but she'd lost that already.

19

"Here we are, baby." Chet smiled at her and put out a hand to stop her when Jolie unbuckled her shoulder harness and started to reach for the door handle. "No. I'm going to do that for you."

She felt a slow burn of anticipation, knowing that opening her door wasn't the only thing he intended to do for her tonight.

Jolie waited for him to come around and let her out, squirming in her seat as the memory of what he'd done for her in this truck the night before washed over her. She was already growing slick and ready for his touch. Was she going to be able to be discreet, to stay quiet, not give the game away?

The neon sign over the building they were parked near was the only thing that marked it as anything more than a warehouse. It had been converted to a roadhouse, and that was pretty much all she knew about their destination. Chet hadn't been forthcoming with information, promising her only that she'd like losing to him. A lot.

He opened her door and put his hands on her waist to lift her out. When her feet touched the ground, he kept her close. "You've never been to a place like this, have you?"

Jolie shook her head. She could hear music coming from the roadhouse, muted in the parking lot, but the level told her it would be very loud inside. Too loud to talk.

"It can get a little wild. Stay with me. We won't be here long." Chet lowered his head until his mouth covered hers. "Open for me, baby," he murmured against her lips.

She parted them and let his tongue thrust inside. He pulled her closer, rocking his hips into hers as they kissed. His hands slid under her shirt, and she felt him unfastening the hooks to her bra in back, then sliding the straps down her arms, stripping her bra off without disturbing her shirt. He tossed it into the truck behind her.

He broke the kiss to look down at her. Her nipples stood out against the soft cotton of her tank top. "Very nice."

Jolie frowned at him. "You want me to go in there showing off my nipples?"

Chet rubbed his thumb over one hard bud, making it swell even more. "I want you to know that you're naked under your shirt. That you're a naughty girl who didn't wear a bra."

She swallowed.

"I want you to feel the soft fabric rubbing against your nipples and to know that I'm going to touch them in there. You could get caught in a public place letting me play with your nipples."

Her knees were getting weak.

"I bet you're starting to cream for me already." Chet slid his hand under her shirt, stroking the underside of her breast. "I bet if I slid my hand inside your pants until my fingertip touched your pussy, it'd come away wet.

She touched her tongue to dry lips. "We already have one bet under way."

"And I'm going to win it." He moved his hand up to cup his palm directly over her breast. "I'm going to take you inside and dance with you."

"You mean those people who claim dancing leads to sex are on to something?" Jolie asked.

"Dancing is foreplay, baby." Chet moved with her, rocking into her while he squeezed her breast. "But only if you do it right."

She didn't doubt for an instant that Chet knew how to do it right.

He moved his hand to cover her other breast, giving it equal attention. "I like you braless. It's going to be so easy to cop a feel whenever I want one."

Jolie shivered and arched her back, pressing herself into his palm. "Are you going to cop a feel inside?"

"You'll have to come with me to find out." He inserted his free hand into the waistband of her jeans, brushing the sensitive skin of her belly, teasing her, stroking back and forth but not moving lower. "I'm going to make you feel so good. Dance with me, Jolie."

While he moved his hand inside her pants, the hand up under her shirt was still busy. Chet caught her nipple between his thumb and forefinger, tugging on it. "Do you trust me?"

"Yes." She did. If she didn't, she wouldn't have picked him to play with, wouldn't have stayed the night with him, wouldn't have agreed to this bet.

He bent his head to hers and drew her lower lip into his mouth, raked it with his teeth, then released it. "Dance with me," he said against her lips.

Jolie nodded.

He slid his hands out of her clothes and wrapped an arm around her waist. He guided her forward, away from the partial privacy the truck door had given them in the parking lot, and closed the door behind them.

It shut with a very final sound.

Chet pressed a kiss against her temple. "You're not chickening out, are you?"

"No."

He tightened the arm around her waist, hugging her closer as they walked. "When was the last time you went out dancing?"

"I don't know," Jolie admitted.

"Know how to do the Texas two-step?"

"What's that?"

"That would be a no, then." Chet matched his stride to hers, shortening it so she didn't have to work to keep up with his longer legs. "I'll show you."

"Like you talked me through blow job basics?" Jolie asked, feeling her body relax into his as they moved together.

"Yep. You picked that right up. You can handle the two-step."

She wasn't so confident, but she figured she could at least fake it well enough to get by. And it wasn't like they were here for a dance contest. Well, a contest. And it apparently involved dancing. But dancing together was a means to an end, foreplay.

They were here for sex.

Jolie leaned into his side and slid her arm around his waist. It felt good to be close to him, to touch while they walked, and in spite of the fact that she probably wasn't going to be terrific at country dancing, she wanted to dance with Chet.

Chet walked her through the door check, paid their admission, and held her hand out to get a little cowboy boot stamp on the back of her hand. He put his lips against her ear and murmured, "Now we have matching tattoos."

They did. It gave Jolie a little jolt, even though they were temporary and would wash off.

Inside, he took her hand in his and drew her along behind him, walking in front of her to make a way through the crowd. He led her to the dance floor, worked his way near the center, and turned to pull her into his arms.

Chet put her left hand on his shoulder, settled his opposite hand on her waist, then moved down to cup her hip. He took her free hand in his, touching their palms lightly together, elbows bent as he demonstrated the position. He started to move and used his hold on her hip to show her where to go, indicating that she should take a quick step back first as he stepped forward, then another quick step. The next two steps were slow, Chet's booted feet gliding forward as she slid her feet back.

Jolie followed his lead, found the rhythm, and relaxed as she realized how straightforward the dance step was. It really was a two-step, and the simple pattern just repeated, two fast steps, two slower.

They started off with a little space between them, and then gradually Chet began to close the distance, drawing her into his arms as he two-stepped her around the floor. Her nipples brushed his chest as they moved, back, forward. His thighs moved against hers, pursuing as she back-stepped.

If they got out of synch, Jolie realized, their knees would bang together and they'd come to a halt in a tangle. But they moved together easily, and the dance became a sensual game of retreat and pursuit.

Foreplay.

The music changed, George Thorogood and the Destroyers wailing about being bad to the bone. Chet moved with her, guiding her to a corner next to some tall speakers, and turned her in his arms so that her back was resting against his front. She found herself facing an empty nook behind the angled speakers. The way the crowd pressed around, Jolie realized nobody could see beyond their partner's head.

They were functionally alone and private in the middle of a crowd. She felt her sex clench with anticipation, felt liquid heat throb between her legs.

Chet continued to move with her, swaying her body from side to side, as his hands moved up her hips, along the line of her waist, the curve of her rib cage. He brushed his palms lightly over her nipples, then settled his hands on her shoulders, stroking her. He moved his hands with deliberate slowness, matching the beat of the music, finally cupping and squeezing her breasts while his hips rocked with hers.

Touch me, she wanted to tell him. But even if she'd said the words, begged, he couldn't hear her over the music and the noise of the crowd.

One hand moved down, massaging her belly, and Jolie let her head fall back onto his shoulder in abandon.

He smoothed his hand up inside her shirt and began tugging at her nipples under the fabric. Her knees went weak as she remembered him telling her he was going to play with her nipples in public. His fingers felt so good on her bare skin, the pressure on the tight buds both a pleasure and a torment, because she wanted more. Needed more.

Chet moved his free hand down her body, settled it over her mound, cupped and squeezed. She moved her thighs apart a little and thrust her pelvis forward, aching for more pressure, a more direct touch.

She thought he would slip his hand into her jeans, or even unzip them, but he didn't. He continued to hold her sex while he moved with her, rubbing his cock against her, playing with her nipples.

The sensations built on each other, and Jolie felt a wave of pleasure rising as he moved his hands over her body, touching her so intimately, so possessively. He began to move the hand cupping her crotch in deliberate circles and strokes, stimulating her clit through her jeans, and Jolie felt the orgasm approaching. She hung on the edge of it as he drew it out, and then she was coming on the dance floor while he held her up.

Chet turned her back to face him, pulling her hard against his body. Jolie pressed her cheek against his chest, feeling breathless and dizzy. She let him rock with her, barely dancing, their feet sliding without leaving the floor. His lips moved over her hair and along her temple. Jolie angled her head to move into his kiss as his mouth found hers.

It wasn't a light kiss. It was hot, hungry, and thorough. His tongue thrust into her open mouth, his arms tightened around her, and Jolie realized how close he was to losing control. She understood why he hadn't unzipped her jeans or even slipped his hand inside them. He wanted her. Now.

By the time he ended the kiss, they'd come to a halt and were simply standing there, arms locked around each other. Chet lifted his head and looked down at her, his eyes full of heat and the promise of what was to come.

He let her go only to catch her hand and pull her along behind him as he once again forged a path through the crowd, making his way to the door without pausing. Outside, he continued to pull her toward the truck without speaking. He opened her door and stood back while she climbed in, watching her, not touching her.

The door closed, and he came around to the driver's side, climbed in, put the key into the ignition, and turned to look at her.

"Tell me I won."

Jolie ran her tongue along her lower lip. "You won."

"I'm going to be on top tonight." He settled his hands on the steering wheel and flexed them. "I'm going to drive us home and we're going to go inside, and if you want to be able to wear those clothes tomorrow, you will strip them off before you hit the bedroom. If you aren't naked by then, I'm going to tear them off you."

Jolie swallowed, caught by his urgency. Then she realized he was waiting for her to say something. "Okay." Her hands were trembling, and it occurred to her that it might slow her down. "Maybe I should start now."

"If you don't wait, I won't be able to," he answered.

"Oh."

"Yeah." He gave her a smoldering look. "I want you too much right now. Sit there and be good until we have some real privacy, and then you can be as bad as you want to be."

Jolie sat back and thought about being bad with Chet, being naked with him, alone with him, under him while he thrust into her. She squeezed her legs hard together in an effort to calm down.

It wasn't working.

"Nice weather we're having," she said.

"Summer's nice," he agreed.

"Hot."

"Damn hot."

"This isn't helping, is it?" Jolie asked.

"Nope." He unwound one hand from the steering wheel and held it out to her. Jolie slid her hand into his and felt it close around hers, firm, solid, warm. "That helps."

It did. The contact made her feel grounded, as if the sexual current that ran through them were a form of electricity.

Chet maneuvered the truck through the night, into his drive, and parked. He turned his head to look at her. "Race you to the bed. Loser has to make coffee in the morning."

Jolie smiled at him. "You're on." She tugged her tank top over her head and tossed it toward him before pulling the door open and leaping out to hit the ground running. She heard his booted feet hitting the gravel behind her and ran faster.

He caught her around the waist just as she put her foot on the porch step, and carried her up to the door. While he opened it, she unzipped her jeans and pushed them down her hips, simultaneously kicking off her shoes.

She stepped out of her jeans, bent to pick up her discarded clothing, and was right behind Chet moving down the hall. She saw the yellow fabric of her tank top and the white of her bra dangling from his hand and stripped off her panties, hop-ping on one foot, then the other, so she didn't have to stop.

Jolie let her clothes fall to the floor, dodged around him, and leaped onto the bed, coming to rest in the pillows. She shot him a triumphant smile. "I made it first, and you're still wear-ing clothes. You're making the coffee tomorrow, cowboy."

"I won't be wearing clothes for long." He stripped while she watched, her breath catching at the sight of his body. Chet pulled her down to lie flat on the mattress, pushed her thighs apart, and let his knee rest on the mattress between them while he reached for a condom. "You've had all the foreplay you're going to get for this round," he informed her.

Then he lowered his body over hers and filled her with one long, sure stroke.

"Chet." She wound her arms and legs around him. She held on to him as his lips closed over hers and he began to ride her, fast and furious, driving his cock into her with hard, deep thrusts.

When she felt her sex clenching around his in the begin-ning surge of orgasm, she broke free from his kiss to gasp for air. *"Chet."* She dug her nails into his back and rocked her pelvis up to meet his, needing more, and he gave it to her as he drove them both over the edge.

Afterwards, he kept her under him, his hands tangling in her hair, his lips moving over hers in a kiss so gentle, it built an ache in her chest. "Mine," he breathed against her mouth.

His. Until the bar. The terms of the bet rushed back. Jolie tightened her muscles around him and hugged him tighter, as if she could keep him with the effort, knowing it was impossi-ble, but unable to help herself.

20

Jolie made the drive to Helena with her stomach churning. She wasn't in the mood to sing along with the radio. The roads were clear, Chet had put snow tires on her car and loaded her trunk with emergency supplies. But it wasn't the weather that worried her. It was the three-day exam that made her want to pull over and throw up.

Okay, maybe it wasn't just the exam that had her stomach in knots, but what it symbolized. It represented an end and a beginning.

She'd studied hard. Jolie knew she was prepared. She fully expected to pass. Chet expected her to pass, too. He'd sent her off, full of confidence in her, kissing her breathless and murmuring, "I'll miss you, baby. Call me every night," before letting her go.

It would be ridiculous to drive back and forth each day of the exam, so she was staying in Helena until it was over. And then what? Pack up all the things that had found their way into Chet's house. Put her jeans away. Pull her suits out of storage. It was time to start her real job and the rest of her life.

Tears pricked at the backs of her eyes, and she blinked furiously. Dammit, she wasn't going to cry. She'd known what she was getting into. Chet had never lied to her. She'd chosen him for sex, and he'd given her more than she had any right to expect.

He'd made the past few months fun. Even the intensity of preparation for the bar had been broken by riding lessons, making love, casual meals eaten together while she had her head in a book, mornings in the hot tub while they talked over coffee. She'd started and ended every day with him, even when every minute in between was filled with other demands on their time.

It had made her realize how much she wanted that. Somebody there when she went to bed at night, when she woke up in the morning. Not just anybody. Chet.

She was hopelessly in love with a cowboy, and she had three nights to figure out what she was going to do about it. The days wouldn't leave her any spare brain cells to devote to her love life, but it was during the night that Jolie knew she would miss him the most.

Chet watched Jolie drive away, then went into the house. He knew she thought the last few months had been a carnal indulgence. She didn't realize that he considered it handfasting, a chance for her to see what the real thing could be like. Since circumstances hadn't allowed time to date and let things develop slowly, he'd elected to skip the preliminaries.

She'd had enough time to see that he wasn't opposed to the hours she had to put in, the other demands on her time and attention.

Since they were living together, not dating, he'd shown her that he didn't expect her to be entertaining, to go out with him at night, to make love with him until dawn. Although he had taken her dancing on one other occasion, and there was one memorable night when he'd still been inside her while the first rays of sun broke over the horizon.

Still, he'd proved to her in the routine of daily living that he wasn't one of the impatient men who hadn't seen that she was worth waiting for. And he'd done his damndest to make her fall in love with him.

Today he had an appointment that he was dreading, but it was the next step in winning Jolie for keeps. When she came home, he intended to be ready for her.

"Chet?" Jolie called his name as she came through the front door, but didn't get an answer. She frowned. He'd known when she was coming back.

Well, he had to be around somewhere. His truck was in the driveway. No matter what happened after she told him what she needed to say, it wasn't like he was just going to push her out the door. It'd be more like him to carry her things out, kiss her, and wave while she left.

Jolie dropped her coat and purse and keys on the kitchen counter, then made her way to the bedroom.

It wasn't empty.

White balloons were tied to the bed with long ribbons. Two fluted glasses sat on the bedside table, next to a bucket of champage. Lounging on the bed, wearing nothing but a smile and his Stetson draped over his lap, was Chet.

"Welcome home, baby." He grinned and held his hand out to her, and she took it, letting him pull her onto the bed to join him. He tugged her down for a kiss, his lips warming her. "Did you miss me?"

"I missed you." She put her hand on his chest, giving in to the need to touch him.

"Did you think about me and touch yourself?"

"I wish. It would have been more fun than lying in bed vibrating with nerves."

"Poor baby." His hands found the edge of her sweater, tugged it up, and pulled it over her head. "I have something to help you relax."

"Oh?" She smiled at him. "Is it hiding under your hat?"

"How'd you guess?" Chet tossed the hat across the room. He was naked and obviously very ready for her.

The sight of his engorged erection was irresistible. Jolie bent her head to lick from the base of his shaft to the head of his cock, sucked him into her mouth and drew him deep. He buried his fingers in her hair. "That feels too good. You'd better stop."

She let him slide out of her mouth and raised her head to give him another smile. She kneeled on the bed and balanced her hand on his shoulder while he unfastened her jeans. "Is the champagne for before or after?"

"After. I don't want to wait."

"Me, either."

"Good." Chet stripped her in record time, then folded back the covers. "Get in. I'll warm you up."

"I'm feeling pretty warm already," she told him.

"Well, let me know when you're hot." He pushed her back against the pillows and nudged her legs apart. His hands closed over her breasts as he settled between her open thighs and lowered his mouth to her sex.

Jolie closed her eyes and groaned as he tormented her with the twin sensations of his hands toying with the sensitive peaks of her breasts while his tongue flicked over her clit. He nibbled at her, licked, sucked, and thrust his tongue into her in a way that told her exactly what he wanted.

Since it was exactly what she wanted, too, it sent waves of

heat and anticipation surging through her. "Chet. Hurry," she moaned, tugging at his head.

He kissed his way up her belly. "Want me, baby?"

"Yes. Now."

"I'm going to make you feel so good," he promised. She felt him against her, the hard, hot shape of his cock nudging against her. She was slick and ready to take him. She bit her lip and dug her hands into the sheets while she waited agonizing seconds for him to sheathe himself in latex before he sheathed himself in her.

Chet framed her face with his hands while he thrust slowly into her. "I missed you so much, baby."

Jolie felt herself stretching around him as he penetrated her, felt his weight settling over her, his body heat warming her. "I love you," she whispered.

She'd meant to say it later so there couldn't be any question that the emotion wasn't simply being caught up in the moment. She hadn't meant to say it in the act, but the words had slipped out. She felt her eyes go wide as she realized what she'd said, waited for him to react.

He smiled at her. "Good."

"Good? Is that all you have to say, good?" Indignation fired her. Dammit, she'd just bared her soul and all he could say was *good*?

"I have more to say, but it's hard to think straight when I've got you naked under me." He thrust into her in hard, measured strokes. "Also, I thought it'd be easier to talk after I softened you up with sex and poured some champagne down your throat."

"I'm softening up," Jolie said.

"You're going to cream for me, baby." Chet adjusted the angle of their bodies, and she felt her body go hot, tight, and liquid. She arched under him and let out a wordless cry as the release shot through her.

"Jolie." He thrust deeper and spilled himself into her.

They stayed tangled together while their heartbeats slowed and their breathing steadied. Jolie smoothed her palms over his shoulders and back, and when she cupped her hands over his butt he reacted. "Ow."

"Ow?" She felt her brows shoot up.

"I'm feeling a little sensitive there." Chet caught her hands in his and stretched them over her head.

"Did you fall off another horse? You know, they call it riding," she teased. "You're supposed to stay on."

Through the months she'd seen him go through various bumps and bruises, including a period of carefully taped-up ribs when he'd had to give up missionary and let her be on top. He worked as hard as he played, and breaking horses led inevitably to injuries.

"I didn't get thrown off a horse. I got a tattoo."

"A tattoo?" Jolie tried to peek over his shoulder to see it.

"Yes. Unlike some people who blurt things out in the middle of sex which they may or may not mean, I thought I'd make sure there wasn't any doubt."

Jolie rolled her eyes at him. "Oh, fine, I say it first but it doesn't count because it was during sex. And what's your way? I haven't heard anything from you yet, cowboy. Do you love me or not?"

"I love you, baby." He smiled at her, and Jolie felt her heart skip and stumble. "Wanna see my tattoo?"

"Yes." He rolled off her, and turned so she could see a smaller version of her butterfly on his left butt cheek.

He'd gotten a matching tattoo.

"Very nice," Jolie said, taking it in. "That'll take my mind off waiting for the test results."

"You passed. You do what you put your mind to." The confidence in his voice made her throat tighten. He turned back to her and dropped a kiss on her shoulder. "Pour the champagne while I go take care of this." He moved his hand toward his midsection, climbed off the bed, and walked away.

Jolie watched the butterfly on his backside until he was out of sight. She blinked, shook her head, pulled the champagne bottle out of the ice, and popped the cork, aiming it carefully away from herself and anything breakable. It bounced harmlessly on the floor.

She filled the two waiting glasses and picked hers up to take a sip. The bubbles tickled the back of her throat. The balloons bobbed overhead. One of the ribbons had something weighing it down, and Jolie set her glass down and leaned over for a closer look.

It was an engagement ring, tied into the ribbon.

"Try it on."

She turned her head and saw Chet leaning in the doorframe.

She untied the bow and let the ring fall into her hand. The diamond sparkled as the facets caught the light. It didn't surprise her that it fit perfectly when she slipped it on.

Chet walked over to the bed and knelt beside it. He took her hand in his, admiring the ring on her finger. Then his eyes met hers, and Jolie couldn't look away.

"Marry me, Jolie."

Words failed her.

"This is where you say yes," he prompted her.

"Yes."

Chet let out an exaggerated sigh of relief and stood up. "I thought my knees were going to give out before you made up your mind."

He reached for the champagne, pressed the stem of her glass into her hand, then touched the rim of his glass to hers. "Here's to us, baby."

"I thought we were celebrating me getting through the test," Jolie teased.

"That'll be round two," he informed her. "The first one was

celebrating you being back home. The next one will be to celebrate you being finished with your exam, so I'll let you be on top." He tipped his glass to let a drop of champagne fall onto her nipple and bent his head to lick it off. "Then we'll celebrate our engagement. It's going to be a long night, baby."

Much later, Jolie stirred and felt Chet's arms tighten around her in reflex. "Chet."

"Hmmm?"

"What if . . ." Her voice trailed off into the darkness as she realized it wasn't so much a question as the last vestige of anxiety.

"You're not chickening out on me, are you?" he asked her. He kissed her temple and hugged her closer. "I'll bet you that we live happily ever after."

Jolie relaxed into him. "You always win."

"Hell, yes. I won you, didn't I?" Satisfaction sounded in his voice.

"Yes, you did." Feeling as light and effervescent inside as the champagne and the helium balloons, Jolie closed her eyes and let herself float into sleep, content that they'd both won.

REUBEN'S rules

21

"I can give you what you need."

The words, spoken in a low Western drawl by a man's mouth so close to Laura Jamieson's ear that his breath feathered across her skin and made her shiver, would have gotten her attention even if the man in question hadn't been standing so close behind her that she felt him all along her back. His arms on either side of her caged her against him as he offered her the large bag of coffee beans she'd been straining to reach bare seconds before.

Was she imagining the sensual promise in those words? That didn't seem likely. If he'd only wanted to help her by bringing down the bag when he'd seen her struggling to reach the too-high shelf, he could have done it without putting them both into this position.

It was more than suggestive. She could feel the heat of him warming her. If she moved back just the slightest bit, would it press his erection into the soft flesh of her denim-covered butt?

Laura imagined it would. She imagined him, hard and hot, pressing into the crease between the full globes of her rounded behind and shivered again in spite of the summer heat.

She put her hands on the bag of coffee and tried to take it from him, but his hands didn't release the burden.

"Think about it," he advised.

Oh, she was thinking about it. And had been for some time. She had a lot of needs, and she'd been more and more aware of them every time he came into her coffee shop. The first time she'd seen him, Laura thought he looked like something out of a Marlboro Man ad in his jeans and boots and cowboy hat. The kind of man women noticed. She certainly had.

Earthy. Male. Muscles hardened from hours and years of labor. Skin tanned and weathered from the same hours of exposure to sun and wind. Strong hands that she'd imagined moving over her body more than once. Shaping her ass. Cupping her breasts. Settling between her thighs.

Laura looked down at Reuben Black's hands and wondered how they would feel on her naked flesh. It seemed he was offering her a chance to find out. Did she have the nerve to take him up on his offer?

It might be awkward if she slept with a customer. Missoula, Montana, wasn't like a typical big city. It had more of a small-town attitude in a city setting. People gossiped. Word got around. She'd known when she chose it for the location of her coffee shop that the atmosphere would be very different from the anonymity of urban life she'd been accustomed to. It was one of the attractions, one reason she'd believed Lemon Espresso would succeed here.

Missoula had a unique cultural mix made up of the newcomers, the artists who'd made it their home and who blended with the conservative old-guard population like oil and water, along with the transient university population. A business like hers, designed to attract and serve the newcomers and students, was already looked on with a touch of suspicion by the locals.

Reuben was a Montana native, and he fascinated her. He had from the first time he'd walked through her door. It might have been the differences between them that made him impossible to overlook, but Laura suspected it had more to do with a deep sense of what they had in common.

He was a rancher, which meant they were both essentially small business owners, although his business was larger than hers.

Before buying his ranch, he'd been in the military. She would have known that even if she hadn't been told. It was in his bearing, his watchful gaze. A person who'd had combat training saw the world with different eyes and moved through it in a way no civilian would.

As a survivor of one of America's more dangerous professions, Laura knew what it was like to experience physical conflict. She knew how living with danger developed a person's ability to read a situation and evaluate any potential threat almost to the level of instinct.

Experiences like that changed people. A peculiar sort of innocence lost that could never be regained. Laura knew she would never again view people in the same light she had before she'd discovered how violent they could be, how personal and immediate a threat they could pose.

Most people lived with a sense that violence was something that happened to somebody else, a report in the local news. Laura knew better. It made her almost an outsider in casual relationships. There was a part of herself she could never share, a part most people couldn't relate to.

Except, possibly, this man, whose eyes shared the same caution and knowledge hers held. They had both eaten the bitter fruit of the knowledge of humanity's capacity for good and evil and were forever exiled from the Eden of blissful ignorance.

Standing with Reuben's arms and his body surrounding her, Laura knew he didn't pose any physical threat. Sexually . . . that was a different story.

She thought about what he'd said. *I can give you what you need.*

What she needed was something she didn't think anybody suspected. She needed somebody she could share the deepest part of herself with. A man who might understand and know how to satisfy her desires. Her desire for domination and submission, for a relationship that offered a deep level of sexual intimacy and trust.

Was he offering her that?

"What do I need?" Laura asked, her voice too soft to be overheard.

"You need to be taken," he whispered in her ear. "You need to be dominated and mastered in bed. You need me."

Her breathing stuttered and weakness stole through her limbs.

"If I'm wrong, if you don't want that, tell me to go. Otherwise, I'm going to wait for you. And when you're finished for the night, I'm going to get started."

A wave of heat and need surged through her, and Laura knew she wasn't going to say the words that would send him away. He gave her a chance to speak, to tell him he was wrong, she didn't want him, she didn't need what he was offering her.

When she didn't say anything, his lips brushed the sensitive skin below the lobe of her ear in the lightest of caresses, invisible to anybody around them. To all appearances, he'd simply helped her reach something too high for her and then leaned in to speak to her. But Laura felt the first touch of his mouth and trembled.

Then he let go of the bag, leaving it in her hands, lowered his arms, stepped back, and walked away. He returned to his table, angled so that she was in his side view but not watching her directly. Discreet. But letting her know unmistakably that she had his attention.

Could she handle the attention of a man like Reuben Black? She wanted it, badly. Reuben had been starring in her darkest erotic imaginings for weeks. Still, fantasy was one thing. Reality was something else. She'd never experimented with the kind of sex she wanted before, the kind Reuben offered to let her experience with him.

Laura set the bag down on the counter before she dropped it, fumbled it open, and set to work by rote, grinding beans, making coffee, the rich aromatic scent of the blend released into the air to tease the palate of nearby patrons.

The work steadied her, and Laura acknowledged silently that whether she could handle it or not, she was about to find out what it was like to be the focus of his attention. To be taken by him.

The thought of Reuben, hard, naked, in control, and taking her, nearly made her spill the open bag across the counter. He hadn't even really kissed her. He'd barely spoken to her. And already she was breathing fast, too warm, aware of a slickness between her thighs and an ache in her breasts. Aroused so easily by him. What state would she be in when they progressed to actual foreplay?

Wanton. Needy. Ready to beg him to fuck her.

She went through the motions for the rest of the night, but her mind was not on work. It was on the man who waited for her without calling attention to the fact, who watched her from his peripheral vision, who had made an outrageous offer that she was going to accept. Had already accepted, her silence giving consent.

He didn't scare her. At least, not physically. He was calm and controlled, and she knew that he would keep that control while he stripped away every last remnant of hers. He was a

man who understood discipline and knew how to control the
force his body was capable of. She could trust him to be methodical, careful. He wouldn't hurt her by accident, by mis-
judging his own strength, or by acting without thinking.

The way he'd approached her let her know he'd been
thinking about this for some time before he decided to act. Not
the behavior of a man driven by impulse or whim. He wouldn't
get carried away in the heat of the moment. He would, as he
promised, let her experience her erotic fantasy.

Laura wanted that. She wanted him. She wanted to experience his sexual domination enough to take the risk that she
could lose her heart to this man without any hint that he was
willing to offer her his in return. He'd been very clear about
what he was offering her: his body.

He hadn't made any promises beyond tonight. But she
wanted him enough to take him any way she could get him. If
all he did was lower his zipper, she'd work with that.

There were people all around them now. Background
noise, music, the low murmur of multiple conversations going
on in the distance, the gurgle and hiss of coffee in progress, the
amplified voices of the poets reading overlaying the other
sounds. But soon the crowd would dispel, the shop would be
closed, and it would be just the two of them giving in to what
they needed.

Sex. As basic as eating, breathing, or sleeping. The touch
of a lover she craved, the need to touch and be touched. So
simple. So complicated. Sex changed things, and the kind of
sex Reuben offered her in particular would change things
even more.

Would he continue to be a regular at the coffee shop afterwards? Would she see him again? Would it be the start of a relationship, or the end of the casual one they'd had up until now?

There was only one way to find out.

Reuben sat next to his friends, far across the room from the object of his attention, but soon enough he'd have her to himself. He'd taken his time before he approached her. Before he'd even decided that he would approach her. He'd seen her on the street one day and followed her to see where she'd go. The line of her body, the graceful way she walked, the alertness in her posture had caught his eye, and he'd been curious. Who was she?

He'd found out she owned and worked in the coffee shop. He became a regular, and they exchanged impersonal daily pleasantries. He liked so many things about Laura, her voice, her calm manner. He liked the spark of awareness when their hands brushed, the interest in her hazel eyes. More, he saw the way she moved and positioned herself, the things she paid attention to, and it made him wonder what had taught her to be so wary.

Laura didn't exactly relax with him, but she was becoming less guarded. She didn't flirt, and neither did he. But the one day he'd been tied up and unable to come by, she'd asked him the next morning what had happened, her eyes dark with concern.

He'd made himself a fixture in her days, slowly, subtly, giving her time to become accustomed to him when he understood what they were leading up to. He didn't want her to feel like he was a stranger.

And he wanted to take his time before he took the irrevocable step of making their relationship more personal. Time to be certain the attraction was more than surface. Time to be sure that she was as aware of him physically as he was of her. To observe her, study her reactions, and be certain that his approach was the right one.

He wanted Laura to trust him completely, with her body,

with her emotions. He wanted to get past the guard she kept up against the rest of the world and get inside her, all the way inside her, to know the secret self she didn't share with anybody else. He wanted her to share all of herself with him, nothing held back, and he'd settled on dominating sex as the key.

Tonight, he would begin to make her his.

She hadn't said no. Hadn't told him he'd misread her. Reuben didn't assume that meant she had no qualms. He would take it slowly, step by step. But he intended to take her to the limit of sensation, to build the bonds of trust and shared pleasure that would pave the way for her to form a lasting bond to him.

He wanted all of her, and if she agreed to play by his rules, he would have her. First for tonight. Then if he was successful, for good.

22

By the time Lemon Espresso was empty except for the two of them and everything was shut down for the night, Laura felt like one giant exposed nerve. When she dropped her keys for the third time, Reuben picked them up. Her hand touched his as she reached for them at the same time, and she drew back as if burned by the contact.

She winced at her own reaction and tried to recover herself by straightening up. He stood, too, and held her keys out, waiting for her to open her hand to take them. Her hand stayed stuck down by her side for a long, awkward minute. Reuben didn't say anything; he just waited.

Laura gave him a rueful smile. "I'm not usually this clumsy."

When he still didn't say anything, she added, "You're not making this any easier."

"Did you think it would be easy?" he asked.

Well. When he put it that way . . . She finally held her

hand out for the keys, closed her fingers carefully around them when he laid them in her open palm so she wouldn't drop them again and turn the moment into a complete farce. "Thank you."

The words were automatic, the result of years of ingrained polite habit. Reuben gave her a slight nod in acknowledgment.

She stood there a minute longer, trying to think of the next step. If he wasn't here, what would she do? Turn the lights off. Leave the shop. Lock the door. But to walk to the light switch, she'd have to go around the man standing in front of her, looking like the proverbial immovable object. She didn't consider herself an irresistible force.

Laura started to move around him, and his raised arm stopped her. She halted before she ran into it and looked at him, head tilted, waiting for an explanation.

"Ask."

She frowned, unable to make sense of that. "Ask what?"

"Ask me to move."

"You put your hand out to stop me so I'd ask you to move?"

His lips curved in the faintest of smiles. "Yes."

"Okay. Please move."

He lowered his arm and moved aside, clearing the way to the light switches without her having to circle around him. Laura had flipped the switches off before it crossed her mind that Reuben had to have known where they were and that he was in front of them. Had he positioned himself deliberately so that she'd have to brush against him, go around him, or ask him to move?

"Why did you do that?" She asked the question while she stood there, facing the wall, her hand still touching the light switch plate.

"You wanted me to move, but you didn't ask. You tried to go around me instead. You can't go around me tonight, Laura.

If you want me to stop doing something I'm doing, you have to say the word."

She hadn't heard him move, but he was suddenly there behind her, his hands settling on her shoulders. She swallowed. "You're talking about a safety word."

"That's right."

A faint tremor went through her. A safety word was something a couple used when they played BDSM games, a signal that things had gone too far, were passing outside the comfort zone or veering over the edge of pleasure and into pain. That he was telling her to use one with him made what they were about to do seem very real.

His hands moved over her bare arms, his touch light. "That scares you."

"A little."

"And excites you."

"That, too," she admitted. No point lying to him about what did it for her.

"I think you need two words." His hands moved over her arms, gathering them against her body, folding them into her waist as he wrapped his arms around her. "One to tell me you want more, one to tell me to stop."

Laura closed her eyes, amazed at the intensity of feeling in simply being in his arms. He'd never held her before. The almost-embrace earlier had given her a hint of how it would be, his body so much larger than hers, so much harder. Stronger. She felt small and fragile. Vulnerable. Protected. That was it, she thought. The way he wrapped himself around her was protective.

It felt so good to be closer to him. She wanted to be even closer. And when they were closer, would she be able to think clearly enough to remember what word to use?

"I think that's too complicated," she told him. "You distract me. You make me nervous. I dropped the damn keys three times, I don't trust myself to remember a code word for stop when it's not something I'm used to saying."

"Then keep it simple," Reuben suggested. "More. Stop."

"Oh." She let out a soft laugh, surprised that she hadn't seen the obvious solution. "Of course."

"Let's practice that now." He slid his hands up to cup her breasts and squeezed, a gentle pressure at first.

"More," she whispered. She knew nobody would see the two of them in the dark if anybody passed by on the street. Only she knew that Reuben Black was pressed up behind her, the hard ridge of his erection unmistakable, his hands fitting over her breasts, touching her intimately.

The pressure increased by degrees, until it approached the limit of what felt good. "Stop."

"See how easy that was?" Reuben's voice was soft.

Laura nodded, then realized he might not read the gesture in the dark. "Yes."

"Don't try to go around me again." His hands moved back down to her waist, and Laura felt bereft, wanting his hands on her breasts again, supplying that exquisite pressure and relieving the ache in her flesh. The ache for touch. For his touch.

"I won't." She touched her tongue to her lips, feeling unsure. "Reuben."

"Yes?"

"I want you to touch me again." She wondered if that was specific enough and decided to make sure. "My breasts. I want your hands on my breasts."

"You ask very nicely." His lips brushed against her earlobe. "No."

"Why not?"

"Because you aren't in charge tonight."

That sent another tremor through her. She felt unsteady as the reality of what she'd agreed to struck her again. "Reuben, what if I can't do this?"

"Then you can't." He sounded so matter of fact, so calm. How could he be so calm when her heart was racing, her breathing had sped up, and a fine trembling in her limbs had her unsteady?

"No, really, tell me what happens. If I can't." She leaned back against him, needing the support.

"If you can't, we stop. I take you home, or we do vanilla sex." His mouth brushed her ear again, a light, teasing kiss, a brush of heat that made her want more. "I don't want vanilla, Laura. But I want you, and I won't make you do something you don't want to do."

Laura thought that through, what he was saying and what he left unsaid. He wanted her, wanted to have sex with her. Wanted it to be dominating. He was willing to leave that part out of it if she couldn't surrender control to him, but she knew that would be cheating them both of something vital, and herself of the opportunity to experience her fantasy.

"It won't be the same," she said. "You'll hold back and so will I."

"No. It won't be the same."

Laura drew a deep breath, letting it steady her. "I don't want you to hold back. And I don't want to hold back, either. I want it all."

His mouth touched the soft skin below her ear. "I'll give you as much as you can take, then."

As much as she could take wasn't the same as all, but logic slipped away as his lips traced the curve of her neck. So warm. So tantalizing, making her ache for more.

"Come home with me, Laura."

"Yes."

Reuben walked her to the door with one hand on the small of her back, held it open for her while she went through it, closed it behind them. She fit the key into the lock, turned it, and dropped her key ring into the bag that hung over her shoulder. She looked up at Reuben, feeling unaccountably shy all of a sudden.

His eyes met hers, and the heat she saw in them reassured her. She looked away, not certain she could meet the sexual intent in his eyes and keep from tripping over her own feet. Somehow she managed the mechanics of walking with him, intensely aware of his hand at the small of her back.

She could feel the warmth of his touch through the thin fabric of her tank top and wondered how it would feel when his hand slid lower, touched her more intimately, without the barrier of clothing.

When she realized he'd guided her to her own car, she gave him a questioning look.

"I want you to know you can leave any time you want to," he said in answer to her unspoken question. "If you have your car, you have a way out.

That made sense. Laura nodded and retrieved her keys from her bag. She hesitated once she had them in her hand, then held them out to him. "If we're going to do this, then we should do it all the way. You drive."

Reuben took them from her, sliding his fingers along hers in the process. "So you're ready to be my submissive, Laura?"

She gave him a half smile. "I reserve the right to admit I'm in over my head later, but yes."

"You always have the right to stop." His face was serious. He touched her cheek gently. "Say the word, and it doesn't matter where we are, what we're doing. Stop means stop."

Laura turned her face just a little, so her lips brushed against his hand. "Okay."

"And I didn't give you permission to do that."

She met his eyes again and waited for more explanation. His hand traced the curve of her cheek. "I touch you. If you want to touch me, you have to ask. I might say yes. I might say no. That's part of the control you're giving me tonight, Laura."

"Oh."

"If you want to kiss me, that counts as touch. When you break the rules, there are consequences."

She wondered what the consequences for touching her lips to his hand without asking might be, and the uncertainty added to the sensation of having surrendered control. She wasn't in charge tonight. Reuben was.

"Since I didn't know about this rule, does it apply?" Laura asked him.

"Do you think it should?"

"Yes and no." Laura thought it over. "If you're in charge, it's up to you to tell me the rules. You can't blame me for not knowing them if you don't tell me. But I also agreed to let you be in control, so if I broke a rule, even one I didn't know about, I guess there should be consequences. Because otherwise we're not serious about this."

"I'm very serious about you, Laura." Reuben's hand moved down and back, cupped the back of her head, urged her forward. She realized he was about to kiss her. She watched his mouth move toward hers, closed her eyes, felt his lips brush against hers, once, twice, before settling into firm contact.

He didn't take the kiss further, didn't open her mouth, or touch her in any way besides the hand behind her head, keeping her in place while he kissed her. And yet it rocked her. When he raised his head, she blinked at him, amazed at the power of something so simple, so ordinary as a kiss.

"That was a very serious kiss," she said, since nothing else came to mind.

"Liked it, did you?"

"Yes." She started to move toward him to initiate another kiss and checked herself, remembering.

He smiled at her. "You learn fast."

"Are you going to tell me what the consequences are for kissing you without asking?"

"So you can decide if it's worth trying it again, in case you ask and I say no?"

His lips twitched, and Laura realized she'd never heard him laugh. He was closer to it now than she'd ever seen. She wanted to see his face relaxed and open, hear the laughter inside him.

She grinned at him. "Maybe."

"I'll let you wonder what the consequences are until we get someplace private."

"Your place," Laura reminded him. "I want to see where you live, Man of Mystery."

The trip to his ranch turned out to be a long enough drive to give her plenty of time to consider a number of possibilities. In one scenario, Reuben withheld kisses. In another, he brought her to the brink of orgasm and stopped. In a third, he left her alone, and that one made her stomach knot.

"Laura?"

She looked up at Reuben, realized they'd arrived at their destination while she was lost in thought, and saw the concern in his expression.

"Tell me what's bothering you."

She tried to think of a way to say it without sounding ridiculous and gave up. "Okay. It's stupid. I know it's stupid."

"Anything that makes you look like that isn't stupid." He reached out to touch her hair, smoothing it back. "You look like you're scared. Like you're having second, third, fourth, and fifth thoughts about doing this. Tell me what scares you."

"Don't leave me," she blurted out. She closed her eyes. "I know how dumb that sounds, but while we're doing this, while you're in charge, don't leave me. You have rules; that's my rule. You can't handcuff me or something and then just leave me alone."

"I would never do that." He undid her seat belt and his,

then pulled her into his arms. "That isn't safe. I would never leave you helpless without being there in case you needed me."

"I wasn't thinking about just physical safety," she mumbled into his shirt. "Though that's pretty important. I never thought you'd let me get hurt physically."

"Emotionally," Reuben said. His hand stroked along her hair, smoothing it down her back. "Emotionally it scares you to think about me taking away your control and leaving you alone."

"Yes."

"I wouldn't do that to you." He held her as close as he could within the limited space, but the car wasn't made for cuddling. Still, the contact was enough to reassure her.

Laura sighed against his shoulder. "Sorry. I started thinking about consequences, and I thought of some fun ones, and then . . . sorry. Maybe I'm too much of a wimp to handle BDSM."

"You're not a wimp. You're a small business owner, a successful one. That's not easy to achieve." She felt his lips touch the top of her head; then he set her back into her seat. "It's a bit cramped in here. Let's get out and we can talk. I'll show you around."

She smiled at him. "That sounds so normal. Maybe we should just have sex so I can stop being nervous about it."

She was only half-joking.

"Anticipation is part of the pleasure."

Well, that was true. And anticipating his hands on her, his body moving against hers, even the possibility of him stopping her from peaking when she was close—it all excited her.

Reuben wouldn't leave her alone. Laura hung on to that thought and knew it was true. She also knew why she'd never been tempted to act on this particular fantasy before, or with any other man. She'd thought about it, fantasized about it, but never had any true desire to act on it until Reuben had offered her the chance to experience it with him.

It was because the emotional vulnerability of sexual surrender was the true risk, and it wasn't one she'd been willing to take with any other man. There were plenty of men who wouldn't mind a little role-playing in the bedroom. If she'd wanted to experiment before, she could have asked a boyfriend to accommodate her. She never had.

Reuben walked around to open her door for her. He held his hand out to take hers. She slid her hand into his, felt his fingers close around hers, and stepped out to join him. "So. Here we are," she said, stating the obvious.

His lips curved in a faint smile. There was just enough light from the stars overhead and the porch lights he must have left on to see by, the angles of his face shadowed. He looked at home in the night, dark and dangerous.

And she'd said yes to him. She should have her head examined.

"Here we are," Reuben agreed. He bent his head to brush his lips across hers again, a slow, careful kiss. He closed the car door behind her, then slid his other arm around her, holding her in a loose embrace.

Then again, he was the one she wanted. It was his arms she dreamed of being in, his hands she wanted on her body, him she wanted to belong to. Reuben drew her closer until they were pressed together, and then he deepened the kiss and Laura sank into it, into him, and there was no hesitation in her response.

23

He tasted like forbidden fruit, Laura thought hazily as his tongue swept into her mouth and slid along hers. Tempting, delicious, enticing. She let Reuben direct the kiss, following his lead, clinging to him because she didn't trust her legs to hold her up. When he raised his head and looked down into her eyes, she felt her body go tight. He looked intent and hungry.

"I want you, Laura."

"I want you, too," she managed to say.

"Enough to agree to everything I want?" He let go of her clasped hand and raised his to cup her chin. "Enough to let me take you the way I want to?"

She started to say *within reason* and thought better of it. She wanted him unreasonably. She nodded instead.

"I want you to submit to me, Laura. I want to dominate you, claim you. I want you to belong to me." Reuben slid his hand down to touch her throat. "I want to collar you. Do you know what that means?"

Her mouth went dry, and she felt slickness gathering between her thighs. "Yes."

"It will mean I own you, Laura." He traced the sensitive hollows of her collarbones, touched his thumb against the pulse leaping in her throat.

It meant more than that. It was a symbol of the power exchange they agreed to, of her trust in him, and his commitment to her pleasure. It could mean a permanent relationship. It could mean something temporary, also, but much more meaningful than one night of play. It meant he didn't take her lightly, that even if it was only for tonight, he wanted her to wear the symbol of his possession.

"For how long?" Laura asked.

"Twenty-four hours," Reuben answered. "Enough time for you to see how it feels. Tomorrow night we'll talk about it again."

Twenty-four hours of belonging to Reuben. Part of that time she'd spend at work, but then, he'd have work to do, too, presumably. Ranchers didn't usually have weekends off. But if she wore the collar when they were apart, it would be a very tangible reminder of her status. That until he took it off, she was owned by Reuben Black.

The idea of having a hidden symbol of Reuben's sexual possession under her clothes excited her, and she also liked the thought of remaining bound to him while she went away and did her job, ran her business. It meant she would see him again, even if it was only for him to remove the collar and take it back.

"All right," she said softly. "And maybe you should tell me the rest of the rules now."

"You look like you already have enough to think about." Reuben bent his head and brushed his mouth against hers again. "I said I'd show you around and we'd talk. If you want to after that, we'll discuss the rules."

"I'll want to."

"Then a few minutes won't make any difference." He took her hand and drew it into the crook of his arm, tucking her into his side in the process.

"You raise sheep, right?" Laura asked as they made their way toward the front porch.

"That's right. Icelandics."

"What are Icelandics?" She was genuinely curious and unfamiliar with the different breeds, although she did know the Montana sheep industry was important in the state's economy.

"They're from Iceland. Hardy, disease resistant, less reliant on stored feed in winter. The breed produces one of the best fleeces for felt, very popular wool." He slanted her a look. "Tell me when I'm boring you."

Her lips twitched. "Is that a rule?"

"It might not be a rule in my favor." Reuben pushed her slightly ahead of him up the steps and followed her. Laura waited while he unlocked and opened the door.

"You sound very knowledgeable."

"I did a lot of research before I decided what direction to take."

She'd done her research, too. Failure to study the market, to plan and truly be prepared caused a lot of business failures. She couldn't afford to fail, so she'd taken her time in the research and planning stage. "What decided you on Icelandic sheep?"

"The breed's characteristics make them very profitable. I wanted the ranch to be self-supporting, independent of an outside source of income. With careful planning and hard work, I could earn back the initial investment in the first couple of years."

"And did you?"

Reuben guided her into the foyer, closed the door behind her, and took off his hat. His dark hair was cropped military short, drawing attention to the angles of his face and setting off his dark eyes. He seemed even larger in the small space of the foyer. Laura watched the play of muscles in his arms as he hung up his hat before he answered her.

"I did it in the first year."

Laura didn't doubt it. He seemed to personify masculine strength and determination. The thought of being the object of his determined concentration made her feel slightly giddy. Even if it was only for one night of sex, she knew it would be a night she'd never forget.

Looking away from him, she took in the foyer with its stone flooring, the hardwood floor that began beyond it, the collection of hats and jackets that hung on neat hooks by the door in preparation for any kind of weather.

"I'll show you the house."

Reuben placed his hand on her shoulder and guided her past the entryway. She let him direct her steps, nodded as he pointed out the kitchen gleaming with its tile and brushed aluminum surfaces, the stone fireplace that occupied the center of the living room, the comfortable-looking pieces of leather and wood furniture scattered about. There was a guest room with a bear-paw quilt covering the bed. And at the far end of the single-story ranch house, the master bedroom.

A low wooden dresser occupied one wall. A chair sat in one corner, angled to face the room. And dominating the room was a king-sized sleigh bed, covered with what looked like soft, fleecy blankets. Laura stepped forward and touched the fabric. "Is this yours? From your sheep, I mean?"

"Yes. There's a shop in Missoula that sells looms and weaving supplies, and there are local people who make felt. I had some of the wool made into felt blankets for my own use, although I sold most of it." Reuben's lips turned up at the corners.

"You don't think I look like a typical representative of the wool industry, do you?"

"No," Laura admitted. He looked like he wore his close-fitting jeans and T-shirt like a uniform. Hard muscles. Hard features. The softness of the wool in contrast was a little mind-boggling. It was easy to picture him shooting coyotes that threatened his flock, less easy to imagine him in the world of wool textiles.

"Well, there's more to a person than their job. You, for instance. Why coffee?"

"I like coffee." She smiled at him.

"There's more to it than that," he prompted her.

"Yes, there's more. It's a business I like, the profit margin meant I could get the loan I needed, especially after I studied locations and picked one that had the right demographics. Location is really the key to success with an espresso shop. The numbers worked."

"And why the drive to run your own business?"

Laura wondered if his questions were another way of keeping her from going around him. "I had to do something else, besides what I'd trained for. I didn't want to go back to school and start over. I didn't want an entry-level business position. I didn't want a nine-to-five kind of job that I had no control over. I wanted to be self-employed."

"We have that in common."

Laura nodded. "I imagine after being an elite member of the military and being trained to lead, working for somebody else wouldn't appeal to you."

"No." He tilted his head to look at her more closely. "I like to be in charge."

His words made her very conscious of where they were and what they were going to do. He was going to be in charge tonight, with her. On this bed.

"Are you ready to let me be in charge of you, Laura?"

Yes. No. She took a steadying breath and answered him. "Yes."

"Then here are the rules." He settled his hands on her waist and drew her toward him, looking down into her eyes as he spoke. "I'm in charge. You do what I tell you to, no hesitation, no questions. You'll have to trust me."

Laura nodded her agreement.

"If I tell you to do something you don't want, if something goes too far, you say the word. I'm trusting you to know your limits. I'll respect them."

She nodded again, since he seemed to be waiting for a response.

"If you have any questions, ask them now. Once we begin, the time for questions will be over."

"What, any questions? Like, what was it like when you were growing up?" Laura asked.

"Personal questions, I may or may not answer. Other questions, questioning what I'm doing or why, those you can't ask."

Because it would go against the nature of the game they were setting up. That she could understand. If she questioned him, it meant she wasn't trusting him, wasn't really willing to let him direct their sexual activities.

She asked the question that had plagued her earlier. "What about consequences? I think it's fair for you to tell me what will happen if I go against the rules. And please keep in mind that if I enjoyed pain, I would've stayed in my former career."

"Tonight is all about pleasure. Yours and mine." Reuben's hands on her waist were warm, strong. "I have no desire to hurt you. Consequences might mean I don't let you come when you want to, make you wait for it."

"You're big on anticipation, aren't you?" She smiled at him, reassured by his answer and the gentle pressure exerted by his hands. "Okay, I can live with those kinds of consequences. Not that I'll deliberately break the rules, but a delayed orgasm isn't scary or painful."

"Well, you may feel differently about that later." His lips curved in a half smile, and Laura realized he was teasing her.

"I might," she admitted. She could well believe that this man was capable of inciting her to the height of physical need, of arousing her to the point where any delay in relief would seem like torture.

"All right, then." Reuben's hands dropped away from her. "Take off your clothes. You can have them back when I give them back to you. In the meantime, you'll wear nothing but my collar."

Well, thought Laura. The moment of truth. Could she take off her clothes and get naked for him? If she couldn't do that, she wouldn't be able to do anything else.

Be brave. She reminded herself that she'd survived armed assaults. She could handle a night in bed with Reuben.

She grasped the hem of her lemon yellow tank top, pulled it up, baring her midriff, then her lacy yellow bra as she drew it up. Over her head. Off. She almost let it fall to the floor, then realized that didn't send quite the right signal. She handed it to Reuben, and he took it, heat flaring in his eyes at the gesture.

Encouraged by his response, she reached behind herself and unhooked her bra, then drew her arms free of the straps and handed that to him, too. Next, she unsnapped her jeans, lowered the zipper, tugged them down her hips. She slipped off her shoes, then pulled the jeans off, raising one foot at a time to step out of them, folded them neatly and passed them over to Reuben, who was watching her every movement.

Down to her socks and panties, Laura debated what to take off next and chose the socks. First one foot, then the other. And then she was nearly naked, standing in front of him wearing nothing but a wisp of Lycra and lace that matched her bra.

It suddenly dawned on her that he might be looking at her breasts, right that moment. Laura felt a blush sweep over her face as she bent her head, her hair sliding forward, although it wasn't long enough to cover her breasts.

"You're a beautiful woman, Laura. And I intend to look at and touch every inch of you, so don't bother trying to hide."

Laura swallowed, nervous and on edge again suddenly. Her hands felt awkward as she tugged at the fabric covering her hips. She decided it was like ripping off a Band-Aid: best just to do it and get it over with.

She stripped her panties off in one quick motion, stepped out of them, and gave them to Reuben to hold. He walked over to the closet, opened it, put her stack of clothing inside, and shut it. The gesture seemed very final. The next time she wore those clothes, she would know what it was like to experience a fantasy, to submit to a dominating male in bed.

She would know what it was like to be Reuben Black's lover.

Reuben walked back over to her, and she saw that he held a black leather collar in his hands.

"Lift your hair."

She slid her hands into the silky mass and lifted it up, away from her neck. Reuben wrapped the leather strap around her throat and fastened it.

"How does that feel?"

The leather was soft, the fit comfortable. Physically, not much different from a choker necklace. But emotionally she felt the impact of what this symbol represented. The point of no return. For the next twenty-four hours, she was a man's sexual property. Not just any man. This man, who'd fascinated her from the first time she saw him.

She was Reuben's woman, if only for a little while, subject to his rules. A sensation not unlike riding a roller coaster, a thrill made from the mix of exhilaration and apprehension.

Laura let her hair fall back onto her shoulders and met his eyes. "Exciting."

24

Laura Jamieson was in his home, in his bedroom. Naked. Submissive. Wearing his collar and willing to abide by the rules he'd set out. The trust she'd extended to him was enormous.

She was excited, but he knew she was nervous, too. Her breath was coming a little faster, her nipples were hard, tight buds, and he saw the fine tremor that ran through her. The edge of apprehension would heighten the experience, deepen the pleasure. The collar would act on her imagination, symbolic of her submissive fantasy.

Reuben knew he was well on the way to seducing her mind. He had her full attention. He had her trust. Before the night was over, he would have her body. And eventually he intended to have her heart.

"Are you enjoying your fantasy?" he asked.

"Yes."

"I have a fantasy of my own I'd like to experience."

Reuben gave her a slow smile. "I want you to go to the kitchen and make some coffee."

She blinked at him. "You've thought about this, haven't you? You fantasized about me." She seemed genuinely surprised, as if she didn't think she'd captured his imagination.

"Yes, Laura, I did. And I think this is the closest we can come to acting out the one where I walk into your shop and you're not wearing anything. You make a cup of coffee for me and serve it to me, the whole time knowing I'm watching your naked body."

She licked her lips, her eyes widening in reaction to his erotic words.

"You pose for me, showing off your body. You bend over so I can watch your ass, and you let me see your pussy. You want me to look. You like me looking at you, and you hope that I'll want to touch you."

Reuben traced his finger along the lower edge of the collar, just barely touching her skin. "Go to the kitchen. I'm going to watch you while you walk."

Laura nodded and turned away, moving to the doorway. He followed her a few steps behind, enjoying the slight bounce of her bottom, the way her hair slid across her shoulders. In setting out to fulfill her fantasy, he had the opportunity to play out his own. One hell of a fringe benefit. Although he couldn't afford to get sidetracked and forget about his goal.

His plans for Laura went well beyond tonight. He had her now, but that was far short of the ultimate objective, keeping her. One night was far too tenuous and temporary an arrangement to satisfy him. Reuben was ready to settle down, and he'd set his sights on Laura.

He watched the rounded curve of her ass and knew that soon he would have his hands on her. He was no stranger to delayed gratification, but it seemed like he'd already been waiting a very long time for the opportunity to touch this woman. He couldn't afford to rush it, though. He hadn't left anything to chance, beyond the factors he couldn't manipulate or control. Laura's seduction had been carefully planned, and he wasn't going to screw up now.

He intended to show her what she could have with him. Commitment. Companionship. Sexual compatibility. Laura was too practical to expect hearts and flowers and romantic declarations, Reuben assured himself. He had no reason to believe what he had to offer her wouldn't be enough. It had to be enough, because the man he was had nothing more to give.

In the past it hadn't bothered him too much to lose a woman when he failed to declare his undying love, but he hadn't planned a future with any woman until now. It would bother him to lose Laura.

Reuben saw that his hands were tightening into fists, as if he imagined her slipping through his fingers, and he forced them to relax. Stick to the plan; focus on the goal. It would be enough.

Laura knew Reuben's eyes were fixed on her, and it made the simple act of putting one foot in front of another a challenge. She was naked. Every inch of her, exposed. She could hear his measured footsteps behind her and wondered if everything he did was controlled and methodical. Not mechanical—there was too much intelligence, too much feeling in his eyes for that. But knowing he was in control while she could feel hers slipping away made her wonder what it would be like if the positions were reversed.

Not that she'd want to be in control. But to see Reuben lose his, what would that be like?

She wasn't likely to find out tonight. It was a paradox: she trusted him enough to surrender control to him because she knew he would stay in control. He was a very disciplined man, and men like him didn't let themselves get swept away by emotion.

Laura didn't doubt that he was perfectly capable of sweeping her away on a floodtide of it, however.

Her feet led her down the hall, into the kitchen, and she found it organized in a very logical manner. It amused her that he fantasized about her serving him coffee naked, but then again, he'd spent a lot of time in her coffee shop. It stood to reason that his fantasies had spun out from there. She certainly had a few that involved the two of them using some of the shop's furniture in various positions, for purposes not intended by the manufacturer.

Her lips quirked in a smile as she imagined Reuben's reaction if she told him about the specific ways she'd thought of him taking her.

Making coffee was a soothing task. Familiar, even in this unfamiliar setting. When life handed you lemons, make coffee and get to work—that was her motto. She'd been handed quite a few lemons, but she'd worked her ass off to turn them into something instead of moaning that life was unfair. And now here she was, a business owner in control of her own destiny, naked in Reuben Black's kitchen while she waited for his next erotic command. Not a bad place to arrive.

"How did that happen?"

The tone of Reuben's voice made her turn her head to study his expression. He looked, well, more dangerous than usual. Something had upset him. "How did what happen?"

"This." He closed the distance between them and touched the scar on her left side.

Oh. That. She'd forgotten. Of course he would notice and have questions. He could probably tell just from looking what it was, unlike the average civilian who would mistake it for something more ordinary. The result of an accident, or maybe some surgical procedure.

Reuben was a trained soldier, however. He knew a knife scar when he saw one.

"It happened the night before I quit my job," Laura answered. "I told you, I needed a career change. Selling coffee is a lot safer than nursing."

She saw a muscle in his jaw flex, and she reached up to touch it without thinking, checked herself, and pulled her hand away. "Sorry. I forgot."

"Don't be sorry. If you want to touch me, go ahead."

"Okay." Laura settled her hand against the side of his jaw, soothing away the tension she felt below the surface. "I worked in a big city hospital in Colorado. We called it the Denver Knife and Gun Club, not quite jokingly. Assaults on nurses from patients and from their friends or family members happen—it's one of the risks you run on the job. I found out how dangerous my job could be when I turned my back on the wrong person and ended up with a cracked rib. After that I was very careful, but it turns out, not careful enough."

She held his gaze steadily. "I'm okay, Reuben. I needed a few stitches and a tetanus shot, but I healed. And I'd been planning my alternative career for quite a while because I knew I had to get out. I hadn't saved up as much money as I'd wanted to before I quit, but I took out a slightly bigger loan than I'd planned on, and it worked out. Lemon Espresso won't make me rich, but I have a livelihood, and nobody's going to stab me over a latte."

Reuben's hand came up to cover hers. "Laura, if you want to back out, it's not too late."

"Do you seriously think I want to give up a night with you because some punk gang member got under my guard?" She shook her head. "I did not come here with you, hand over my clothes, and let you put a collar around my neck so I could back out before I even got to see you naked."

"I knew you were guarded," he answered. "I didn't think

you'd been hurt, not like that." He frowned at her. "I'm going to be blunt. Were you raped?"

Laura stared at him, shocked by the question. Well, of course, it was reasonable for him to wonder. "No. Nothing like that. Just a little on-the-job assault with a deadly weapon." She smiled at him and attempted to lighten the moment. "If it had been something worse, I probably wouldn't have the nerve to stand here wondering how long it's going to take you to get out of those jeans and hoping it will be soon."

"You trust me not to hurt you."

"Yes. You're not some street punk. You were a highly trained and disciplined soldier, and now you're an extremely dedicated and focused rancher. You're not high on some base-ment lab chemistry experiment; you're a smart man in control of his faculties." Laura let out a soft sigh. "Maybe too much in control, but yes, Reuben, I trust you not to hurt me."

"I won't disappoint you." His hand stroked down her arm until it reached her shoulder. He placed his other hand be-hind her and drew her forward, into his arms. "This isn't quite what I imagined, the first time I saw you naked. I thought I'd have to explain my scars to you, not the other way around."

"Do you have some? We could compare." She hid her smile in the soft fabric of his T-shirt.

"A few." His lips brushed against her forehead. "But I hadn't planned for us to exchange war stories tonight. I'd rather focus on the present."

"Works for me." She could feel the warmth of his body through his shirt, the rasp of his jeans against her hips and stomach, the soft cotton of his shirt against her nipples. The present was far more interesting than anything in her past.

"Undress me, Laura."

"My pleasure." She slid her hands into the waistband of his jeans, tugged his shirt loose, and reached under it, touching him. She smoothed her hands along the hard muscles of his abdomen, unsnapped his jeans, lowered the zipper.

Laura drew his shirt up, taking in the washboard stomach she'd felt before she could see it, then stopped when she got it up as high as his shoulders. "Um. You're too tall. I can't reach high enough to get it over your head."

"I'll take care of that part." Reuben drew his shirt off and let it fall to the floor. "You work on the rest."

When she'd come in to work that morning, she'd never dreamed that instead of going home alone afterwards she would be easing Reuben's jeans down his hips, freeing an impressive erection in the process, staring at his bare upper torso, and waiting for him to tell her what he wanted next.

She worked the fabric down his thighs and calves; then he helped by stepping out of the jeans. Laura folded them up, stood with them, and set them on the kitchen counter. It gave her a minute to regain her composure before she removed the last item of clothing. He'd taken his boots and socks off already, probably in the bedroom while she started the walk to the kitchen. She was a handful of fabric away from seeing it all.

She'd probably stare. Or drool. Or have to sit on her hands to keep from touching him without permission. *Damn these rules,* she thought. Who knew it would be so difficult to follow them?

Reuben waited patiently while she hooked her fingers into the waistband of his briefs and stripped them off. Her breath caught when she got her first glimpse of his penis, engorged, thick, heavy with arousal. A bead of moisture gleamed on the head, letting her know that he wanted her as much as she wanted him.

He stepped out of the briefs when she got them down to his ankles, and she stayed where she was for a minute, crouched down and looking up at an impressive display of masculine perfection.

"What do you think?" he asked her when she continued to stare.

"I think this is better than Christmas," she answered.

"Like me unwrapped?"

"Oh, yes."

Reuben reached down and took her hand in his, pulling her up to stand in front of him. They were so close, their bodies almost touched. "I like you unwrapped, too."

It was amazing how tantalizing the forbidden became, Laura thought. Since she wasn't free to touch him, to initiate anything, she wanted to so badly that it was an ache. Her hands clenched, her sex throbbed, her breasts felt full and heavy. It was an effort not to lean into him, to brush against him, not to let her hands stroke the length of his cock. The anticipation had her so ready for his touch that she suspected she'd peak quickly and explosively.

Reuben's arm wrapped around her and pulled her against his body. Laura closed her eyes to intensify the sensation of his skin against hers. His hands moved down to cup her buttocks, and his fingers dug into the soft flesh, massaging, gripping, pressing her closer to him.

"I love having my hands on your ass, Laura," he said in a low, rough voice. "I like knowing that you're naked and every inch of you is mine. Do you like knowing that your body belongs to me tonight?"

"Yes." Her voice came out as little more than a breath.

"I'm going to take you every way possible." His hands tightened on her. "I think the first time I'm going to take you on your hands and knees so I can watch your beautiful ass while I fuck you."

She trembled against him, picturing herself in that submissive and receptive position, Reuben hard and hot behind her, thrusting into her.

"I'll be able to touch your breasts, your clit, any part of you I want to touch." His chin rubbed against the top of her head in a rough caress. "I'm going to use your body until you can't take any more."

Goody, she thought, and resisted the urge to giggle. Nerves and anticipation were making her feel almost intoxicated with desire. Reuben felt so good against her, his size, his strength, the warmth of his body. The thought of having him, all of him, and being had by him made her knees weak.

"The collar isn't the only toy I picked up for tonight," he said, and she leaned into him to keep from falling. What other surprises did he have in store for her? And was she going to survive the wait before she found out?

"This really is better than Christmas," Laura said.

"Christmas for naughty little girls," Reuben agreed. "I have something you'll like much better than a lump of coal in your stocking."

Laughter bubbled up in her throat. Of all the things she'd imagined, laughing during sex with Reuben hadn't crossed her mind. It felt good. Free. Funny that she felt free when she was wearing the symbol that marked her as his sexual slave.

"I like hearing you laugh, Laura." His mouth searched hers out, and she lifted her head to meet his kiss. He took it deeper, urging her lips apart, twining his tongue around hers, his body moving against hers in a way that sent her nerve endings into a chorus of sensations.

His hands moved over her butt, her hips, up her rib cage to brush the sides of her breasts. Laura leaned back from the waist in silent encouragement. His fingers brushed over her nipples, then tugged at them, teasing her before finally cupping her breasts in a warm, firm hold.

He kissed her long and hard, rubbing his thumbs over her nipples until she was breathless and on the verge of losing control, ready to beg him to touch her between her legs.

"Spread your legs for me, Laura." He gave the low command against her mouth.

God, yes. She shifted her feet and adjusted her stance.

Reuben moved his hand down to stroke the soft curls that covered her mound. "Are you wet for me, Laura?"

"Yes." So wet, it probably wouldn't be hard for her to accommodate him, even though it had been a very long time since she'd had a lover, and Reuben was long and thick.

His fingers slid down, touching the folds of her sex, finding them swollen and slick. "Let's see how wet you are." He worked one finger into her, testing her. "Hmmm. Almost ready to take my cock."

Almost? She wanted to groan and bit her lip instead. This was no time to earn sensual punishment in the form of delayed gratification. She already felt like she'd waited far too long. Her body was primed for release, aching with need.

His finger thrust in and out of her, then slid up to flick over her distended clit.

"Go to the bedroom and kneel on the bed for me. On your hands and knees, facing the headboard. Legs apart. I want to be able to see your pussy when I come up behind you."

Reuben's hands fell away from her. Laura swallowed, nodded, and managed to follow his instructions without falling on her face.

One foot in front of the other, that was the key. Focus on the individual actions. She climbed onto his bed, felt the softness of the blankets under her hands, against her legs. She positioned herself facing the right way, balanced her weight on her hands and knees, moved her knees far apart, arching her lower back to display her sex.

Reuben was going to take her like this. The thought made her sex clench, made her body go tight. He was going to kneel between her thighs, push his cock inside her, fuck her.

Laura bit her lower lip harder, and wondered if she was going to start coming before he even got all the way inside her.

25

"Very nice." Reuben's voice sounded behind her, full of approval. "You're almost exactly how I want you."

Almost?

Laura waited for him to tell her what else he wanted, but instead she heard soft sounds as a drawer opened and closed. What was he doing behind her? He'd mentioned that he'd picked up some other toys for tonight. Did he have something besides the collar he wanted to play with? And if so, what?

Remembering the mind-boggling array of playthings she'd seen at a bachelorette sex toy party had her on the verge of melting down. The possibilities were endless. The anticipation was going to kill her.

She felt the mattress dip as he joined her on the bed, felt his hand settle on her butt, stroking the soft flesh. His hand followed the curves of her ass, then the dimple at the top, the line of separation between the rounded globes. He wouldn't . . . would he?

Yes, he would. Something brushed against her anus, soft, slick. Not his hand. Too small for his penis. An anal toy. He fitted it against her, applying gradually stronger pressure, and she felt the tissue opening to accommodate the entry.

"Is that a plug?" Laura asked.

"Yes." His other hand caressed her, stroked her, moved around underneath her and traced the folds of her labia. "Very soft, coated with special lubricant. It won't hurt you, but with this inside you, you're going to feel very full when I enter you."

Yes, she would. And it was probably the only form of double penetration she was ever likely to experience in her life. She closed her eyes and relaxed, focusing on the joint sensations of his hand teasing her clit, the slick folds of her sex, and the careful, steady progress of the plug Reuben was inserting.

"Do you like that, Laura?"

"Yes." She arched her back more, pushing back against him, taking more, until she felt his fingers penetrate her while the plug settled fully into place.

"I thought you would." His lips touched her back, then followed the line of her spine, his breath feathering over her skin and sending waves of gooseflesh in the wake of his mouth. "You're going to be so tight when I fill you here." His fingers moved inside her, leaving her in no doubt about his meaning.

She was tight now. She could feel herself clenching around his fingers, the sensation of fullness in her anal passage, not uncomfortable, just . . . full. And all of her felt far more sensitive than usual.

"Tell me you want me."

"I want you." She nearly groaned the words, thrusting her hips back to take more pressure against her labia, push his fingers deeper inside her.

"Soon." Reuben kissed the back of her neck and slid his fingers out of her.

Laura dug her fingers into the blankets and tried to remember how to breathe.

His hands slid up under her to cup her breasts. "These are very nice, did I mention that before?"

"No." Then she frowned, concentrating. "At least, I don't think so."

"Soft. Pretty. And your nipples are so hard." He pinched them, rolled them between his fingers, tugged them by turns, and Laura squirmed in reaction, unable to keep still. If he didn't take her soon, she wasn't going to be able to stand it. The joint stimulation of the plug and his hands on her nipples had her inner muscles clenching in need.

"Please, Reuben," she gasped out.

"Please what?"

"Please. Fuck me."

"Do you think you deserve to be given my cock?" He reached down to stroke his finger over her clit. "Is this pussy hot and ready for me?"

"Yes." She was hotter than the sun, so ready, the first stroke would be ecstasy.

"I'm so hard for you, Laura." His hands left her body, and she heard a tearing sound as he opened a condom packet. "Feel how hard I am."

The head of his cock nudged against her sex, pressing into her folds. He felt larger than she expected, hard, hot. He gave her the head, and she felt herself stretching to take him, felt the fullness of the plug, and then he thrust all the way into her in one long stroke, and she was filled completely.

When he withdrew, she wanted to scream in protest, but he thrust into her again and she moaned instead. So good, it felt so good. His fingers dug into her hips as he held her positioned for his thrusts. Each long stroke had her gasping, trembling, reaching for more. He held her to a slow, deliberate pace, letting the tension build.

The knowledge that he could keep up the erotic torture as long as he wanted to, that he owned her body, was taking her, triggered the breaking point. Laura felt her back bowing as the orgasm hit hard, the intensity stealing her breath. She was dimly aware of him thrusting harder, deeper, finding his own release and drawing hers out in the process.

She collapsed onto her stomach on the bed. Reuben moved with her, covering her with his body, staying deep inside her for a long minute. Then he withdrew, removed the plug, and she felt the bed move as he climbed off. She was beyond moving, almost floating in the aftermath of pleasure. He wasn't leaving her, she knew.

Laura closed her eyes and drifted until she felt his hands close over her shoulders and roll her onto her back. She lifted her lids halfway to look up at Reuben, bending over her.

"Laura." He touched her breast, stroked her belly. She stretched like a cat, enjoying his hand on her. "So lovely. And this lovely body belongs to me."

Yes, and it was incredibly smart of her to agree to that because he certainly knew what to do with it. She hadn't been doing her body any favors recently. It was better off under Reuben's control.

Reuben stretched out beside her and slid an arm around her, hugging her against his side. Laura laid her cheek against his chest and listened to the steady beat of his heart. She felt his hand stroking her hair, her side, the curve of her hip.

This was the best part of sex, she thought, settling into him. Being held close, feeling the touch of her lover's hand moving over her, bodies resting twined together. Somehow she hadn't expected the closeness, the contentment. As if this was where she belonged, as if they had a bond that went beyond the temporary agreement the collar symbolized.

What would it be like to belong to Reuben permanently? Laura drifted in his arms and let herself imagine that she was truly his, that he loved her, that she was cherished by him. It hurt, a dull, distant pain, and she realized that until that moment she hadn't truly known she wanted to be his love as well as his lover.

Don't think about it now, she admonished herself. She had one thing she wanted, and it was more than she'd ever had before. The experience of being taken by Reuben was worth the risk of getting hurt. She'd known that she would give him more than she'd given any other man, known what that could mean to her emotionally. She'd agreed to this with her eyes open, aware of the potential consequences.

She just hadn't known that she was already achingly, painfully, a little bit in love with him before he'd made his irresistible offer, and now she was falling further, helpless to hold back or stop the process.

By the time he removed the collar, she wouldn't need it anyway, because she would be his on the inside.

"You're very quiet." Reuben smoothed the length of her hair with unhurried fingers.

"I think I forgot how to talk," Laura answered.

He laughed, a low, velvet sound. "Then I guess I don't have to ask if it was good for you."

"Not unless you're just looking for praise." She smiled against his skin. "Which you deserve," she added as an afterthought.

"So do you. Such a passionate woman." He drew light patterns over the sensitive skin of her back. "So responsive to my touch."

"You're very good with your hands," Laura said.

"I like having my hands on you."

"Did you like having your hand in me, too?"

"Very much."

Reuben tugged her up on top of him, and she pillowed her chin on her hands so she could look at him, enjoying the feel of him under her and the relaxed, open expression on his face.

"Probably not as much as I enjoyed it," she informed him, picking up the thread of the conversation. "I think I got the best end of this deal."

"We'll see if you feel that way tomorrow." Reuben moved his hands down her back, kneaded her ass. "I'm not done with you. I intend to use you hard and thoroughly."

"If that's supposed to be a threat, there's something wrong with this picture," Laura sighed. She rocked her hips into his and felt his cock twitch against her belly.

"No threat. Just a promise." Reuben pushed back against her, then pulled her up higher until his shaft pressed into her sex. "I like feeling you there, wet and willing against my cock."

"Mmmm." She closed her eyes and shifted her weight onto her knees so she could slide herself along his rapidly hardening length. The contact felt so good, so warm. She wanted to raise her hips and align herself so that the head of his cock pushed against her opening. Wanted to feel her sex open for him, wanted to take him deep inside. It was so tempting that she stilled and shifted away a little.

"Get another condom," Reuben said, watching her closely. "From the dresser."

Laura nodded and rolled off him, stretched her legs out until her feet touched the floor, and stood. She saw another packet lying on top of the dresser's smooth, polished surface and picked it up. He must have laid it there when he got the first one, ready for them to use the second time, and she felt her sex throb in reaction.

It excited her, knowing that he'd planned this, that he'd taken her the first time while he was already thinking of the second.

She picked it up and went back to the bed, climbing up to straddle him again. "I'm assuming you want me back where I was? Or did you want something else?"

"I want you to put that on me." Reuben stretched under

her and reached up to tuck his hands behind his head. "But first you'll have to show me you want my cock again."

"How should I do that?" Laura licked her lips and waited for his answer, feeling desire coiling through her.

"Put your mouth on me."

Reuben watched as Laura slid down him, her silky hair spilling across her shoulders and onto his belly and thighs as she moved. She settled herself at a comfortable angle and took his shaft in her hands. Small hands, but so capable. He'd watched them often, making quick graceful movements as she worked, deft, sure. Seeing her hands on him was a pleasure all its own.

She explored him with her fingers, gliding up and down his shaft, then settling one hand at the base and cupping his balls in the other. Her mouth touched his head, and he felt the first touch of her tongue, swirling around him, tasting him. She used her lips and tongue on his head and shaft, then began a series of soft hickeys down the length of him.

Finally she closed her lips over him and drew him into her mouth, adjusting her position to take him deeper. The hand cupping his balls stroked the sensitive skin that covered the sac, and her hand at the base of his cock tightened and moved up and down just a little, in rhythm with her mouth swallowing his length.

The way her body moved as she sucked his cock told him she found it arousing, that she was enjoying the opportunity he'd given her to play with him.

He was certainly enjoying it. Her soft mouth and clever hands had him almost painfully hard, but he hated to stop her. If he didn't stop her soon, however, he would have to wait awhile before he could have her again. Reuben didn't want to wait.

"That's enough." He speared his fingers into her hair and tugged her head up. "You've shown me you want my cock, but I need to see if you're ready for it."

Reuben drew her up to lie beside him, turned to face her, and touched the soft curls that covered her mound. She parted her thighs for him, and he slid his hand down to cup her, pressing his palm against her clit.

"How ready is this pussy?" he asked her.

"Very." Her eyes were half-lidded, a blush of arousal spread over her cheeks and breasts, her nipples budded into hard points. Her body was ready for him, but he wanted more.

Reuben let his fingertips stroke the soft folds of her sex, dipping just barely inside her, finding her slick and receptive, opening for his fingers easily. It felt so good to touch her, to know that she was his, that she trusted him to give her pleasure. He wanted to give her so much that she was drowning in it, so that her body would cling to his like a life raft.

"I like this pussy you've given me," he whispered, leaning over her to brush his mouth across hers. "I like fucking it. Maybe I'll fuck it again."

He felt her quiver in reaction, knew the way he reminded her of her status as his sexual possession excited her further. He thrust his finger into her, drew it out, thrust it in again, and felt her hips rise to meet him, to take more.

"Would you like to be fucked again, Laura?"

"Yes." She was breathing faster, moving restlessly against him. "Please, Reuben."

"I think you're almost ready."

Laura made a low sound of protest when he withdrew his hand, then left the bed, but she waited to see what he'd do next. He took out the small toy he wanted to use on her, a tiny bullet of a vibrator, just the right size to fit against the sensitive bundle of nerves at the apex of her sex.

It had been fun shopping for this night, although not

nearly so fun as using the toys to heighten the experience for Laura was proving to be. He'd never gone in for artificial enhancements before, but he'd also known that it would take extraordinary measures to overwhelm Laura's defenses.

Already she showed him such trust, such passion. When he was finished, he intended for her to be thoroughly his.

"Let's see if this makes you ready for me." Reuben rejoined her on the bed, turned the tiny vibrator on, and touched it to her clit. She let out a strangled sound and clutched the blankets in both hands. "You can touch me if it helps."

Laura dug her hands into him, gripping his waist. She buried her face against his chest while he brushed the vibrator around and over her sensitive flesh, along her labia, back to her clit, while she groaned and shuddered. So close, almost there . . . He turned it off when he knew she was on the verge.

"Put the condom on me, Laura."

"Right." She was breathing hard and fast. She let go of him, sat up, and felt frantically around them on the bed. "Dammit, I lost it. Shit, shit, shit!"

"Here." Reuben spotted the package, pressed it in her hand, and resisted the urge to laugh as she tore it open and rolled it on him with record speed. He'd intended to have her on top of him the second time, but she was too far gone to follow his direction.

He pulled her down onto him and claimed her lips in a hard, hot, openmouthed kiss while he rolled her onto her back, moved between her thighs, and thrust into her. He swallowed her gasp, and then her keening wail as she tightened around him, stiffening, jerking, coming while he rode her down.

When she went still under him, he continued to thrust into her in long, steady, slow strokes, taking her, spilling himself into her and feeling her open herself even further to take that, too.

He softened the kiss, making the contact gentle, before he

ended it and raised his head to look down at her. She looked up at him, her eyes wide and dark, mouth swollen from his kisses.

"I like having you under me," he said. "Almost as much as I like being inside you."

He felt her tighten around him in reaction, but she didn't say anything. He brushed his lips against hers one more time, savoring the taste and feel of her, knowing he'd have to move off her in a moment before the weight he rested on her became too much.

"Laura." He kissed the soft curve of her lower lip, slid his tongue along it, rocked deeper into the cradle of her hips. It was harder than he'd imagined it would be to stop, to lever his weight off her, withdraw from the tight clasp of her body. His body simply didn't want to leave hers.

Reuben forced himself to move away, off the bed, gathering up the toys he'd used on her and taking them to the bathroom to clean them before putting them away. He disposed of the condom, cleaned himself up, and splashed cold water on his face to help clear his head.

"Remember which one of you is supposed to remain in control, and which one is supposed to lose it," he told the man in the mirror.

It might be sound strategy, but it was proving harder to implement than he'd expected.

26

"Laura."

Reuben's voice penetrated the haze of sleep she'd slid into. Laura blinked awake and turned her head toward him.

"Hmmm?"

"The coffee's ready now." He held a cup out to her, his lips curved in humor. She smiled back, realizing how long ago they'd forgotten it.

"You're a lot more stimulating than caffeine," she said. But she sat up and took the cup he handed her. She had the rest of her life to sleep, but one night with Reuben. She didn't plan to waste it.

Reuben joined her on the bed and settled against her, hips and thighs touching. He slid one arm behind her. "So stimulating, you went right to sleep."

"After that much stimulation, I was spent." Laura leaned into him and sipped her coffee. It wasn't great, but it was hot and it would wake her up. "Where did you get this stuff?"

"The kitchen."

She made an exasperated sound. "And before that, where? It was just in a container on your counter, no label."

"You think I need better coffee at home?" Reuben stroked her shoulder in a lazy caress as he smiled down at her.

"Well, that might rob you of an excuse to take a trip for the good stuff, so forget I mentioned it."

"The coffee isn't the only thing worth the trip to Lemon Espresso." Reuben trailed his hand down to her breast, running his finger along the upper curve.

"I can't give you that in the middle of the day," Laura pointed out.

"You'll be wearing my collar tomorrow. I could come in and order you to show me your breasts." His hand moved lower to brush over her nipple. Laura felt it tighten at his touch.

"You could. The stockroom has a locking door," she said, thinking it through. Jolie would cover for her. They could go into the back, and she could do anything he told her to do with nobody the wiser. Their secret. Like the collar she'd hide under her clothes.

She realized she was plotting out ways to have a clandestine encounter in the middle of the workday and laughed out loud.

"What's so funny?"

"Me. I'm really enjoying this." Laura smiled at him over the rim of her cup and took another swallow of wake-up juice. "Not the coffee. The dominance-and-submissive deal. You. Sex."

"I hope you're enjoying it. No man wants to hear that his performance needs work." Reuben slanted a look at her. "I can live with you finding the coffee lacking, but not the sex."

"The sex is mind-blowing, and you know it." Laura snuggled into him and sighed happily. "I can't believe you bought sex toys. Where'd you get them, anyway? It wasn't anyplace local."

"The Internet brings the world to your doorstep."

"Aha. You let your browser do the walking."

"Yes, and it was enlightening. So many choices, shapes, styles. Sizes. I didn't think you looked like the type to keep an arsenal of self-pleasure products under your bed, so I stuck to items for beginners."

"Good call." Laura was waking all the way up, feeling a little drowsy still, but alert. Aware of her body and the various twinges and aches that told her she hadn't been using it to its full potential. It was a sad statement on her sex life.

She also felt good, undoubtedly due to the sea of endorphins swimming in her bloodstream. Nothing like a few good, hard, roll-your-eyes-back orgasms to send your body chemistry into a natural state of sex-induced high.

That last orgasm had been something else. The first one had been off the scale, too, now that she thought about it. She'd been collared, dominated, double-penetrated from behind, and vibrated. By Reuben. It was like coming off a diet and binging at an all-you-can-eat dessert buffet.

From a long dry spell to twenty-four hours of excess. You do not know how to do things in moderation, Laura told herself. Well, excess had worked for her so far. Pouring her energy into her business had made it successful. If she'd put in only the minimum hours the doors were open, it would be a different story.

"Feeling okay?" Reuben took her empty cup from her and set it aside with his.

"Fine. A little sticky." She squeezed her thighs together and grimaced. "I should go clean up."

"A good submissive would ask permission."

"Oh." She felt her nipples tighten at the reminder of her status. "May I go wash myself?"

"Would you like me to do it for you?" Reuben asked, pulling her into his lap.

"That would be more fun, but not necessary." She nuzzled

his neck and inhaled the distinctive blend of soap, musk, and leather that was his scent.

"I like to see you having fun." Reuben shifted her weight to cradle her in his arms and climbed off the bed, carrying her to the bathroom.

"You must be a really happy man tonight, then." Laura laid her head on his shoulder and enjoyed the feeling of being held by him. "I can't remember the last time I had this much fun."

"That's not saying much." Reuben set her on her feet and turned on the water in the sink, letting it warm up. "You were hit and stabbed in your first career, and now you work about seventy hours a week. You were probably in high school the last time you did something completely frivolous."

"Look who's talking." Laura let out an inelegant snort. "I read up on Ranger school, you know. And then you had all those years of active service before retiring to work around the clock making your sheep venture profitable. When did you last have fun?"

"Maybe that is my idea of fun." Reuben gave her an in-scrutable look and ran a washcloth under the warm water. He added soap and made a come-stand-here gesture with his hand.

And yet he'd spent God only knew how many hours driving back and forth to get a cup of coffee and say good morning to her every day, not to mention the time invested in shopping for sex toys on the Internet. Why, when he could have had any woman he asked? For that matter, he could have simply asked her on a date and then tried to persuade her to get horizontal, like a normal man.

But then, Reuben wasn't like any other man she'd ever met. It was perfectly in character for him to have planned this down to the last detail. Like the way he'd researched his Ice-landic venture, deciding on the outcome he wanted, studying, planning, choosing the course of action that would get him the results he wanted. Although what he could possibly want from her beyond the chance to play dominant bedroom games, Laura couldn't guess.

It was a mystery, but she wasn't going to question her good luck. With a mental shrug she moved to stand where he wanted her and let him wash away the evidence of their debauchery. It was nice of him to volunteer for such a personal chore, the kind of thing she should probably be doing for him, since she was in the submissive role.

"This seems wrong," Laura said.

"You're having second thoughts now?" Reuben gave her a surprised look.

"No, it just seems wrong that you're doing that for me. Shouldn't I be doing it for you?"

"You just want to get your hands on me again." Reuben smiled at her, the humor softening his features, making him seem warmer, more approachable. Come to think of it, he'd shown her a definite tender side in his role as sexual dominant. The combination of dominance and tenderness made for a heady mix.

"I wouldn't mind getting my hands on you again," Laura admitted. "But I like your hands on me, too." Especially now, with the warmth of the cloth rasping against the sensitive skin of her inner thighs and the folds of her sex. The indirect touch was very stimulating, knowing that his hand was separated from her by a layer of fabric.

"You like being my property to handle, don't you?" He dropped the cloth into the sink and then petted her mound with casual familiarity.

"Yes. I'm not likely to have many chances in life to be a sex object." She smiled at him and shifted her feet farther apart to give him better access if he wanted to continue touching her.

"You don't think it's politically incorrect?"

"What do politics have to do with fantasies? Besides, it's you."

"Me?" Reuben gave her an inquiring look.

"Yes, you. You're my fantasy. It's probably very juvenile to admit that, but then again, I'm sure it was obvious without me saying anything." Laura shrugged. What the hell, if she was worried about keeping up a dignified front with Reuben, she wouldn't be walking around naked and wearing his collar.

Dignity and reality could wait for tomorrow night, and that would come soon enough. Right now Reuben's hand was stroking her pubic curls, and it wasn't like he couldn't tell she enjoyed it. When his fingertips pressed inside her and came away wet, her reaction to him was impossible to mistake.

"You're certainly fulfilling my fantasy," Reuben said. He ran his fingertip along her labia. "I have you naked and submissive, and any time I want to touch you, I can. If I want you, all I have to do is say the word. If I told you to sit on the counter and spread your legs so I could fuck you again right now, you'd do it, and you'd like it."

She felt a wave of heat roll through her at his words and knew she was making his fingertips even wetter. She loved the idea that he could order her to spread for him, that he might want her again already. That he found her desirable, saw her as sexual, when for so long she hadn't been able to guess if he even saw her at all.

He thrust his finger into her, then added a second. "What do you think, Laura? Should I use this pussy again?"

"If you like," she said, trying not to sound too eager or too bossy.

"I want you to go lay on your back on the bed with your feet flat on the mattress, knees bent, legs spread wide apart." Reuben twisted his fingers inside her, watching her face as she reacted to his touch and his words. Then he slid his fingers out, leaving her free to obey.

Her legs felt weak, but she managed to walk the short distance without being awkward and lay down in the position he'd described. It was a very submissive pose, she realized, one that left her body exposed and displayed in an open invitation.

Reuben came up to the bed and looked down at her. "Very nice, Laura." He sat beside her, facing her, and rested his palm over her sex. "Here you are, so open and ready for me. What should I do first?"

"Whatever you want to do," she said, her voice low and husky with desire.

"I want to make you come while I watch." Reuben pressed his palm into her, then rubbed back and forth, teasing her with the light pressure and the indirect stimulation. "I want to play with this pussy until you can't take it anymore and you have to come."

It sounded like he was planning to take his time and draw it out. Laura bit her lower lip and closed her eyes, hoping he'd stroke her clit or penetrate her with his fingers again soon because the hand covering her sex without going further was driving her insane already.

"Maybe I'll play with your nipples while I do it." He suited action to words, pinching one nipple between his fingers while he took his time working one finger into her tight sheath. "I like touching your nipples, making them hard."

He released the first nipple and pinched the second, applying enough pressure to almost hurt, stopping just at the limit of what felt incredibly stimulating and what would edge over into pain.

The combination of his hand between her thighs and the stimulation of her nipples had her inner muscles quivering, her sex growing soft and wet in readiness for more penetration. Each time he pinched a nipple, it sent a jolt from her breast straight to her sex as if live wires ran between the two places and each touch sent off an electrical impulse.

"Such a lovely body," Reuben said. He bent down and drew her clit into his mouth, thrusting two more fingers inside her at the same time. Laura let out a low moan of pleasure.

His mouth on her escalated her reaction. She felt her lower

body going tight, coiling, her hips rising involuntarily to meet his invading fingers and the hot suction he was applying to the tight bud of her clit.

"Reuben," she gasped. She twisted her hands in the blanket to keep from reaching for him, threading her fingers through his hair and holding his head down to her.

He released her clit, then flicked his tongue over it, back, forth, hard, quick thrusts while his fingers moved in and out of her, hard, deep, demanding.

She couldn't stop, couldn't hold it back. She was going to come. She felt her inner muscles squeezing, felt the liquid heat spiraling through her. "I can't—I'm going to—," she choked out, unable to frame the thought coherently.

Reuben raised his head and pinched her clit with his free hand to replace the pressure his mouth had been providing. "Come for me, Laura. I want to watch you come."

He twisted the fingers inside her and stroked her clit and Laura felt her body bow and buck as she found release. When it ended, she drew in air and fought to relax, to slow her breathing, to let her body come down. She opened her eyes and found Reuben still watching her, his hand closed possessively over her mound, his fingers still buried deep inside her.

There was something more intimate about him watching her while she reached orgasm when he wasn't pursuing his own that was vaguely unsettling. She'd been lost to sensation, out of control, while he directed her response and watched. He'd made her physically vulnerable, witnessed her vulnerability, and now she felt exposed in a way that went beyond nakedness.

She stared at him, caught by the realization that he could hurt her so easily, with a word, with a look. If he ridiculed her, if he showed her that he found her less than he'd expected or wanted in any way. Something of her apprehension must have shown in her eyes because he kneeled between her spread thighs and lowered his body over hers.

"Laura." He framed her face with his hands, keeping her from looking away. "So lovely. And mine.".

She could feel his erection pressing against her, hard, ready to take her, proof that he found her desirable. She needed that, needed him to show her that he wanted her, that she was his because he wanted her to be. "Take me," she breathed out, a whisper of sound. "Please. Take me now."

"I need to get protection."

She bit her lip and closed her eyes, feeling the delay like a rejection. Logically she knew better, but emotionally, she felt him moving away from her.

"Laura." Reuben's body moved over hers, pressing her down into the mattress. "I have to. I won't take a risk with you."

Of course he wouldn't, why would he take the risk that she might get pregnant, why would she want him to, even for a moment? "I know," she whispered, but she felt tears burning at the back of her eyes and clenched them more tightly shut.

"Laura." Reuben's arms slid around her, held her tight. "I want you. I won't do this to you, though. If we ever do this, it has to be your choice. What you want. Not the heat of the moment, a real choice. And it wouldn't be right now. You know that."

"I know," she said again, her throat too tight to let her speak normally so the words came out choked.

"I won't leave you." His body moved on hers, the hard length of his cock pressing into her belly. "I promised you I wouldn't leave you alone."

Laura nodded, still refusing to open her eyes, to look at him. She felt him rocking against her, sliding his erection along the soft skin of her stomach, thrusting hard. Then she understood what he was doing, what he meant.

Rather than risk her feeling emotionally abandoned while he left her long enough to retrieve protection for them, he was stroking himself against her, finding his release without intercourse. Keeping his word.

She felt her heart clutch along with her stomach, felt her breath go. Reuben surrounded her, on top of her, his arms wrapped around and under her, his legs between hers. She felt the velvet skin of his penis thrusting against her, the heat of his body against hers, heard his harsh breathing and knew how close he was.

Reuben. Like falling into space, she felt the world drop away below her and knew it would never be the same. She would never be the same. She was his, irrevocably, forever. He held her heart that beat and ached for him.

She felt him shudder, felt the liquid jet as he spilled himself against her, and sank her teeth into her lower lip again to stop herself from saying the words that would tell him she was breaking the rules.

27

Laura pressed her cheek against Reuben's shoulder, breathing in his scent, savoring the feel of his weight on her, his arms around her, the liquid of his release spilled across her belly like a brand.

"All right?" he asked her.

"Yes." She burrowed into his embrace, feeling embarrassed by her reaction now. "I'm sorry I lost it there for a few minutes."

"Don't be sorry, Laura. I made you lose it." His lips brushed across the top of her head. "I need to get up so I can clean us both up now."

"I'm know. I'm okay," she assured him. "And thank you. For, well. Thank you." She left unsaid, *For not leaving me. For not having unprotected sex with me when I might have regretted it later. For finding an alternative.*

"It's a good thing I know what you mean," he said, his

voice full of amusement. "I'll be right back. Stay right where you are. Don't move."

She blinked up at him as he levered himself off her and stood. "Do you think I'm going to bolt while your back is turned now?"

"Maybe." Reuben looked down at her, his face impossible to read.

"I'm not going anywhere." She touched the collar at her throat. "You own me until you take this off. I agreed to that. I wanted that. I still do."

Laura thought she saw his shoulders relax as a tension left him. "I'll be back."

She felt her mouth twitch in a smile. "You sound like the Terminator."

"I'm glad I amuse you." Reuben bent and kissed her breast. "I've decided that I want you where I can see you. You're coming with me." He slid an arm under her knees, another under her shoulders, and scooped her up.

"I really wasn't going to bolt," Laura said, but she didn't waste the opportunity to snuggle into him.

"I know." He carried her to the bathroom and set her on the counter next to the sink while he turned the water on in the tub and stopped the drain. She watched as he squirted liquid soap into the stream of water.

"A bubble bath," she said out loud. "For me?"

"For us." He came back to her and retrieved the washcloth from the sink, using it to clean her stomach and his. "It'll be a tight fit, so we'll have to get very close."

"I'll endure," she said solemnly, fighting to keep the smile off her face.

"I'll probably have to rest my hands here." Reuben palmed her breasts, cupping them in his hands to demonstrate. "No place else to put them."

"What a shame." She grinned at him and arched into his hold, rubbing her nipples against his palms.

"Shameless," Reuben corrected her. He squeezed her breasts, then bent his head to kiss his way along the upper curves. Laura let her head fall back, giving herself up to the pleasure of his hands and mouth on her. So many nerve endings, so much exposed skin for him to touch, all of her finely attuned to him.

He raised his head and slid his arms around her, pulling her forward, off the counter, standing her so close in front of him that their bodies touched. "I didn't ask if you like baths, but I thought it would relax you."

"It sounds wonderful," she admitted.

"Let's find out." Reuben turned and kept one arm around her, using it to draw her toward the tub. He climbed in first, settled against the back, then made a space for her between his legs. "Come here."

Laura stepped into the tub and settled with her back against his chest. His hands made lazy patterns over her arms and upper body with rivulets of water and lacy bubbles of soap.

It felt good to rest against him, feeling his body supporting hers, the warm water soaking away tension and soothing long-unused muscles. Safe. She felt safe here with Reuben. She frowned, trying to remember the last time she'd felt such a strong sense of safety and contentment, then gave it up as unimportant.

Now was what mattered. Here, now, floating in her lover's arms. Laura let her eyes drift closed and simply floated.

Reuben listened to her breathing grow deep and steady, felt her body relax fully into his, and knew that Laura slept in his arms. Extricating them from the tub without waking her proved a challenge, but he managed it. He grabbed a towel and draped it over her, carried her back to the bed and laid her on it, then got a second towel to dry himself and her more thoroughly with.

That done, he picked her up, pulled the top sheet and blankets back, placed her in the bed with her head on a pillow, and took the damp towels back to the bathroom. Once they were hung up to dry, he padded back to the bed, climbed in beside her, and slid his arms around her to hold her close.

She made a soft, sighing sound but didn't wake. Reuben stretched one leg over hers, as if having her in his arms wasn't enough. He wanted to have as much of himself in contact with her as possible.

Laura.

Had he won or lost tonight? It was too soon to say. She trusted him. She'd given herself to him and held nothing back. It might be enough to persuade her to accept his permanent offer.

Sexually they were very compatible. They were compatible outside of bed, too. They had many shared values; they had a good basis for enduring friendship. Marriage to him should make sense to her when he proposed the idea.

He found it very revealing that she'd come so close to having unprotected sex with him. Some part of her didn't find the possibility of having a baby with him unthinkable, at least. He didn't know if she wanted a family. That was something the two of them would have to talk about. Having children with Laura was important to him, but it wasn't more important than having her. If she didn't want a family, he was willing to compromise on that desire.

He'd weighted his case with so many reasons for her to say yes. Commitment, companionship, a family if she wanted one. He'd demonstrated that he could and would satisfy her physical needs. Emotionally, well, she needed a man she could trust. One she could depend on. He'd proved that she could trust him.

Laura was practical, he assured the doubt that whispered in the back of his mind that it wasn't enough, that she might want more. He didn't have any more to offer her.

He buried the doubt in the memory of Laura on the brink of orgasm, then lost in pleasure. His. For tonight, at least, she belonged to him.

Reuben tightened his arms around the woman who slept in his possessive embrace and closed his eyes.

Laura woke up to find herself sandwiched between a hard man and an impossibly soft blanket. She touched the wool with curious fingers and wondered what a sweater made from it would feel like. It would be warm enough for the coldest winter day, she was sure.

"Good morning."

Reuben's voice was husky with sleep. She smiled at the sound of his voice and stretched, feeling him against her back, his erection pressed into her butt, his arms around her. "Good morning."

"Sleep well?" He moved one hand up to cup her breast, stroking the sensitive tissue.

"Yes." It would have been nice to think of something clever to say, but the only things that came to mind when he touched her were variations on *ahhhhh* and *mmmmm*. Not exactly scintillating conversation.

Then again, he hadn't asked her here to talk.

"Do you like spoon sex?" Reuben rolled her nipple between his fingers and tugged gently while he asked the question.

"If it involves you, I think I can safely say I'll like it." Laura stretched again, pressing back against his cock with an inviting shift of her hips. "Should you be asking me my opinion? Doesn't that go against the dominant code or something?"

"Are you questioning me? I could punish you for that." Reuben slid his hand down to cup her sex.

"Just saying." She shifted so that instead of lying on her side with her knees on top of each other she placed the top one a little behind, making herself more accessible to his hand.

"I'm being considerate." He moved his hand against her, massaging her. "If you're not up to a gentle round of morning sex, I'm giving you the opportunity to say so."

"Is spoon sex gentle?"

"Yes. The position makes for a little more restraint. I thought my sex slave might appreciate that after last night."

"I'm not sure we're capable of restraint, but I think it'd be fun to try." Laura smiled as she spoke and moved her hips in rhythm with his hand between her legs, inviting more contact, more direct touching.

"I'm not sorry to hear that you feel unrestrained in bed with me." Reuben kissed the nape of her neck as he stroked her clit. She felt him shift position behind her as he flexed his hips, rocking into her.

"I'm just sorry I fell asleep," she said. "I didn't want to waste precious hours in bed with you being unconscious."

"It was the end of a long day. You were tired."

"Mmm," she agreed. His hand between her legs was stroking her, opening her, tantalizing her with almost but not quite penetration. His hand and her hips moved together. His hips rocked into her, echoing the action. A prelude to sex.

His hands shifted her hips, adjusting her to the angle he wanted. She felt the head of his cock press against her opening, his body spooned up against hers, his hand reaching around to allow him to resume touching her.

Reuben stroked her clit as he pushed into her, slow, gradual penetration by inches. His hips flexed into hers, each rock-ing movement giving her more of his cock until he was in as far as the position allowed.

He held her, moved with her, moved inside her, all the while keeping up a steady rhythm and gentle pressure on the sensitive bud of nerves between her legs.

The pleasure built slowly but surely as Reuben made un-hurried love to her. She felt fragile and precious in his arms, cherished, desired.

"I'm going to come, Laura," he said, his voice rasping as he pushed into her harder, more insistently. "Come with me."

She moved into his thrusts, taking him, feeling his finger-tip pressing into her clit, around it, over it.

Deep inside her she felt him swelling, throbbing, and it triggered an answering throb as her inner muscles clenched around him. The wave built and peaked and broke over her, leaving her calm and still in his embrace, his shaft buried in her, both of them sated.

"I like spoon sex," she said eventually.

"Thought you might." His hand squeezed between her legs, familiar and possessive. "What time do you need to be at work? We might have time for unrestrained before you go."

Laura lifted her head and looked around for a clock, noted the time, and dropped back down. "We have time. Do you want to be unrestrained before or after coffee?"

"After." Reuben pulled her hips into his and ground his cock deeper into her, then withdrew. "You make the coffee, I'll take care of this."

"Okay." Laura rolled over and watched him stand and stretch, seeing him with different eyes.

She knew what his body felt like on hers, wrapped around hers. She knew the weight of him, knew the length and width of his cock sliding into her, the shape of his hands and how they fit themselves on her body. She knew the touch of him, the scent of him, the rasp of the morning growth of beard on his chin against her shoulder.

She knew what it felt like to welcome him into her body, the taste of his mouth, the heat of his skin against hers.

They had been lovers, and she would never see him as a stranger again, whatever else they became to each other. Friends, maybe. Occasional lovers. If he came in for coffee and she handed it to him, there would be a level of awareness, of knowledge, in the simplest brush of their hands.

"Like what you see?" Reuben asked, his stretch ended.

"Yes." His body was big, strong, well muscled. It had been trained as a weapon as well as a tool. He was beautiful in a raw, masculine way. Since there was no telling when or if she'd have another opportunity to feast her eyes on him, Laura drank in the sight of him, committing his naked form to visual as well as sensory memory.

She watched the flex of muscle beneath the skin as he walked away, then sat up and stretched her feet to the floor. Waking up to a bout of morning sex with Reuben was a far cry from a basket of lemons, but it was still time to make the coffee.

It didn't take long, and with a mug in each hand, she retraced her steps to the bedroom. Reuben was waiting for her, sitting up against the headboard.

"Yours," she said, handing a mug to him.

"Yes, you are." He took the mug with one hand and used the other to fondle her breast. "Glad you haven't forgotten."

"Sex with you could make a lot of things slip my mind, but that isn't one of them," Laura assured him. She perched beside him, facing him, and sipped from her mug.

"I like having you there, naked." Reuben eyed her breasts, then let his gaze go lower. "Spread your legs apart."

Laura let her legs fall open, exposing herself to him fully.

"Very nice." He reached out to stroke her mound while he drank his coffee, fondling her casually. "I may have to see this sometime during the day. If I come in and tell you to show me your pussy, will you do it, Laura?"

"Yes." She felt her breath catch at the idea of submitting to him in her shop, spreading her legs at his order, offering herself to him for whatever he wanted. To look, to touch, to take. If he wanted to fuck her in the back of the shop, he could order her to strip and spread, to take his cock with no further preliminaries.

Reuben thrust a finger into her. "You're getting very wet, Laura. Are you thinking about me ordering you to give me this pussy in the middle of the day?"

"Yes."

"And that excites you." He added a second finger, worked them in and out of her in slow strokes.

"Yes." She opened her legs wider for him.

"I'm going to drink my coffee," he said, working a third finger into her. "If you don't come, I'll fuck you when I finish."

Laura groaned and bit her lip, knowing that telling her not to come was going to push her further toward orgasm.

She wanted him, wanted his cock inside her, wanted to take him all the way, as deep as he could go. *Don't come, don't come . . .*

Her awareness shrank until it centered on the movement of his hand between her legs, his fingers thrusting into her, stretching her, filling her but not quite enough.

"You're getting so close," she heard him say.

"Yes." She couldn't seem to find any other words to say, but it didn't matter.

When he took his hand away, the sudden empty sensation was a shock. "Give me your cup and lay on your back with your legs spread."

Laura complied, pushing her nearly full mug into his hand and sliding down to position herself for him.

He set their mugs on the dresser, sheathed himself, and came back to stand over her, looking down at her.

"Is that my pussy?"

"Yes." She arched her back, thrusting her breasts upward, emphasizing her sex. "Yes, it's your pussy, Reuben."

"I want to fuck my pussy now, Laura. And I'm not going to be gentle. I'm going to fuck you hard."

Oh, good. She felt herself clench at his graphic promise. She was so close. It was going to feel so good when he entered her. She was ready enough to take him hard and deep, and she wanted to.

Reuben lowered himself over her, positioned his shaft at her entrance, and thrust into her, all the way inside, burying himself in her to the hilt in one swift, sure stroke.

"Take me, Laura," he growled. His mouth closed over hers in a bruising kiss as he ground his pelvis into hers.

She kissed him back, wound her arms and legs around him, arched her hips up to take as much of him as she could, straining to take him deeper.

Reuben raised his head and looked into her eyes. "I'm going to fuck you so hard, you'll still feel me inside you next week." He began thrusting into her, hard, fast, unrestrained. She moved with him, gasping, panting, needing to be taken by him.

"Reuben." Laura dug her fingers into him as she felt the orgasm begin. "Reuben."

She gave up on words and moaned and screamed and bucked underneath him, coming violently while he drove into her with relentless intensity. When he finally came inside her, she clutched at him and wished it could last forever.

His mouth took hers again, his kiss hard at first, then gentling, his lips moving over hers, seducing her into opening for his tongue. When Reuben finally ended the kiss, she felt bone-less, spent, unable to move.

Laura rested underneath him, feeling him buried deep in her core. She would carry the memory of him inside her next week, next month, twenty years into the future.

For now, the clock was ticking and her day of belonging to him was slipping away. Already she knew it was time to get up, shower, dress, go to work, pretend that nothing had changed, that it was simply another day.

"I told you it would be unrestrained," Reuben said finally, levering himself up to look down at her.

"You didn't hear me complaining." Laura let her hand slide along his back, stroking him.

"I heard you making a lot of noise, but nothing that sounded like complaints," he agreed. "You might have complaints when you try to walk, though."

"I might." She gave him a slow, satisfied smile. "I'll take the risk."

"I'll be more restrained the next time." He placed a final hard kiss on her lips. "If you can take me again later. If you can't, you have to say so."

"How are you going to make me?" she asked.

"I'm in charge. I own you. You have to do what I tell you, including telling me when you need more gentle play or a rest."

"All right," she sighed. "The damn rules. I agreed to them. I'll follow them. If you want me again later and I'm too sore, I'll admit it."

"Thank you." Reuben pulled out of her and rolled onto one side, facing her. "I'm not sadistic. I don't like the idea of you feeling any pain."

"I'm feeling very, very good right now." Laura smiled at him, sprawling on her back, too relaxed to move just yet.

"That's the way I want to keep it." Reuben settled one hand on her belly, his fingertips just brushing her pubic curls.

That made two of them, Laura thought. In the pleasurable haze of afterglow, she could forget that when it was over, the ache in her heart would pierce her.

28

The collar posed a problem, Laura realized later. It was very visibly displayed by her usual lemon yellow tank tops. In the winter, she switched to long-sleeved T-shirts with scoop necks. Nothing with a high neck to cover up the evidence of her current status as Reuben's sexual property.

She didn't want to take the collar off. Dammit, she'd earned this, she deserved this day of being his. She wasn't going to miss out on a minute of it. So, she had to find a way to cover the evidence.

Laura rifled through drawers and finally found a tank top with a turtleneck, a style she'd tested out when she was deciding on uniform shirts for Lemon Espresso. She'd decided against the high-necked tank in the end, but kept the sample. Good thing she had; it was going to come in very handy today.

She'd showered and dressed in yesterday's clothes at Reuben's, then driven home to change into fresh undies and figure out a solution to the collar problem before going to work for the day. Reuben had work to do, too, and it was probably for the best that they had a few hours apart before their bargain concluded.

Her attraction to him had always been intense. The sex was even more intense. Her feelings for him ran deep, and a little space to come to terms with it all would give her a chance to regain her emotional equilibrium.

I'm in love with Reuben Black, she thought, and turned to look at herself in the mirror with a critical eye.

The turtleneck hid the flat leather band around her throat. Her face looked a little flushed but composed. No outward sign revealed the state of her heart, or the fact that she'd spent the past several hours playing kinky sex games. No different from the face she'd seen in the mirror before she agreed to be Reuben's submissive lover for a day, or before she realized she was in love.

Funny how a thing like that could take you by surprise, she thought. She knew how to watch for signs that a person was strung out on drugs, subtle cues that indicated a person could be dangerous or unpredictable, but Reuben had circled around and slipped under her guard, into her heart, and she'd never seen it coming.

And now, well, she'd see. The rules remained in place until tonight, and then maybe a different relationship would be possible.

No sense overthinking it or trying to guess what would come next. If she had an opportunity for a future with Reuben, she'd take it. If she didn't, she'd be glad to have the memories. It would be pointless and dumb to rob herself of the present, enjoying the time she had left to be with him.

"Time to get to work," she informed her reflection.

Keeping busy kept her from dwelling on what might or might not happen in the next few hours, although in spite of her best efforts to focus on what she was doing, her attention wandered.

Jolie was in the same state, both of them making small mistakes. Since Jolie had left with Reuben's friend the night before, it was easy to guess why she was distracted.

The day passed slowly. At closing Reuben reappeared along with the cowboy she now thought of as Jolie's man, and Laura had the sense that time was about to speed up.

Reuben put his hand on the small of her back. The gesture was both intimate and possessive, although not in any way inappropriate in public. Such a small thing, to cause such a strong reaction in her. It was a touch that said *mine*, and she wanted to melt into him in response. For a few more hours, at least, she was his.

"Are you still wearing my collar?" Reuben asked after Jolie and Chet left together.

"Yes." Laura smiled, pleased that she'd found a way to keep wearing it without raising questions. Well, not entirely, Jolie had asked about the high-necked tank, but she'd thought it was disguising something far more innocuous than a collar. Remembering Jolie's expression when she'd told her what she had underneath made Laura want to laugh. That look had been priceless.

"I'm pleased to hear it." Reuben's hand on the small of her back felt warm, strong. He applied a light pressure, guiding her toward the door. "I'll be even more pleased to see it, and you wearing nothing else."

"And where would you like this to happen?" Laura asked.

"I want to take you home with me again." He bent his head and brushed his lips against her temple. "I want to watch you undress, and know that you're mine, that I have you alone, and then, Laura, I'm going to have you. Any and every way I want to."

Her legs felt unsteady, her breath and her heart rate uneven as she pictured Reuben taking her again. "I hope you're planning to drive fast."

"I'll get us there." Reuben trailed his lips lower, until they touched her cheek. She turned her face toward him and he kissed the corner of her mouth. "Let's go."

Laura shut off the lights and locked up in a dreamy haze of anticipation and emotion. Laura the business owner was off-duty. Laura the woman who was Reuben's lover was free to enjoy herself.

She let Reuben guide her to her car, seat her in the passenger side, and drive her to his home. He kept one hand on her as they drove, stroking her thigh, touching her arm, smoothing back her hair. Nothing overtly sexual, and yet all of it made her want more.

By the time he'd ushered her back to his bedroom, she was feeling the heat, and it had nothing to do with the summer temperatures.

"Undress," Reuben said, letting his hand drop away from her. Laura obeyed and made a striptease of it this time, drawing it out, revealing her bare skin inch by inch, sliding her tank top up, holding it in front of her after she'd taken it off, reaching behind herself to unhook her bra.

"Tease." His eyes turned even darker, watching her. "Show me your breasts, Laura."

She let the shirt fall but kept the bra, letting it slip down to show her curves but keeping her nipples covered.

"Show me your nipples."

The wisp of her bra fell away and she stood in front of him, naked from the waist up, his collar around her throat marking her as his.

"Take off the rest, Laura." His voice was deep, a little rough, his eyes full of heat and intent.

Knowing she had his attention and his interest so completely captured was a heady sensation. It made her feel awake to herself as a sexual creature, aware of the feminine power she had to attract this male. Laura undid her jeans, slid the zipper down, moved her hips side to side as she wiggled out of them and stepped free of the denim.

"Turn around," Reuben said.

She did a slow half turn, ending with her butt toward him and waited for his next command.

"Take the panties off. Let me see your ass. Then bend over, spread your legs, and show me your pussy."

Knowing that he was watching her every move made each small movement she made sexually charged. She felt intensely aware of herself, of what he was seeing. She slipped her panties down her hips, down her thighs, knowing his eyes were fixed on her bare ass. With the panties gone, Laura set her feet shoulder-width apart and bent forward, exposing her sex to him.

"Stay just like that."

She heard soft sounds of fabric rustling, the metallic whisper of his zipper, and knew Reuben was stripping behind her. Then she heard the sound of foil tearing and felt her breath catch in her throat, knowing what it meant.

Reuben's hands closed over her hips. She felt his shaft probing between her legs as he pulled her back and thrust into her simultaneously. She was slick with anticipation but just unready enough that it was a tight fit. She felt every inch of him, felt her body working to accept him, the sensation of his entry heightened by the suddenness of it.

"Brace your hands on your knees," Reuben said.

She did, and then closed her eyes as he thrust deeper, withdrew, thrust deep again, taking her. His hold on her hips kept her steady. Her spread feet and braced hands did the rest, but she knew if he let go, she would fall. He didn't let go. His hands were hard and demanding, his thrusts urgent and insistent as he took her standing from behind.

When he stopped as abruptly as he'd started, she nearly did fall over, but his hands kept her from losing her balance.

"I want to see your face when I come inside you," Reuben

said. His hands moved from her hips up her waist, her rib cage, lifting her torso until she stood upright, pulling her back against him. He cupped her breasts in a possessive hold, stroking her nipples. "I want to watch your face while you come, too."

He released her and gave her a light slap on the ass. "Get on the bed. Lay on your back, legs open."

Right. No problem. All she had to do was walk. Just a couple of steps—she could do that. Laura made it to the bed, onto it, and arranged herself in a wanton sprawl.

He looked down at her in approval. "Very nice."

Reuben took his place between her thighs and lowered his body over hers. His mouth claimed hers in a hot, possessive kiss, tasting and taking her with his lips and tongue. The full body contact, the weight of him pressing into her and the raw, carnal kiss had her squirming under him, trying to align herself so that his shaft could slide back inside her. She felt empty, needy, burning for him to fill her, but he made her wait for it.

His hands pulled hers above her head and pinned her wrists to the mattress while his body rocked into hers in a tantalizing prelude of what was to come. His tongue penetrated her mouth in an erotic echo. And then finally he shifted himself so that the head of his cock pressed into her. He held her down, giving her only that much, no more, while she writhed under him and made low, urgent sounds that were muffled by his kiss.

Finally, when she didn't think she could stand it another second, he drove forward, filling her completely. She clutched at him, arched into him, moved with him while he pounded into her until they both broke, coming together in a fierce spending.

Reuben rolled onto his back, taking her with him, keeping himself buried in her while he held her on his chest. Laura collapsed against him, panting, waiting for her heart to slow down.

"So how was your day?" he asked her.

Laughter bubbled up and out of her. "It started off really well and it just got better."

"Better?" Reuben toyed with her hair. "I think this morning set a pretty high standard. If you start raising the bar every time, I'm going to be in trouble in a hurry."

"This morning was good. This was good, too. Different kinds of good. I liked waking up for a nice, slow bout of morning sex. I liked being dragged off to your bedroom, ordered to strip and then taken with no further preliminaries, too." She let out a happy sigh and traced an aimless pattern on his chest with her fingertips. "I'm not saying I'd like that all the time, but it's one hell of a way to end the workday."

"If you hadn't been primed for that by lots of sex in the last twenty-four hours, you probably wouldn't have enjoyed it," Reuben said. His hands moved over her back with long, hurried strokes. "I don't want you to think I'm going to throw foreplay out the window."

Tomorrow that wouldn't matter, Laura thought. Or would it? She raised her head to look at him, wondering if he was just talking idly or if it meant something. If he was thinking of a future between them.

He caught her look and put one hand over hers on his chest. "Wondering if you've earned disciplinary action in the form of withheld foreplay?"

"What? Oh." Laura looked down at her hand, trapped beneath his. "You said I could touch you last night and never took it back, so technically this doesn't count as me initiating anything."

"I didn't, did I?" Reuben's hand stroked hers. "You've done a good job of sticking to the rules."

Well, she had stuck to the letter, if not the spirit, of the rules she'd agreed to. "Harder than I thought it would be," she said out loud. "I mean, not that I ever wanted to back out or quit, but it's not easy to keep to a submissive role when you're used to being the one in charge."

"That's the point of the fantasy," Reuben said. "Not to have to be in charge—to have permission to take a vacation from it."

"Some vacation." Laura turned her head to the side, resting her cheek against the warm, smooth skin of his chest. "Most people just rent a time-share on the beach."

"Would you like a time-share on the beach?"

"Hmm." Laura stretched, luxuriating in the feel of him under her, in her, while she contemplated that. "I don't think I'd want to go by myself, to tell you the truth. I always associate it with those ads that show the couple hand in hand, walking along the shore at sunset. The beach is for romantic getaways. I think it would feel lonely to go alone."

She spoke without thinking, then realized too late it could be misinterpreted. Or correctly interpreted, revealing too much. She relaxed again when he continued to talk, his tone light.

"Imagining that you're not going alone, what beach would you go to?"

"I've never been to Hawaii," Laura said. "I think a trip to the beach should include palm trees and those lethal drinks with the little umbrellas in them. Water warm enough to swim in. And there are all sorts of interesting things to see in Hawaii, lava, waterfalls. So, Hawaii."

"Palm trees. Little umbrellas." Reuben slid a hand through her hair and stroked the nape of her neck. "The beach at sunset, warm enough to swim. Anything else on your list?"

"Well, you know." She moved under his hand, sighing in pleasure as he began to massage from her neck up to the base of her skull. "There's that beach scene in *From Here to Eternity*."

"Not familiar with that one."

"The beach scene in *Wild Orchid*, then. At the end."

"Do either of these scenes involve hand-holding?"

Laura smiled. "They involve body parts touching, but not the kind of thing you can really do in public and not get arrested."

"I'm very good at things you can't do in public without getting arrested."

"Very good," Laura agreed. "Good enough to risk getting sand into delicate places for."

"That's high praise." Reuben shifted under her, put his hands on her hips and lifted her up so he could slide out of her. "Rest your sand-free delicate parts here for a minute. I'll be right back." He kissed the top of her head and settled her beside him before sitting up and getting to his feet.

Laura watched him walk away, too comfortable to want to move, glad that he was taking care of all the pesky details involved in contraception and disease prevention. Not that she'd expect him always to be the one to handle that if the relationship continued. But for now, as part of the unconventional vacation she was on, it was nice to know that he was taking charge of that, too.

When Reuben returned, he sat beside her and rested a hand on her hip. "Hungry?"

Now that he mentioned it, she hadn't had dinner. Her stomach growled as if to speak for her. He smiled at her. "I guess I have my answer."

"Guess you do." She rolled onto her side and levered herself up on one arm. "How do we do this? Cook? Go someplace?"

"I don't think you can go anywhere dressed like that." Reuben ran a possessive hand along her side, up to her breast. "Not that I'm complaining. Dinner is waiting in the oven."

"No kidding?" Laura sat all the way up. "What's for dinner?"

"Steak. Baked potatoes."

"Sounds like what a cowboy eats." She grinned at his description.

"Women have been known to eat meat and potatoes, too."

He ran a finger over her nipple. "I cooked them earlier and left them warming."

"If you keep that up, I'm going to be pretty warm, too. And dinner will dry out."

"Hussy." Reuben bent his head to kiss her. "No more sex for you until you clean your plate."

"That should make dessert interesting."

"You have no idea." He gave her a look that positively smoldered with masculine confidence and sexual intent. Then he held out a hand to her, helping her up when she took it. "Now that we've taken the edge off one appetite, it's time to pay attention to more mundane hungers."

"Somehow, I don't think sitting across from you stark naked after you've just finished ordering me to spread my legs for you is going to be mundane."

"Maybe I'll order you to keep your legs spread while we eat," Reuben said.

Laura swallowed. "Like I said. Not mundane."

29

Reuben didn't tell her to display herself during dinner, but the knowledge that he could kept Laura in a state of heightened awareness. They sat across from each other on polished wooden chairs, the kitchen table between them. An ordinary scene if she ignored the fact that they were both naked and she was wearing a collar around her neck.

The steak and baked potato disappeared from her plate in spite of the charged atmosphere. Between running the coffee shop and moonlighting as a sex slave, she'd worked up an appetite.

It felt surprisingly comfortable to have dinner with Reuben. The sexual tension was off the charts, but he was good at making her feel at ease. He'd always had a knack for that, Laura thought. She looked forward to his visits to the coffee shop not just because she liked the way he looked and was drawn to him, not just because repeat customers were good for business, but also because he was one of those people who knew how to make other people feel competent.

That was probably the result of his training. It wouldn't pay to make the people around you nervous and likely to make mistakes when your life might depend on their performance. Instilling confidence in the troops was a sound tactic.

Even if he hadn't had a starring role in her fantasies, even if she hadn't been attracted to him, she would have enjoyed his company and wanted him for a friend. An odd realization to have while she could still feel the faint throbbing between her legs from the vigorous bout of sex they'd just had.

"Finished?" Reuben asked.

Yes, they nearly were. The clock had overtaken them. Out loud she said only, "Yes."

"I'll take the plates." He stood and cleared the table, carried the dishes to the sink and ran water over them. He came back to her, stopped by her chair, and held out a hand.

Laura slid her hand into his and scooted her chair back, letting him help her stand. They stood close together, almost touching, looking at each other. Reuben raised his free hand to her throat, tracing the outline of the collar.

"Come on," he said finally. He drew her into the living room, over to the couch. He sat down and pulled her into his lap, his arms cradling her. "Did you enjoy your fantasy, Laura?"

"I did." She leaned into him, far from relaxed now, focused on his thighs underneath her bottom, his hands on her, all the places their bare skin met.

"It's been twenty-four hours." He ran a hand over her breast, circled her nipple. "Are you ready for me to take it off?"

She didn't have to ask what it was. The collar. Once he removed it, she wouldn't be his anymore. She had to swallow before she could say it, but she managed to get the word out. "Yes."

Reuben's hands caressed her torso, moved up into her hair, slid it over one shoulder so he could unfasten the collar. The band of leather came away, and left Laura feeling truly naked.

"Fantasies don't last," he said, touching the hollow of her throat. "But reality does."

"And what is reality for us?" Laura asked, not sure she wanted to know the answer.

"What we want it to be. What we make it." He looked into her eyes and deliberately placed his hand on her breast again. "We're sexually compatible."

"That's an understatement," Laura said.

"We have a lot in common."

She nodded. She'd thought that herself when he first offered her what she wanted, what she needed. They did have a great deal in common. Including war stories and scars, although he hadn't told her the tales behind the few marks she'd spotted on his body.

"I know you're a very practical woman," Reuben went on.

Not exactly words she longed to hear, Laura thought, but she couldn't argue with the statement. It was true.

Although maybe she wasn't all that practical. She'd agreed to be a sex slave for twenty-four hours. A more practical woman probably would have said, "No, thank you," and gone home to watch *Wild Orchid* again instead, making sure to replay the beach scene at the end a few times.

"Have you ever thought about having a family?" Reuben's hand moved down to cup her belly and Laura looked down at it, wondering what it would feel like if her belly was rounder with their baby and his hand was resting there, waiting to feel first faint kick.

"I hadn't until just now," she said.

"And what do you think of the idea?"

"It's a big commitment. It would mean cutting down on

the hours I work, hiring another employee," Laura said, thinking it through out loud.

"That's work. What do you think of it outside of work?" He rubbed his hand in a circle, massaging her belly.

"It's a nice idea." She watched him touching her, thought about the kind of man he was, and was sure he would stay with her through labor, massaging her to help her relax and rest between contractions.

He'd stay for the rest of it, too. Reuben Black was not a man who shirked his responsibilities. That would extend to fatherhood. Although parenting was a lot of work and it would be nice to have time as a couple first, maybe even time to walk hand in hand on a beach. "I wouldn't be in too big a rush to get started, though," she added.

"Very wise." He smoothed his hand along the curve of her hip, his fingertips brushing her thigh. "What do you think of that for reality? The two of us together permanently. Sexual compatibility. Common grounds, common goals. A family in a year or two."

That sounded right. So why did it feel wrong? What was missing?

Laura felt something go still inside her. "And?"

"And what?"

"Are you proposing to me, Reuben?" she asked, point blank.

"Yes, Laura, I am."

"What about love?"

His hand on her hip stilled. "What about it?"

"Do you love me?"

"Laura." Reuben's hold on her tightened. "There's no need to get off track, here. I'm offering you reality, not a fantasy."

And in this version of reality, he didn't love her. She felt her heart ache, literally ache in her chest.

"I love you," she said, the words forcing their way past the tightness in her chest.

"I'm glad." He held her closer. "I'll be a good husband. If we have a family, I'll be a good father. I won't leave you."

"I know that." Her throat was burning, closing up. A heavy weight pressed down on her chest. "I asked you a question, Reuben. Do you love me?"

He didn't answer, and that was answer enough. "I see," she said.

She sat there in silence for a few minutes, unable to move, her limbs turned to lead. "You planned this. Didn't you? What was it, Reuben, did your biological clock go off one day, you decided it was time to settle down, and I was handy? Did you think I was so lonely, so hard-up, so *practical*—" She nearly choked on the word. "—that I'd be too grateful for any kind of offer to say it wasn't enough?"

Fury shot through her and gave her strength to stand, to move away from him and meet his eyes. "It's not enough." Her legs somehow carried her away from him, to the bedroom where she'd left her clothes. She picked them up and the visceral memory of how she'd dropped them washed over her, along with the vivid realization of what she was giving up.

But it wasn't enough. It wasn't.

She dressed herself, fumbling, hands shaking, and retrieved her car keys that he'd set on the dresser after driving them both here. His truck was here; she'd seen it when they pulled into the drive. He must have gotten a ride with Chet, which meant she didn't have to worry about driving him back to collect his vehicle. She didn't think she could face that and was quietly grateful that she didn't need to.

Laura paused by the couch on her way out, where Reuben still sat. "I love you," she said again. "That's why it isn't enough. I need you to love me back." She brushed at something burning her cheeks and stared at her hand, unable to understand why it came away wet. "Come and see me when you can give me what I need."

She left him holding the collar in his hands. She paused once when she reached the door, listening for him. He didn't try to stop her, didn't tell her not to go.

She closed the door behind her, very carefully.

Laura drove home on autopilot, glad that Missoula didn't have heavy traffic. She remembered to lock her car, a big-city habit she'd never relaxed, and let herself into her apartment.

For some reason, she found herself thinking that it would be nice to live in a house. Nice, but not practical. She'd rented an apartment so she wouldn't have to take care of maintenance, yard work, the many chores couples shared that would simply overload her in the first few years when all her energy needed to go into her business.

It didn't change the feeling that she'd come back to something temporary, the place she lived, but not her home.

Home, she was afraid, had come to mean the place where she'd left Reuben.

Ridiculous. Irrational. Too bad her heart didn't listen to reason. Laura sighed and padded off to her bedroom. Not that she expected sleep to come any time soon, but she was tired and she wanted to curl up with her pillow, bury her head under the covers, and stop thinking for a while.

She undressed with automatic motions, let her clothes fall in a heap, and crawled into bed. Once there, doubts crowded into her mind.

Had she done the right thing? Was it wrong to turn down a good man who'd made an honest offer because he wasn't ready to make a declaration of love?

Maybe he would have come to love her in time.

She thought about that, rolled over, punched her pillow, flopped back restlessly. Maybe. And maybe he would have remained a decent man, good in bed, who simply didn't love her and never would. And maybe after living with that for a few years, feeling the hope die, they'd end up in divorce court.

Because she didn't believe she could live with it for the rest of her life, knowing it was one-sided and he didn't return her love. If she hadn't been in love with him, it probably would have sounded like a pretty good bargain. She knew she was getting older. She knew if she ever wanted a husband and a family, the longer she waited the fewer options she'd have.

Even putting aside the consideration of whether or not she'd regret not having children, there was a lot to be said for companionship. Friendship. Somebody to come home to. Somebody who might, from time to time, bring out a leather collar and invite her to play the sex-slave game.

It was a tempting offer, even now. And she would probably have more than a few regrets that she couldn't have just accepted it and been glad to have that much.

I wanted him to love me, she thought. She rolled over again and stared up at the ceiling. Was that too much to want?

No. It wasn't. But if she couldn't change how she felt and neither could he, they had an unsolvable problem.

It hurt. It would probably hurt for some time. But she'd made the right choice. Better a clean break now with good memories on both sides than dragging them both down into a nightmare of pain and recriminations and eventual bitterness.

Which didn't make it any easier.

"Sometimes doing the right thing sucks," she said out loud.

It took all his control not to go after her. Reuben wanted to grab Laura, hold her, stop her from leaving. But she had a right to leave if she didn't want to stay, and he hadn't offered her enough to make her want to.

He'd planned his strategy carefully, done everything right, but it hadn't been enough.

If he lived to be a hundred, Reuben didn't think he'd ever recover from the way she'd looked when she said it wasn't enough. She'd looked wounded. He'd promised not to hurt her, and he'd put that look in her eyes.

But what option did he have? He lived by reason, by rules, by making careful plans and following them. A smart man didn't allow himself to be ruled by emotion. Emotion could get you killed, cause you to make a fatal mistake.

After a while, it occurred to Reuben that love and war did not follow the same rules. He'd set his sights on her like a target to be acquired, studied her weaknesses like an enemy to be defeated. But she wasn't his enemy. She was his heart. How could a man fight his own heart?

And he'd thought he was adjusting well to civilian life.

The realization came slowly, but it did come. If he didn't love her, why wouldn't any other woman do? Why did it have to be her and no other? If he didn't love her, why was he willing to do anything, give anything, to have her back here with him?

It went against everything he'd lived by for his adult life, but one thing became perfectly clear as he sat there alone. The only way to win her was to wave the white flag and surrender.

By the time he went to bed, he'd begun to formulate a new plan.

30

"I can give you what you need."

The words, spoken in a low Western drawl by a man's mouth so close to Laura Jamieson's ear that his breath feathered across her skin and made her shiver, would have gotten her attention even if the man in question hadn't been standing so close behind her that she felt him all along her back. His arms on either side of her caged her against him as he offered her the large bag of coffee beans she'd been straining to reach bare seconds before.

Was she imagining it? Laura closed her eyes, breathed in the soap and leather scent of him. Hallucinations didn't usually come with a sense of smell, although it was easier to believe that she was dreaming or hearing things than it was to believe that after a week of silence and absence, Reuben had come back to say the one thing that would persuade her to say yes.

She hadn't heard him come in. It was closing time. Lemon Espresso was empty; Jolie had just said good night and left. The door hadn't opened again, and Laura realized Jolie must've let Reuben in and locked the door behind them, leaving them alone to work things out.

"Laura?"

She could feel the heat of him warming her. If she moved back just the slightest bit, would it press his erection into the soft flesh of her denim-covered butt?

Laura imagined it would. She imagined him, hard and hot, pressing into the crease between the full globes of her rounded behind and shivered in spite of the summer heat as she remembered him taking her from behind standing the last time, taking her the first time as she kneeled.

Was he really ready to offer her what she'd asked for, what she needed? She was afraid to believe it and unwilling to risk any misunderstanding.

"What do I need?" she asked him.

"You need to be loved." His breath touched the soft skin below her ear a second before his lips did, brushing the lightest of kisses there. "You need me. And you need to let Jolie run Lemon Espresso for the weekend, because you need to get on an airplane."

Laura leaned back into him, melting into his body. He set the bag of coffee on the counter and folded his arms around her, holding her in a hard, tight embrace. "Why an airplane?"

"Because Montana is landlocked. No beach."

The prosaic answer made her laugh.

"Come to Hawaii with me. Hold hands with me, walk on the beach at sunset with me. We'll drink things with umbrellas in them, and you can tell me what happens in that beach scene you like so much. Or better yet, show me."

"It's a very long flight to Hawaii," Laura said. "Plenty of time to describe that in full detail."

Reuben turned her in his arms and looked down into her eyes. "I love you, Laura."

She stopped breathing, was silent so long that he added, "Say something."

"I love you, too."

It was the last thing she said for a while. His mouth covered hers, and words weren't needed. It was a hungry kiss. His lips devoured hers. His hands cupped her butt, lifted her off her feet. Laura wound her arms around his neck, locked her legs around his waist and held on while he walked her back to the stockroom.

That would work, Laura thought through a haze of lust and need. There was a table back there, about the right height . . .

It was torture to feel the hard wall of his chest against her breasts with all those layers of fabric separating them. His erection pressed into her sex as they walked, the movement rocking him deeper into the cradle of her hips.

Reuben got the door open and set her down on the edge of the table. He took hold of the lower hem of her shirt and pulled it up, breaking the kiss just long enough to tug it over her head before his mouth came back down on hers and his tongue thrust inside.

She worked to yank his shirt free from the waistband of his jeans, briefly fought with his snap and zipper, then began the process of getting his pants down his hips while he unhooked her bra and freed her breasts. His hands closed over them, cupping, squeezing, stroking. He rubbed his palms over her nipples, then rolled them between his fingers and applied a steady pressure while she arched into his hands and moaned into his mouth.

He broke the kiss again to trail his lips down her throat, taking her nipples into his mouth by turns as his fingers moved down to unfasten her jeans and spread the fabric open.

Reuben lifted his head and said, "You'll have to stand up for a second."

Right. It'd be a challenge for him to peel her out of her jeans when she was sitting on them. Laura slid off the table and then Reuben had her jeans down to her ankles, panties included, in record speed. She used his shoulder for balance as she stepped out of them, and then he lifted her again and replaced her on the table, naked.

"Spread your legs wide for me," he said.

Laura complied readily, bracing her hands behind her for support, displaying herself to him.

"God, you're beautiful." He knelt between her thighs and closed his mouth over her clit as if he was hungry for the taste of her, his tongue delving into her folds, flicking over the sensitive nub of her clit, sweeping lower to thrust into her and taste her deeply.

He kissed, licked, and sucked at her sex, and then he opened her and pushed two fingers into her tight sheath.

"Reuben," she groaned, thrusting her hips toward him to take more. "That feels so good."

But it wasn't enough. She wanted more of him inside her, wanted to take all of him.

He toyed with her, petting and stroking and licking her while she moaned and squirmed, penetrating her with one finger, then two, then using only his mouth and his tongue until she was ready to scream.

When he stood up and retrieved a foil packet from his jeans pocket, sheathing himself, Laura was trembling, aching, desperate for him to thrust inside her and fill her.

He positioned himself, guided his cock to her opening, and drove home in one sure, fast movement. Laura locked her ankles around his waist, wrapped her arms around his back, and strained to open her thighs wider, to take him deeper.

He took her hard, driving in and out of her, while she moaned and then screamed and bucked against him, coming so hard, she thought she might actually pass out. She felt him throbbing inside her, swelling, and then he thrust faster, coming as he seated himself so deeply that he touched the opening of her womb.

Afterwards, he leaned his forehead against hers and held her while they rediscovered how to breathe.

"I missed you," she said finally.

"I missed you, too." His arms tightened around her. "But I thought I'd better be prepared when I came to see you."

She let out a soft, helpless laugh. "Don't tell me. You had to make plans."

"As a matter of fact, I did. I wasn't going to come and tell you I love you in some half-assed way."

Laura let her hands run down to his ass. "Doesn't feel like you're missing anything," she said, enjoying the feel of his muscled butt under her palms.

"Funny."

"Well, I can laugh now. Nothing seemed very funny yesterday."

His body rocked into hers. "But me fucking you blind in the stockroom is hilarious?"

"No. Well, it'll make Jolie laugh," Laura said, thinking about that.

"Glad I'm entertaining somebody." He withdrew, and Laura felt the loss like a shock.

"I wasn't finished with that," she complained.

"I'm not finished, either." He palmed her sex. "Just getting started, in fact."

"That sounds very promising." She tipped her pelvis to push herself against his hand, enjoying the contact.

"I do owe you dessert," Reuben reminded her. "We ran out of time before."

Heat flashed through her as she remembered the burn of anticipation she'd felt, seated naked across from him while they ate, knowing he could do anything at all to her that he wanted to do.

"Which reminds me. I bought you something." Reuben gave her pussy a last pet and bent down to go through his pockets. He straightened up and said, "Hold out your hands."

Laura held them out to him, palms up. He laid a necklace into them and she had to look at it for a minute before she understood what it was. A collar-style piece of Southwestern jewelry, a combination of overlapping metal pieces shaped like coins with stones set in the center, and a leather strap that fastened like a buckle.

It wouldn't look like anything more than a necklace when she wore it, but the two of them would know what it represented.

"I thought you should have something you didn't have to hide," Reuben said. "When you want to be dominated in bed, put this on and be prepared to follow the rules or suffer the consequences."

Laura laughed. "I'd better be good or you might not let me come again." She lifted it to her neck and searched for the catch.

"I'll do it."

She swept her hair out of the way and bent her head while Reuben fastened it around her throat, then settled it into position. His warm fingers caressed the soft skin just below the necklace. He looked down at her with clear appreciation and a light of laughter in his eyes. "What a nice view. A naked, submissive woman wearing my collar."

"Not just any woman," Laura pointed out.

"No." His face went serious and the teasing light left his eyes. "I knew that before I knew why. You accused me of planning it when I made you my offer, and I did. But it wasn't what you thought. I didn't just decide one day that it was time I settled down and I thought you'd be convenient. I saw you, and decided it was time I settled down."

Oh. The meaning of that sank in while he continued, "I

didn't want any other woman. I wanted you, just you. I came up with all sorts of logical reasons to justify it to myself, but when you left I had to admit that there wasn't anything logical about it. You weren't part of some master plan. I came up with the plan because I wanted you."

Laura looked up at him and asked, "When did you figure out that you loved me?"

"About half an hour after you walked out." His lips twisted in a half smile, half grimace. "I may have made a mistake with you, Laura, but I do learn from my mistakes."

"Fair enough." She slid off the table and stood up. "How long do we have until we need to be at the airport?"

Reuben consulted his watch. "Not long. You'd better get dressed and get your wallet and ID. We need to get through the security check, and we're booked for the last flight out."

"What about packing?" Laura gathered up her clothes and started to scramble into them.

"We'll get whatever you need for the weekend there. Which shouldn't be much. Toothbrush, bikini, condoms."

"Planning to keep your sex slave naked and in bed?" She smiled at him and made a show of putting her bra on slowly, covering her nipples one at a time while he watched.

"You can wear a bikini to walk on the beach," he allowed.

"You actually booked a room at the beach," Laura said, shaking her head as she tried to take in the complete change in direction her life had just taken.

"A time-share condo. Oceanfront. Beach out the back door. A hotel within walking distance with a restaurant in case we don't feel like cooking and a bar for those umbrella drinks you wanted."

"Sounds perfect." Dressed, Laura held her hand out to him. He took it and pulled her into his arms.

"Nothing in life is perfect, Laura, but this is pretty damned good." He kissed her, and she had to agree.

———

"We're here." Reuben parked, then turned to look at Laura, who was half-leaning out the window of their rental car, trying to see everything at once. A necklace made of fragrant blossoms hung around her neck. "You got 'leid' at the airport. Time to get laid at the beach."

Her laughter floated to him on an ocean-tinged breeze. "Such a romantic."

"I'm romantic. We could have stayed home and had sex. I brought you to Hawaii to have sex," he pointed out.

"Yes, you did." She pulled her head back inside the car and looked at him. "Why'd you do that?"

"Because you wanted to go to the beach, but you didn't want to do it alone." He reached over to touch the necklace that collared her throat. "You had another fantasy to fulfill, and I'm the man for the job."

Her lips curved in humor. "You certainly are."

"The sun's just coming up," Reuben said. They'd spent the night flying over the Pacific, landed on the Big Island in the wee hours, and picked up the keys to the rental car and rented condo. He'd stopped at a convenience store to pick up essentials for them, and they'd pulled in to their destination as the sky lightened and the first rays of morning sun broke over the horizon. "It's not sunset, but we can walk on the beach and pretend."

"I've learned something about fantasy," Laura said solemnly. She leaned toward him and whispered in his ear, "Reality is better."

Reuben agreed fully. The reality of Laura back in his arms, naked in the stockroom of Lemon Espresso, slick and open and ready for him was better than any fantasy. Thinking about that was making his jeans uncomfortably tight. Time to get them both into more appropriate dress, or undress.

"Let's go change." He reached behind the driver's seat to

snag the shopping bag he'd left on the floor, hooked his fingers into the handle, and climbed out of the car, carrying it. Laura hopped out and slammed the car door behind her, smiling at him while the wind blew a strand of hair across her face.

She was so beautiful, it nearly hurt him to look at her. Laura. His.

He got the condo's front door open, and before they went inside, Reuben scooped her up and carried her across the threshold.

The sun was well up by the time they'd changed into bathing suits and went out the back door to the beach. A little path led through the yard to the sand. Palm trees towered over them. The sound of the surf made a rhythm almost like music. Laura felt Reuben's hand around hers, warm, strong, and wondered if it was possible to be any happier.

He'd done all this for her. Scheduled airline flights, found and rented a beachside getaway, arranged for Jolie to mind the coffee shop while she was away. All so she could experience walking hand in hand with her lover in paradise.

"Thank you," Laura said out loud.

"For on the table in the stockroom last night, or against the wall in the living room just now?" he asked.

"Well, that, too." She grinned at him. "But I was talking about going to all the effort to plan this for me. For us."

"There are benefits to having a man who's good at making and carrying out plans." He reached out to touch her nipple. "This power can be used for good."

She found his fingertips stroking the tight bud of her nipple through the thin fabric of her flowered bikini top very good. They had the beach to themselves for now, although she didn't doubt that it would be very crowded soon. Otherwise she'd be tempted to slip the bikini top off and walk half-naked

with him, letting him look and touch without anything interfering.

His hand moved to her other nipple, and there was suddenly too much space and too much material between them.
Laura stopped and turned to face him, pressing into him, burying her face against his shoulder. Her breasts were crushed into
his chest as his arms locked around her.

"Laura?"

"I want you," she said baldly. "And we're in a public place
wearing too many clothes."

"You're hardly wearing anything." His hand played along
the edge of her bikini bottom. "I can have you naked in about
two seconds. Although we can't act out your beach scene without getting arrested."

"Two seconds, very specific. Spoken with military preci-
sion. Should we time it?" She smiled against his bare skin and
then quivered as he stroked her butt, then lower. She felt her
sex clench in anticipation, already growing soft and slick and
ready to take him again.

"I think you should run." Reuben released her and stepped
back, his face hard and intent. She dashed down the beach, her
feet digging into the soft sand, heading toward the condo's
back door and privacy.

Laura heard him close behind her and knew he was going
to catch her. That was fine; she really didn't want to get away.
His arm caught her around the waist a few feet from the door
just as she reached the patio. Side walls blocked them from
view unless somebody happened to be directly in front of
them. Fairly private.

She felt his fingers hook into her bikini bottoms and strip
them down her legs. He untied the string between her shoulder blades and then the one at the nape of her neck, letting her
bikini top fall to land next to the bottoms.

"Naked. Mine." She heard him say in a satisfied tone. His

hand landed a light slap on her bare backside. "Get through that door before I take you right here."

It wasn't much of a threat, but then, she really didn't want to be seen. Or risk giving a senior citizen who happened to go out for a walk a heart attack. Laura hurried through the patio door and then turned to face Reuben as he followed close behind her.

"I want you on the bed," he told her. His hands went to his waist, hooked into his swim trunks, and stripped them off. She eyed his erection, full, thick, bobbing slightly toward her as if it had a mind of its own and knew what it wanted.

Laura forced herself to look away and pay attention to where she was going. She didn't want to stub her toes on something in this unfamiliar setting. *The bed,* she told herself. *Focus. You can make it to the bed.*

The condo was one open living space, with the kitchen, dining room, and living room all flowing together. The bedroom was the only room with four walls and a door, aside from the bathroom. Laura went through the open doorway, pulled the covers back, and threw herself onto the bed. She rolled onto her back and smiled at Reuben as he placed his knees on the mattress and then lowered himself over her.

"Get a condom," he said. "I put the box in the drawer beside you."

"I hope you bought a really big box," Laura said. She felt around for the drawer, pulled it open, found a packet, and got it open. She rolled the condom down his shaft and then held him around the base, enjoying the feel of him hard and hot in her hands.

"Big enough."

"You certainly are." She stroked her hand up and down his length.

"I meant the box."

"That, too." Laura adjusted her position beneath him and

then let go of him to get her hands out of the way as he pressed into her.

Reuben reached for her hands, pulling them above her head, pinning them to the mattress. Then he kept pushing forward until he was all the way inside her.

"Take me," he growled as his mouth closed over hers.

And she did.

Read on for a preview of Charlene Teglia's
upcoming erotic romance

Satisfaction Guaranteed

Available from St. Martin's Griffin
in February 2008

The Capture Agency is a dating service unlike any other. Men and women sign up to live out their most forbidden fantasy: for the male to capture his partner and make her a slave to passion. At The Capture Agency, pleasure is a must and satisfaction is always guaranteed. . . .

"You work too hard. You should take more time to play."

Chase Hunter glanced from his monitor's flat screen panel to the open doorway of his office, currently decorated by Mark Lewis. Mark's flair for men's fashion was accentuated by a pose any male model would envy.

"Don't tell me, let me guess. You want to take me shopping again."

Mark rolled his eyes. "You make it sound like such a bad thing. I'm just trying to save you from your stuck-in-the-nineties look. But I didn't come in here to debate the merits of the latest winter fashions. I came to show you this."

Mark straightened up to wave a computer printout he'd had tucked behind his back. He sashayed across the office and placed it on Chase's desk with a flourish.

Chase knew what it was before he picked it up. He should. He'd designed the client information sheet printouts for The

Capture Agency, along with the state-of-the-art compatibility matching software. He just didn't expect to see his name on it.

"Mark." The tone of his voice said it all.

"I know, I know. You don't mix business and pleasure. You run the business, you don't date the clients. But this is a hard match, Chase. We had nobody in our database that came close for compatibility. We were going to lose the sale."

"So we lose a sale. We have plenty of other clients." Chase kept his voice level with an effort.

"Yes, but when in the five years you've owned this place have you ever had a match?" Mark persisted.

"I don't know. I don't check. I don't date clients."

"Well, I check for you. Once a month. Once a week if you're moodier than usual."

"I am not moody." Chase balled up the printout and tossed it into his wastebasket. "Leave. Go search the Internet for the perfect sweater. I'll be here doing something radical called working."

"You know what they say." Mark placed his lips closer to Chase's ear and whispered, "All work and no play makes Jack a dull boy."

"So go worry about Jack." Chase focused on his monitor again, ignoring his assistant and right-hand man.

"I'll take care of Jack later, don't you worry. For now, let's talk about you. It's not just your wardrobe that's stuck in the nineties. You need a new interest. A new woman. This woman, for instance. She's a perfect match." Mark produced a second, pristine and uncreased copy of the printout. "The computer says so and *you* should know it's never wrong."

In fact, Chase did know the computer was never wrong. His fuzzy logic software was revolutionary and incredibly accurate. Which still didn't mean he was going to date a client.

"Thank you, Mark." Chase took the second copy and folded it into a complex paper airplane before sending it after the first. It landed nose-first in the trash. The sight gave him a brief sense of satisfaction. The plane's design was aerodynamically sound and his aim had been accurate.

"You're just being stubborn." Mark retrieved the paper airplane and smoothed it out. "I signed her up. I took her money. I promised her a compatible date. You're compatible. So if you don't want to date her, you're going to have to tell her yourself."

He dropped the paper onto Chase's keyboard and headed for the door.

"I'm not going to call her," Chase said.

Mark held a hand up behind him. "Talk to the hand."

"That's very mature. I mean it. I don't date clients. I don't care how perfect she is."

Mark's silencing palm answered for him. Then he shut the door, leaving Chase alone with the printout.

He scowled first at the closed door, then at the sheet of paper covering his keyboard. In order to go back to work, he'd have to move it. Mark had left it that way to force him to look at the client sheet. Chase grudgingly admitted the strategy was sound. Annoying, but sound.

Behind the annoyance he felt a vague curiosity. Who was this perfect woman? Since he had to pick it up anyway, Chase took the printout and leaned back in his chair to read it.

Rachel Law. Hotshot sales professional, career woman, single. Smart. Chase looked over the section that showed her IQ and the special notes section that detailed any requirements a client had that didn't come up in standard compatibility testing. It told Chase at least part of why Mark hadn't come up with any other matches in the system. Ms. Law had an IQ of 130, which meant that only two percent of the population could meet her special request.

He read the note a second time and entertained himself briefly by calculating the odds that she'd find a compatible man anywhere outside this agency. A man who fit her other personality profile requirements for basic compatibility, shared interests and tastes, and equal or greater intelligence, who had a desire to experiment with dominating sex. The odds were astronomical.

Chase knew he was going to regret it, but he flipped the page over and looked at the photocopied image of her face.

It was her eyes that caught him. Direct, with a hint of humor as well as the intelligence he'd expected. Her eyes were set off by a very nice face, with what his mother would call good bone structure. Blond hair worn in a fairly conservative style, not old-fashioned but not riding the edge of any fashion trends, which Chase supposed made sense in her line of work.

She looked polished and professional, but not unapproachable. Direct, not the type to waste time or words. She'd probably be impatient with the games most people played in the dating scene.

Judging by her personality profile and her appearance, she'd appreciate being told the straight truth about her lack of a match, and the sooner the better. She really was a lot like him, Chase noted, abandoning the photo to read her results again. If he'd decided to sign up for a fantasy date, the sooner he knew he was following a dead end, the sooner he could begin to plan an alternative to reach his objective.

He leaned back in his chair and thought about Rachel Law planning an alternative course. Might she experiment with one of those BDSM-lifestyle clubs? Those attracted some pretty fringe characters. A woman who was new to playing around could find herself in a bad situation with a stranger who might not be trustworthy.

The idea bothered Chase. A lot. So, Mark would win. He'd deliver the news to her personally that The Capture Agency couldn't match her, warn her about taking risks outside of the agency's safety measures, hope she met some nice man with a high IQ who could surprise her as she'd requested.

Chase had an IQ of 140. He could surprise her.

The thought was unwelcome, and Chase squelched it. He was a match, no question. And he could surprise her, but that didn't mean he should break his policy of mixing business and his personal life. There were lots of good reasons for that policy.

Ms. Rachel Law had gotten along fine without the services of The Capture Agency until now, and she'd manage without them in the future. Unless she elected to stay in the system until another match came up. That was an option and he'd be sure to point it out to her. Then he could tell Mark he'd done his best to save the sale.

Although Chase knew Mark's real goal wasn't to keep the client. Evidently Mark worried about his personal life. That worried Chase, because Mark was nothing if not persistent.

As if to confirm that realization, his intercom beeped and Mark's voice came over it. "She's waiting in Conference Room B."

Chase blew out a breath but otherwise didn't answer. He might have known Mark would keep her there, using her presence to push him into talking to her.

The office suite included several small conference rooms that could be used for first client meetings. The agency recommended that each matched pair of clients meet for the first time in a neutral, public setting to preserve their privacy and give them a chance to decide whether they wanted to pursue a real date. Conference rooms could be scheduled for that purpose, or they could choose to meet for coffee if they preferred to size each other up away from the business atmosphere of The Capture Agency.

There was nothing suspicious about Mark showing a new client to a conference room to meet with a match. It might

seem like amazing luck or too-good-to-be-true timing to Ms.
Law that her candidate happened to be on hand. Knowing
Mark, he'd answered any questions she had about that and left
her waiting with the honest expectation that she was about to
meet her agency date.

Chase wasn't looking forward to being the one to disappoint her.

Rachel shifted in her chair, toyed with the cup of coffee sitting on the table in front of her, and let her eyes wander
around the small room again. Soft beige walls, fluorescent
lighting, framed photographs of Mount Rainier capped with
snow and the Space Needle lit up at night. The berber carpet
was thick, well-padded, and a mix of earth tones that went
well with the room's neutral furnishings. She could have been
in any office of any business in the Seattle area.

Well, what had she expected, red curtains and velvet wall-
paper? Rachel suppressed a grin at the idea of mixing a bor-
dello's décor with an office suite.

The Capture Agency didn't scream "sex" in any way. It
looked like any typical office suite, with employees dressed in
business casual and computers at every desk. A professional,
high-tech environment.

Rachel hadn't felt at all uncomfortable coming in to fulfill
all the requirements to become a client. She'd been treated
politely and respectfully. The man who'd ushered her into this
conference room to await her prospective date had practically
bent over backwards to make sure she had everything she
needed to make the experience positive. And not because he
was flirting. She was clearly the wrong gender to appeal to
him.

The policy of having clients meet for the first time in one of
the agency's conference rooms made perfect sense to Rachel. If
she didn't like the look of the man she'd been matched up
with, she didn't have to date him. He'd never have any way to

contact her outside of the agency, since no personal information like an address or phone number was given out. She'd never have to worry about unwanted pursuit from a rejected candidate.

The closed door gave them privacy, the office setting gave them anonymity, and the office staff on the other side of the door ensured that if the meeting didn't go well, it could be ended quickly, with assistance if need be.

The lengths to which the agency had gone to create a safe environment for what could be a risky kind of fantasy to act out impressed Rachel. Whoever had created this business cared about people, or at least cared about avoiding lawsuits and creating positive word of mouth.

This was a good idea, she thought, settling back in her chair. She'd had a few doubts about it, but two things had prodded her to go through with the process. One was that nagging sense of something missing. The other was the realization that the type of man she'd always wanted to meet might remain forever out of reach unless she used some method to look for him other than trusting to random chance and hoping they'd wind up in the same place at the same time.

It struck her as funny that they had, in fact, ended up in the same place at the same time. But then, if a man was looking for the same things she was, this was a logical place for him to try.

The door opened and she didn't have time to wonder if it had been a mistake to wear the navy blue skirt and sweater set, styles that might have been called classic but could also be called boring, because the man who entered the room made it impossible to think about anything but him.

He had brown hair and brown eyes, a square jaw with a dent that Rachel found herself wanting to touch, broad shoulders, and a general sense of solid masculinity. Rachel thought he'd look equally at home behind an office desk, at the head of a conference table, or sailing a boat. She blamed Sabrina for planting pirate images in her head, but she could see this man carrying out pretty much any role with capable ease.

He was dressed conservatively, like herself, but he didn't seem like the type who considered casual wear to mean not wearing a tie. She could see him wearing jeans and a sweater and looking comfortably at home. In fact, she could picture him sitting outside on her patio drinking coffee and orange juice, reading the paper, having breakfast. The image was so unexpectedly ordinary that she blinked.

"Hello," he said, regarding her with steady eyes. "You must be Rachel Law."

She nodded.

"My name's Chase."

The name suited him, she thought. It was a solid kind of name but not boring. "Hello, Chase."

He walked over to join her at the small round conference table, pulled out a chair and sat across from her. "If you don't mind me saying so, you don't look like a woman who has any trouble getting a date."

"No," Rachel agreed. "The trouble is getting one worth the time and effort."

"Sex isn't worth your time and effort?"

The question was asked in a matter of fact tone. She didn't get the sense that he was trying to shock her or make her feel uncomfortable, just stating the obvious. People became clients of The Capture Agency for a very specific reason.

"It hasn't been," Rachel answered, matching him for directness. "Not bad or anything. It's just that sex was never very exciting. Not fun. No surprises."

She looked down at the tabletop as if the designers at Ikea could help her search for the right words. "The men I dated, the relationships I had, I knew what they were going to do before they did it. Everything was predictable and it seemed so pointless."

Rachel gave a slight shrug and continued, "I know I could have made an effort. If I wanted something different in bed, I could have shown up with a can of whipped cream and handcuffs. But the problem was on the inside and I didn't think adding props would change anything. I thought—" She broke off and then looked up at him, meeting his eyes. "I thought if I met somebody who was whipped cream and handcuffs on the inside, then whether we used any props or not, it wouldn't matter. It'd be exciting and different because he'd be different."

"Capable of surprises."

"Yes." She smiled at him. "Exactly."

He studied her as if she'd presented him with a puzzle. Something gave her the idea that he was very good at figuring out puzzles. Finally he said, "Stand up."

"Excuse me?"

"Stand up." He smiled at her, and it reached all the way to his eyes. His expression was warm, reassuring, with a hint of humor. "I want to see if you're really ready to do this."

"What, here?" Rachel felt competing surges of anxiety and anticipation. "Don't we talk first, get to know each other a little?"

"I'm not going to ravish you on the table," he said. The smile widened just a little. "Although that's certainly an interesting idea."

"Oh." She folded her hands primly in her lap and made no move to get up. "Then what?"

"An exercise. Ever been in theater?"

Which had what to do with her sex life? "No," Rachel answered cautiously.

"This is an exercise that casts often do together. Putting on a production means people will be working closely together for some time, playing roles. They have to trust each other to do their part well. It makes for the right environment for creativity and cooperation, for good performances."

She could see how having the right environment could foster the level of comfort needed for the best possible performance and how that could transfer to this kind of sexual roleplaying. Rachel nodded her understanding. "I see. And you do this exercise standing up?"

"Yes." Chase stood and extended a hand to her. Rachel slid hers into his grip. His hand felt warm, strong. He helped her to her feet, then let go, not using the contact to try to prolong any kind of physical intimacy.

"How do we do this?" she asked.

"You stand here." He indicated a spot farther away from the table, with more empty space around. Rachel took her position and gave him a questioning look. "Okay, what next?"

"I stand here." He took up a position behind her. "Your job is to relax, let yourself fall backwards, and trust me to catch you."

She felt her whole body tense up at the very idea. "I don't think I can do that."

"You can if you relax. If you trust me. I'm right here behind you, Rachel. I won't let you fall. I won't let you hit your head or get hurt. I'll catch you."

His voice was deep, reassuring. Rachel took a deep breath and tried to relax. "I think you're too far back," she said. "I don't want to fall that far."

"We'll start smaller, then." She heard him move behind her, taking a step forward. "Now I'm just behind you. Only a few inches, less than a foot of distance. Enough that you have to actually let go to fall into my arms, but not too far. Think you can try it now?"

That was okay, Rachel thought. Even if he didn't catch her, at that distance she'd fall into him and then she could right herself. "Yes."

"Close your eyes."

She did and felt her heartbeat accelerate at the thought of

falling in the dark. But she knew he had the right idea. They could talk for hours and it wouldn't help convince her that this would work. That he was the man who could surprise her. Although he was already surprising her with his insight and his practical approach.

If she could do this, if she could fall into him, then she could feel comfortable letting him capture her. She could trust him with her body and her physical safety. This test would prove it to both of them.

Rachel took another deep breath and leaned backwards, letting herself go past the point where she could recover her balance, falling into Chase. Her shoulders hit his chest, breaking her fall. His arms closed around her, catching her easily. He held her for a second, then helped her return to her standing position.

"Good," he said. "Now do it again. I'll be farther back, but I'll be right here, Rachel. Just let go. You can do it."

It was both harder and easier the second time. Harder because she knew he was farther back and if he didn't catch her this time, she really might hurt herself. Easier because they'd already done it once.

Think of it this way, she told herself. *If he doesn't catch you, you'll know within the first fifteen minutes of meeting him that the sex isn't going to work.* As a way to screen potential dates, this technique could be a real time-saver.

The fall seemed to last forever and she had a panicked moment when she thought she'd fall all the way to the floor, but in reality only a split second passed between the time she went beyond the point of no return and landed in Chase's sure embrace.

The relief made her sag into him. Her pulse was pounding and she felt very aware of his size and strength behind her, supporting her. His arms held her securely. He didn't let her go immediately as he had the first time, but he also didn't make any attempt to turn his hold into something more. He just held her, waiting for her to signal him that she was fine on her own two feet again.

Her balance was restored on one level. On another it was rocky, so Rachel delayed for a minute and stayed where she was. She liked the feel of his arms around her, his chest supporting her back. There was a level of tension in the air and all her senses were alert to the man behind her. It was all too easy to imagine his hands sliding up to cup her breasts. She could feel them swelling in anticipation of his touch.

The test was a success. So was the agency's matching, thought Rachel. This man had her attention and her interest, and she didn't know what he would say or do next.

Chase breathed in the mixed scent of light floral perfume and woman and knew he was going to regret this. But he'd regret it even more if he let her walk away to find the satisfaction she sought from some other source.

If she had her fantasy date with him, he wouldn't have to worry about whether or not her curiosity led her to take foolish risks, or that some other man simply wouldn't appreciate what she was trusting him with.

His arms tightened around her briefly. "I'm going to capture you," he stated. "I'll contact you through the agency with the time and place. You'll go there, but you won't know what to expect. I'll take you by surprise. Be ready."

She nodded. "It's a date." Her voice was a little less than steady.

Chase let her go and left the room, still wondering what had gotten into him, but committed to following through. As far as Rachel knew, he was just another client. He could fulfill her fantasy and she'd never know anything different.

He'd opened the door with every intention of telling her the truth, then sending her on her way. Instead, he'd taken one look at her and hadn't wanted to end the conversation before it even began.

That was where he'd gone wrong, Chase decided. He'd talked to her. The competent, intelligent blonde with the Madonna face sitting there in navy business casual blithely telling him she wanted a man with whipped cream and handcuffs in his soul had flipped some atavistic switch inside him.

He'd had a sudden overwhelming desire to see her wearing both items and nothing else. Then he'd decided to conduct a little test to see whether or not she meant it, if she trusted him to be the one to play captor—and captive games—with.

Well, she'd meant it, and now the game was on. He'd caught her and he wasn't ready to let her go.